THe RISe OF RYNN

Prequel to The Rita Series

Bianca Rowena

Bianca Watson Publishing

Rowena, Bianca The Rise of Rynn / Bianca Rowena.—2nd ed.

Summary: Previous to his reign as the mighty Takano Rynn, Bryn was a Student at the Academy for the new Ruling Order under Master Dukath. Can he conquer his emotions and commit to the Master's Rule of No Attachments? Or will an unprecedented bond he forms with the little girl Rue keep him from becoming the ruthless Dark Lord he's destined to become?

ISBN 978-1-9992041-5-0 (Softcover : alk, paper)/978-1-9992041-5-0 (e-book) [1. Sci-Fi—Fiction. 2. Fantasy.] I. Title.
Designed by Uzichu | Printed in Canada | Second Edition

10 9 8 7 6 5 4 3 2

First Published in Canada in 2019 by Bianca Watson Publishing
The Rise of Rynn/978-0-9948513-9-0 (Softcover)/
978-1-9992041-0-5 (e-book)

contents

To Emily, for always encouraging me

MASTER DUKATH

"TODAY'S TEST," MASTER DUKATH says, "is to bring me the heart of a forest animal." He leans back in his chair and clasps his fingers together. His stare is unnerving, as always.

I frown. Each day the tests have been getting harder. Yesterday's was to make somebody cry. I don't enjoy making people cry, since it reminds me of when I would hurt people with my Gift powers and I didn't mean to.

Randon stands beside me, by far the most ruthless student in our Ruling Order training program. He succeeded in making someone cry on his way out of Master Dukath's study yesterday. It took him no time at all to accomplish the test. He told one of the child boarders at the school for the summer, that her parents died in a spacecraft malfunction on their way out of the planet's atmosphere. She ran away crying and calling for her grandfather, who is one of the instructors here.

I glance at Randon now. He has a stupid grin on his face and I imagine he's already planning some gruesome way to get the heart of an animal. All the tasks are easy for him. He has no conscience.

"Go ahead then," Grand Master says, dismissing us.

Randon turns and walks briskly out of the study, seeming eager to get started. I'm not as fast and get stopped at the door.

"Rynn," Grand Master says.

"Yes, Your Leadership?"

"Come and have a seat. I wanted to tell you this in private."

I walk back into the study and sit down, my heart pounding.

"Randon isn't ready to hear of this yet. He believes he is my favorite student," Grand Master says. "And I admit that I do find his enthusiasm... commendable. But he is not Gifted and doesn't possess any real power, like you do."

I nod, not sure what to say.

"Our new army, the Ruling Order, will be all powerful. You and Randon will rule the galaxy together, but you will be the leader."

I sit completely still. Did he say I would be the leader? I'm two years younger than everyone else in the program. Grand Master has always believed in me, when no one else did and when even my brother Morlin was beginning to give up on me. But Master Dukath told me he'd foreseen it, that I would become great and powerful if I joined him in building up the new Ruling Order.

"You have your grandfather's strength and Gift within you," Grand Master continues. "I will help you use it and you will become the most feared and most powerful ruler in the galaxy."

My chest fills with pride and it's hard to breathe.

"Your brother has taught you well," Grand Master nods and I frown. Morlin only held me back, always telling me to repress my emotions. But Grand Master encourages me to embrace my anger and rage.

"What are his thoughts on your returning to summer training?" Grand Master asks.

I shift in my seat. "I didn't tell him."

"Good. He would only discourage you. When he returns to find that you are the true leader that you were always meant to be, he will be ashamed for holding you back."

I stifle a smile. I don't want to seem too eager for praise, which would be unfitting for a future Master. But I'm still too young to be a leader, aren't I?

"I have high hopes for you my boy," Grand Master continues. "You will become a powerful, Dark Master."

"I will?"

"All in good time." Grand Master nods slowly, his eyes never leaving me. "Stay focused on your daily tasks. You must find your darkest emotions to truly become a Master, and I believe you will."

"Thank you, Your Leadership." I bow slightly then step back.

"And Rynn?"

"Yes, Your Leadership?"

"Tonight you are not permitted to sleep."

My chest deflates. "Am I being punished?"

"For asking me that, you will be, once I think of a suitable punishment."

My shoulders slump. I've said the wrong thing again.

"It's not a punishment, but to help you master your body and have greater self-control. In battle you don't sleep, for days, or even weeks at a time, not until there is victory. One night should be simple enough, even for you."

I nod. It's anything but simple, especially with how I feel the day after I get no sleep. For some reason Randon never has to do any of the self-mastery disciplines like staying up all night. Maybe Grand Master thinks he's already good at self-discipline. But I know there's nothing further from the truth. Randon lies and cheats and has no control over his temper or anything else that has to do with his emotions, or desires. I shiver at the last thought.

"Very well then, go on." Grand Master dismisses me with a small wave of his hand and I get up immediately. My head is still spinning with all that he's told me. Randon won't like it.

Now I have to go get the heart of a forest animal. I can't disappoint Grand Master. He's the only one who's ever believed in me.

THE LITTLE GIRL IN THE FOREST

I LOOK OVER MY shoulder to the school building in the distance. From here it simply looks like a pile of ancient ruins, abandoned at the end of an open field. The forest is dark and unforgiving, even in the daytime. Cool air wafts out from the dense trees which form a wall where the field ends and the forest begins.

I step over the thick roots of the old trees, heading into the forest. Above me the white clouds are obscured by gnarled branches and leaves. For a moment I wish I could fly—away from the daily tests and from Randon, and from Aurah the only girl on our summer training team.

She leans over the lunch table in front of me so I'll notice her breasts. I try not to look but I always do and I hate that it works every time. I'm not supposed to like girls or think about those kinds of things. Master Dukath says those things are for the weak and undisciplined, that Dark Masters don't allow such things into their minds or lives to distract them.

The wind rustles the leaves and I shiver. I came out here to find an animal but they all seem to be hiding, like they know I want their hearts.

"I can do all things through the Gift which strengthens me." I whisper the mantra my brother taught me as I walk through the trees. I can't tell if it actually helps to use the mantras but it's become a habit now.

A sound catches my attention and I stop walking to listen. It's coming from my left and sounds like a child crying. I head in that direction and see a little girl through the trees. She's kneeling in the dirt, mud on her light colored clothes. She's the same girl Radon made cry yesterday. She's holding something in her hands.

The leaves crunch beneath my boots and she looks over to me, her eyes wide and full of tears. I'm not supposed to talk to anyone outside of our summer training group, not even my mom over the comm unit. Not until the training is over. But I can't help but be curious about what the girl is holding. I'll just add this to the list of everything else I'm going to be in trouble for anyway.

"She fell out of her nest," the little girl says. Her voice has a high child-like pitch that I'm not used to hearing. I never had younger siblings, and I was taken out of regular schooling, early on.

"Can I see?" I ask.

She gets up and walks over to me. I step back, thinking she might accidentally touch me. I'm not allowed to touch anyone. When I do, Master Dukath seems to know instantly and I get punished for it. He says it will spoil my training and I'm to have no physical contact with others.

But he never seems to notice when Randon pushes me or hits me. That's also contact. But Randon is Grand Master's favorite student, or at least I thought he was, until today.

Am I really his favorite? He said I'd be a Dark Master someday and the leader of his new army, the Ruling Order.

"She's still alive!" The little girl holds up her hands to me and I see a tiny baby bird. I pick it up, careful not to touch her fingers as I do. The baby bird's tiny heartbeat flutters in my palm.

"My name's Rita-Rue," the girl says. "My grandfather calls me Rue. He lives here. I'm staying with him."

I watch the bird struggle in my hand and don't respond.

"How old are you?" the little girl asks.

"Fifteen."

"I'm five." Rue holds up her palm and spreads out five chubby fingers to show me the number.

"Oh, I thought you were like... three."

"I'm not three!" she yells. Her high pitched squeal makes me jump. I step back.

"I'm not supposed to be talking to you," I say, wrapping my fingers around the baby bird. I have what I came for and I should head back, before someone finds me talking to this five year old.

"I'm turning six soon you know," she says, clasping her hands behind her back and standing up on her toes. I nod and start to walk away.

"Wait!" she runs after me and grabs my cloak. "We have to put the baby bird back in its nest." She points up into the tree. I look up too, but I don't see the nest.

"I'm taking the bird," I say. There's no point in letting her think I would ever be her friend.

"Why?" she demands, putting her hands on her hips.

I frown. Usually kids are scared of me, like they can sense that I'm dangerous, but Rue is different.

"Because I have to take my Master the heart of a forest animal."

I look down at her round, little face, expecting her eyes to go wide with fear at what I've said. But she only nods, as though this is logical.

"Okay," she says. "The baby bird has a heart inside. You can take her to your Master." She crosses her arms. "But you have to bring her back when you're done and climb in the tree and put her back with her brothers and sisters after!" She purses her lips and tears fill her eyes. "You have to promise or give her back to me right now!"

"I promise," I say.

"Okay. But she'll miss her brothers and sisters. She'll be scared."

"She won't be scared. She's resting, see." I open my palm to show her the bird, then quickly close it again. "My hand is like a nest. She likes it."

Rue nods and wipes her eyes. "Okay. I have to go back to grandfather, but can I come play with you after lunch?"

"No," I say.

Rue's face turns red and my chest tightens. Is she going to cry or scream? I've never met anyone so emotional. Maybe if I lie to her she'll go away.

"I'll come find you after I put the baby bird back and then we can... play."

She smiles. "Okay. What's your name?"

I almost say Bryn, but stop myself. "It's Rynn."

Rynn's the new name I was given when I started training with Grand Master. And now everyone calls me Rynn. I just forget sometimes.

"Bye, Rynn." Rue runs off through the trees, like a little bird herself, her light frame moving fast. I'm tall and lanky and not a very good runner. I watch her go, wondering if she actually knows the way out of the forest, or if she'll just get lost deeper in it.

Should I follow her? The forest is scary at night and lots of people have seen the spirits of the dead Masters roaming about. They say if you look them in the eyes, you'll die.

I open my palm and look down at the baby bird, Rue's words still running through my mind. *She'll miss her brothers and sisters.* The bird's tiny heart still beats. I want it to live and I want to return it to the nest, like I said I would. But I won't.

I sigh, closing my hand again, then hurry back to the school.

Failure

I WALK INTO MASTER Dukath's study and Randon is already there. We're the only two who are part of the personal training with the Master. The other kids that are in the summer training for future commanders and leaders of the Ruling Order don't do the daily tests that we do.

I stop at the door, wondering if I should just wait until Randon leaves. I hate him. He always says something to make me look bad in front of Master Dukath, and sometimes he even makes stuff up. Then I sound stupid when I say it's not true, like I'm the one who's lying and trying to cover it up.

"Rynn," Grand Master says from inside the study.

I freeze.

"I know you're out there. Come and join us."

I step inside, the baby bird sweating in my hand now. Randon glances at me when I walk in. He has a stupid smirk on his face and his hands are all red with blood. He looks me up and down.

"Nothing to show for yourself, *Rynn?*" he says. "As usual?"

I ignore him and walk to Master Dukath's large wooden desk and set the bird down. It moves but has lost most of its energy, like a fish running out of air.

Master Dukath looks down at the sad, little creature and I can tell he's disappointed. I hold my breath.

"I asked for the heart, my dear boy, not the entire animal."

I don't answer and Grand Master looks up at me.

"You know all of these... creatures, are for our use, do you not?" he says. "They exist to help further a greater purpose, our purposes. Today it is for the purpose of your training, that this bird will be killed." He studies me a moment. "Do you feel sorry for the bird, Rynn?" he asks.

"No, Master."

"Then perhaps Randon could bring us a knife?"

My shoulders stiffen but I don't say anything. The bird moves again, trying to get up from its side but unable to. I close my eyes, angry at the little girl in the forest for making me promise to take it back. It just makes this harder. I'll tell her tomorrow that I killed it, and I'll make her cry, like Randon did. Then she'll leave me alone and not ask me to play with her anymore.

I hear Randon's hurried footsteps approaching from the hall and I open my eyes. How did he find a knife so quick? He's breathing fast when he walks in. Did he run? There's an evil grin on his face that makes my stomach tighten. He holds out a large kitchen knife to me. I take it and look at Master Dukath. He nods for me to continue.

"Don't be afraid," he says, putting his palms out. "Go ahead. The bird may be innocent, but sometimes we have to kill the innocent, to show those in power that we are serious and will use any means to achieve our goal. You will not be able to save the lives of many, if you cannot end the lives of a few. Go on. The bird's sacrifice is your growth in the powers of the Gift."

He's right. It's just a stupid, little bird. I clutch the knife handle, turning it in my hand. The bird is still alive. Why couldn't it have just died already, like a fish?

Suddenly Randon grabs the knife out of my hand and slams the blade down over the baby bird's neck.

"You lose," he whispers to me, then reaches in front of me for the bird. I turn away, unable to watch. I know what I should do. I should push Randon away and do it myself and get the heart, but I can't. I've failed again.

"You've failed again," Master Dukath says, echoing my thoughts.

I turn to face him. "And for that I know I will be punished," I say. It's the response I'm supposed to give if Grand Master says I've failed. I used to try and give explanations as to why I failed, but it doesn't matter. I know Grand Master approves more of this simple response, than anything else I'd have to say.

"For your punishment, you will stay out in the forest for the entire night. You must not sleep or even sit down, but wander deep into the forest and think about all the life around you, the life that is there to serve you, to serve all of us, feeding us and giving us air. We do not serve the creatures and plants, they serve us."

"Yes, Master," I say.

"You may both leave now."

Randon and I bow then walk out. I brace myself for Randon's ridicule, once we're in the hall. But he doesn't say anything and hurries ahead of me instead.

I frown. He's either in a really good mood or has something bad planned for me later.

I look down at my cloak. There are spots of blood on it from the bird. I don't care what Randon says. I haven't lost. I won't lose my chance at being a leader in the Ruling Order. I don't want to give him the satisfaction of taking that from me.

RANDON

T HE FULL MOONS SHINE through the trees of the forest, casting ghostly shadows all around. My breath puffs out into the cold air and I pull my hood over my head to keep the chill away. I've spent the night roaming the forest before, as punishment. The first time was the worst and I had nightmares for days. But I never saw any ghosts, although I thought I heard them, and now I think I hear them again.

"I can do all things through the Gift, which strengthens me," I whisper. My words get lost in a gust of wind. A tree branch moves like the arms of a giant, with gnarly fingers silhouetted against the starry sky. I walk faster, heading for a clearing up ahead.

The snap of a branch behind me makes me stop. I turn, my adrenaline pumping. Visions of ghostly Masters with dark hoods and no faces invade my thoughts. But it's too dark in the trees to see anything.

Probably just a forest animal. I pull my hood lower over my head and keep going.

My boots crunch the leaves and branches as I hurry to the forest's edge. The tall trees sway wildly overhead and the wind lifts the leaves up around my feet.

Another branch snaps and I stop to listen.

Suddenly, a dark shape jumps out at me and I scream, falling to the ground. Two hands hold me down and I know by his familiar grasp that it's Randon. The roots of an old tree stab at my side, sending pain shooting up my back.

"Get off of me!" I yell, but my voice is drowned out in a rush of wind. Randon pins my legs down with his bony knees and his hands push on my wrists, making my fingers numb. My heart won't calm down, from the startle of his attack. "You're not supposed to touch me," I say.

"No, *you're* not supposed to touch anyone," he replies, sounding out of breath. "Because Master thinks you're so special. But you're not. And I can do whatever I want."

"Get off!"

Randon leans in close and I turn my head to the side. "I'm the only one that's ever going to want to come anywhere near you," he growls. "Even Aurah would never lay with you."

"I don't even want her to," I say, trying to push Randon off, but he's strong and two years older than me. My heart pounds wildly. I'm not allowed to use my Gift powers or I'll be expelled from the program. The tree roots dig further into my side and I clench my jaw.

"We need each other, Rynn," Randon says, his face close to mine.

I hold my breath, my stomach twisting. "I don't need you. I'm going to be like the Grand Masters who don't need anyone."

"Who said you could ever be a Grand Master?"

"Nobody," I say quickly.

"Well, you'll never be one. You're too much of a coward."

"Why don't you lay with Aurah?" I say. "She'll let you lay with her."

"She'll let anyone lay with her. I don't want Aurah. I'll get thrown out for unclean acts."

I stop struggling and give in, looking out past the trees at the stars in the distance. One day I'll be all powerful and I'll have armies and weapons and battle starships at my command. But for now I have to deal with Randon.

"Why won't you just leave me alone?" I say, defeated. "I failed another test. Isn't that good enough for you? You're passing them all."

Randon seems to consider this for a moment. "You'll never make it through the training course," he snarls, climbing off of me. "Have fun in the forest."

I sit up slowly, my back aching from the fall. Radon is already gone into the dark woods and I'm alone again, my body suddenly cold from his absence.

* * *

"What happened to you?" Aurah asks as I walk by her table in the dining hall. I try not to limp. I don't want to look even more pathetic than I already feel, for being sent out into the forest for the night. Randon's jump attack made me twist my ankle on some tree roots in the ground and now I'm hobbling when I walk.

I ignore Aurah and keep going.

After Randon's assault last night I walked as deep into the forest as I could, not caring about the ghosts anymore. I dared them to come and destroy me. I wouldn't have resisted. Randon's words got to me. I no longer felt sure I'd make it through the training, let alone become a Grand Master someday.

Early in the morning I reached the wide river and considered jumping into it, but the water wasn't deep enough for me to drown in so I came back here instead. Now I'm running late reporting back to Master Dukath and don't have time for breakfast.

"Where are you going?" Aurah calls after me. "Come and have breakfast with me."

I keep going to the next building, connected to the dining hall by a wide archway, leading to Master's study. The sun shines through the long windows, so bright that I feel like I'm walking in a dream, my mind hazy from lack of sleep.

Master Dukath isn't in his study when I get there.

I frown. I'll be in trouble when he returns, for being late. But at least I completed my punishment this time. I'll just have to wait here until he comes back.

There's a movement near the door and I stand up straighter, thinking it's Master Dukath. I look and see the little blond girl, Rue. She's got her hair in braids today and is wearing the same beige pants and a dust-colored shirt she had on yesterday, but now she has a towel hanging down her back, clasped at her neck. She stops when she sees me in the study.

"Did you fall out of the tree?" she asks, her eyes going wide.

"What tree?" I blink, squinting to see her. She's standing in front of the hallway windows with the sun shining so brightly behind her that it hurts to look at her.

"When you took the baby bird back," she says.

I quickly glance at the wooden desk, then let out a sigh of relief. It's cleaned of the bird's blood, and the bird is gone. I look back to Rue again. "If Master finds me talking to you I'll be in big trouble."

She nods then starts to walk away.

"Rue?" I say in a loud whisper.

"Yes?" she replies in an even louder whisper, looking back into the room.

"Why are you wearing a towel around your neck?"

She narrows her eyes at me in an angry glare. "It's my *cloak*," she growls, then stomps off loudly down the hall.

I hear new footsteps approaching and my heart speeds up. *Hurry Rue*. I can't afford any more mistakes. I'm starting to lose count of how many I will be punished for. What if Master Dukath regrets his decision to take me on as his personal apprentice? Randon says the only reason Grand Master tolerates me is because I have Gift abilities. But I know I can be a leader. I'm the youngest one here and everyone treats me like it. But when I'm older, it won't be that way.

Two elderly Masters walk by in the hall, their hoods hiding their faces. My shoulders relax when I see it's not Master Dukath. I'll have to stand here and wait for as long as it takes for him to return, if I can stay awake that long.

YOU SHOULD BE SCARED OF ME

I LIGHT A CANDLE and sit down on my bed. The smell of the sulfur and wax relaxes me. I stare at the flame. I used to miss the modern luxuries of home, but now I've gotten accustomed to the simple lifestyle of the Masters and I almost prefer it.

A breeze blows in through the partially open window, almost blowing out my candle. I look up at the picture of my mom on the dresser. I never did get a frame for it, but for some reason I brought it with me.

I close my eyes, feeling tired. Tonight I'm allowed to sleep, but I can't seem to. I thought I'd be so glad to finally get to bed, but every time I lay down I think of home and of Mom. I don't want to miss her. Her and Dad sent me away and now they expect me to come back on summer break, but I'm staying to do the leadership program. What's the point of going back? Just so they can look at me with pity when I lose control of my powers, then send me away again?

I get up and walk to my bookshelf to take down *The Book of The Masters*. Reading should help me fall asleep, or at least get my mind off of things.

There's a gentle knock on my door and my grip on the thick book tightens.

Please don't let it be Randon again.

I go to unlock the door. At least I won't be alone with my thoughts, even if it is Randon. I don't have the energy to hate anyone today. The hinges creak as I open the heavy, wooden door. At first I don't see anyone, then I look down at a head of blond hair.

"Hi," Rue says, tilting her head up and smiling. I frown.

"Where did you come from?"

"My home planet!" She sticks her chin up and gives me a defiant look.

I grin. "That's not very specific."

Rue seems to consider my words, but I can tell she doesn't understand. "Yes it is!" she finally replies. "My planet is *very* pacific."

"Shhh..." I kneel down to Rue's level. "You can't be here. I'll get in big trouble."

She shrugs, seeming unconcerned about me getting into trouble.

"Actually," I continue. "*You'll* get in big trouble."

Rue crosses her arms and still doesn't move.

"Rue," I give her my most serious look. "I'm training to be an evil Master. I do evil things, things you don't know about. I've always done evil things, like hurt people when I'm mad, even when I was only two years old. You should be scared of me."

Rue gives me a curious look but doesn't respond.

I frown. "I could hurt you," I say. "Or kill you by accident."

Rue uncrosses her arms and her hand comes up and smacks my cheek.

I blink in surprise.

Did she just slap me? Her tiny palm stays against my face.

I take her hand away.

"You can't touch me or you'll get into trouble."

Rue shrugs and I realize she doesn't care about getting into trouble.

"If you touch me you'll get really sick and die," I say.

Her eyes go wide and she shoves her palm in my face again. "Is that why you have the red spots on your face? Because you're sick? And you're going to die?"

"No!" I take her hand away again. "Don't touch my face, or my cloak, or my hands. And don't come to my roo—"

Rue squishes my nose with her palm.

"What about your nose? Can I touch your nose?"

"No." I push her hand away again. "I told you, I can be very mean, and scary."

"You're not scary."

"Yes, I am."

"No, you're not."

"If I get mad, I could kill you."

"No you won't."

"How do you know?"

Rue tilts her head to the side, as thought studying me. "Because I know. Mom says it's my gift. I can tell when people are nice inside or if they are evil inside."

I stare at her for a moment. A sound in the hall makes my heart speed up.

"You have to go now."

"Can I stay here? I'm scared in my room."

"No."

"But I can't sleep."

"Then stay awake, but do it in your own room."

"I want to stay here. I don't want to be alone."

"No Rue."

"Please?"

"It's against the rules."

"Everything is against the rules!" Rue yells.

"Shhh..." I grab her by the shoulders, then quickly let go. She's already made me break my vows.

"You're right," I say. "There are a lot of rules here."

"Why?"

A shadow moves in the torchlight down the hall. Someone is approaching. I hesitate a moment then quickly pull Rue into the room. I turn the handle all the way so it doesn't make a click sound when I push the door closed, then I slowly release the handle.

"If you get me into trouble I'll..." I turn to find Rue pulling out my grandfather's sword from under my bed. "Don't touch that!"

Rue jumps back, letting it go.

"It's mine!" I yell. "You can't just grab my stuff. It isn't yours!"

I push the sword back under the bed. Rue backs away from me until she hits the wall, then covers her face with her hands. I'm still on my knees, having tucked the staff safely back under my bed, and I wait to see what she'll do next. She crouches down and hugs her knees, then she begins to sob.

I groan. "I told you I would hurt you," I say, feeling bad but not wanting her to know that. "Just go back to your room."

"I'm sorry I touched your toy," she says, her voice muffled in her knees.

"It's not a toy."

She keeps crying and I suddenly feel very tired. "Please just go. I want to sleep."

"I want to sleep too," Rue says lifting her head. Her face is streaked with tears. "I can't sleep in my room, it's dark and scary and cold and I can't light the candles by myself." Her bottom lip quivers.

"Why do you cry so much?" I say, trying to sound angry so she won't feel sorry for herself.

"I don't know," she says, crying even more, only now she isn't covering her face and seeing her cry makes me feel like crying. I go over to her and sit down beside her, leaning back against the wall.

"Just... stop crying, okay?" I say.

She takes a few deep breaths and looks at me.

"I just cry at night time, because I always think of my mom and dad." She hiccups, then continues. "In the daytime I forget about home. I can look at the plants and bugs, and play with Mr. Rock... Oh no!" She screams her last words and I jump away from her in surprise. "Mr. Rock! I have to get Mr. Rock! He's going to be so scared! I forgot Mr. Rock!"

"Shhh..." I put my hand over her mouth to stop her from yelling but my palm covers her entire face and she freezes in surprise. I take my hand away and wipe the tears on my palm onto my cloak.

"We have to go get—"

I cover her face again. "Can you stop yelling?" I whisper.

She giggles against my palm and I pull my hand away.

She takes two breaths then yells, "we have to get Mr.—"

I cover her face, but I know that she wants me to this time.

She laughs behind my palm.

"Let's stop yelling and be serious about Mr. Rock. Okay?"

"Okay," she mumbles behind my palm.

I let go slowly. "You should go back to your room and find him," I start to say, but Rue isn't paying attention. She grabs my hand and pushes my palm to her face again, puffing up her cheeks and blowing hard so it makes a funny sound.

She giggles and I pull my hand away, getting up.

"Wait!" Rue grabs the front of my cloak, putting all her weight into pulling me down again. I land on my knees and she throws her skinny little arms around my neck, hugging me tight, her strength surprising me.

"Please can come get Mr. Rock? please, please—"

I try to peel her off of me, but she won't release her death grip on my neck.

"You can go back to you room and—"

"No, it's too scary! You have to come with me!"

"If I say yes, will you let go of me?" I ask.

Rue quickly releases me and runs to the door. "I'll show you the way. I know all the places in the school and I even drew a map. Oh, I'll show you my map! It's in my room, too."

"I'll walk you back to your room and you can be with Mr. Rock, okay?"

"And then will you stay, too?"

I hesitate. I should just tell her yes, even if I don't plan on staying, so she won't start whining again.

"Yes," I say.

Rue's face lights up. "Okay! Let's go!"

GOODNIGHT LITTLE RUE

RUE PULLS HER COVERS off her bed and lets them fall to the dusty stone floor.

"Mr. Rock, Mr. Rock.! Where are you?"

I close her door and look around the room. It's small. There's a tiny bed and a bedside table. That's all. No bookshelf or books or toys.

A lone candle sits on the window sill, bathed in moonlight. I glance around for something to light it with but don't see anything. She'll just have to make do without candlelight, the way she's done yesterday and all the other days she's been here.

"Rue, I'm leaving now," I say, my tiredness coming back with a vengeance.

"Wait! I'll find him," she says, continuing her search.

I turn to leave.

"Found him!" Rue yells.

"Okay. Have a good night." I reach for the door handle and Rue scrambles off her bed to stop me. She trips herself up in the bedsheets and lands on the stone floor. The thump of her head on stone makes me cringe.

There's a moment of silence and I hold my breath. Then a tiny, high pitched sound escapes her and I tense in preparation for the load wailing that is sure to follow any second now.

I hurry over and lift her up into my arms. She's lighter than my folded cloak. I sit down on the bed. "Are you okay?"

She shakes her head no.

"Did you hit your head?"

She shakes her head yes.

"Can I see?"

Rue stops crying. Her breath is staggered as she lowers her hands from her head. Even in the moonlight I can see the bump that is forming there. She's breathing deeply now and her eyelids look heavy. She tries not to close them but they keep slipping down.

My shoulders relax. She'll fall asleep soon.

"It doesn't look that bad. You'll be fine," I say softly.

She starts to say something in reply but her words drift off and her head starts to nod. She falls limp to one side and I grab her before she topples onto the floor. Her head lands heavy on my chest and I hear something clatter to the floor.

It's her rock. It rolls to the middle of the room then spins to a stop in a beam of moonlight.

I pull Rue's knees up to keep her from sliding off. She breathes softly against my shirt and I close my eyes, listening to her gentle breathing sounds. It's so peaceful that I begin to nod off too.

I shake myself awake. I need to put Rue to bed and get back to my room.

Her bed sheets are thrown aside from when she was searching for Mr. Rock. I lay her down gently and pull the blankets up. She mumbles something and curls into a ball.

I step on something hard and look down. It's the rock. I pick it up and set it in her small hand, then wrap her fingers around it.

"Goodnight, little Rue," I whisper, tucking her in tight, the way my mom used to do for me. Then I turn and leave, locking the door behind me.

In Your Mind

"You've touched someone," Grand Master says.

I stop, in mid bite of my bread. Aurah gives me a funny look and Randon stares down at his plate, his brow furrowing.

The morning frenzy in the breakfast hall suddenly becomes still as everyone pretends not to listen. I swallow my last bite of bread. It goes down hard and I resist the temptation to take a drink from my glass. Grand Master has never come to our table before and I'm not sure what to do. I must be in big trouble.

Does he know about Rue? I can't bring myself to look at him. What if he used his powers to look into my thoughts? Usually I can tell when he's doing that, but right now I'm not sure of anything.

He must sense the shift in me. I felt different when I woke up this morning, like I was looking forward to the day. That short time I spent with Rue made me feel less lonely. Though I'm always around other students here, I still feel lonely all the time.

I should have known Master Dukath would notice a change in me. But I can't let him know that I let Rue get close to me, if he doesn't already know. She'll get sent away to who knows where, and I'll get another punishment. If I have to wander the forest all night again, alone, I might just jump off a cliff.

I glance over at Randon, who is also avoiding eye contact with Grand Master. He looks worried.

Of course! Randon jumped on me the other day, no wonder he's worried.

"It was Randon," I say, clearing my throat.

Aurah lifts an eyebrow, as though this information is very curious, but I ignore her.

"In the forest," I continue. "The night before. He followed me and... attacked me."

Grand Master studies me for a moment, and I hold my breath. If he reads my mind now then he'll know I'm not telling him the whole truth. But it's not technically a lie.

"And did that make you angry?" he asks me.

I glance around at the curious faces all turned towards me in the dining hall. Is Master really going to question me here, in front of everyone?

"Yes, it made me angry," I say. But it's not the truth. It didn't really make me angry that time, not the way it usually does. I felt more resolved to my fate, than mad.

"Did you fight back?" Master Dukath asks.

Aurah looks between me and Randon.

"No, Your Leadership," I say.

"I'd like to see you both in my study, after breakfast."

"Yes, Your Leadership," Randon and I both respond.

Grand Master stands there for a moment, then walks away. There is a collective sigh of relief around the table.

"Wow," Aurah says, biting into her bread. "I didn't realize you two were *together*."

"Shut up!" Randon stands abruptly, his chair scraping loudly across the floor. Then he storms off.

Aurah turns to me and I look away. I don't want to talk about the forest, or Rue, or Randon. I push my plate aside, no longer hungry. Grand Master is going to give us another test this morning, and it will probably be something neither of us is going to like, now that we're in trouble.

* * *

"What?" Randon snaps. He's not his usual, composed self around Grand Master today.

Master's eyebrows raise slightly at the outburst. "Is there a problem with my request?"

Randon glowers and shakes his head. "No, Your Leadership."

"Then go ahead, Bryn," he says to me.

I turn to Randon, who looks like he wants to kill me. He's definitely going to beat me up for this later. I take a deep breath and place my hand on his forehead.

"No, Rynn," Grand Master says and I quickly pull my hand away. "You can read his mind without touching him. I've been very clear about physical content being prohibited. Reach out your hand and concentrate."

I nod and step back, glad that I don't have to touch Randon.

I hold up my hand towards Randon. He still looks mad but I see something else in his blue eyes, something that looks a bit like worry. Is he worried I'll see something he doesn't want me to see?

It doesn't matter, I don't have a choice.

I close my eyes and focus. I'm not exactly sure how mind reading works, it just sort of does. No one's trained me on it so I never use it. With Dad it just happens and he always initiates it. Morlin didn't think it was proper use of Gift powers, so he never taught me.

I push aside my uncertainty. I'm under Grand Master's teaching now and he's asked me to do it. I have to try.

I start with Randon's surface thoughts. There's a layer of emotions, but they're not actual thoughts. It's strange to feel someone else's emotions, familiar to my own, but so different. The anger is first and foremost, a feeling of injustice that he has to let me do this to him. Beneath that is the worry I saw in his expression. Or maybe it's embarrassment. I realize I don't know what certain emotions feel like for other people.

I have to push past these emotions to reach the images and words in his head.

I reach further and Randon resists. He's repeating a mantra so I only hear that.

I stop, not wanting to persist because it's hard, and if I'm honest, I'm scared of what I might find.

"He's resisting," I say quietly.

"As he should," Grand Master says. "Try harder."

I sigh heavily. My palms are sweating and I just want to go drink some water. I have to get this over with.

I try again. Randon's anger has subsided and has been replaced by a new found confidence in my inability to read him. I catch a thought. He thinks his resistance is stronger than my abilities, that I'll fail another test once again. But his confidence has made him less careful, and I break through. He's definitely scared I'll see something he's hiding.

"If he is hiding something he doesn't want you to see," Grand Master says, breaking my concentration, "then it will be the most prominent thing on his mind."

Easy for him to say. I focus harder, curious now about what it could be.

Then I see it.

Randon doesn't want me to see how he feels about me.

I let go of my hold on his mind. It's not hate that he feels so strongly, as I expected, but something else. An emotion I didn't think he allows himself to admit.

I drop my hand and open my eyes. Randon's brow is furrowed in a look of anger but I know it's actually embarrassment. I know I violated his privacy.

Our eyes meet for a second and I don't need to read his mind to know that he knows I've discovered his secret.

"Well then?" Grand Master says, bringing me back to reality.

Except now, reality has changed. I know something I was never meant to know. It should have been Randon's choice to tell me, if he ever wanted to, which I'm quite sure he never would.

"What did you see?" Grand Master insists.

"Pardon?"

"You must tell your victim what you saw, so they know you were successfully in reading their thoughts," Grand Master says. "Then it will break down their confidence."

I glance at Randon, who is now red in the face.

"I saw anger," I say. "Randon is mad that I'm allowed to read his mind."

"What else?"

I hesitate.

Randon gives me a look I can't decipher. His lips are pressed together and he has nothing to say for once. He shakes his head slightly, as though telling me not to share his secret.

"I... I couldn't read him very well," I lie. "He was resisting too much."

Grand Master sighs, leaning back in his chair. "How disappointing."

Randon's shoulders relax but his face is still red.

Master Dukath watches Randon for a moment then smiles.

"Now, as for today's test. You will practice mind reading," he says, looking to me. "Then you will return tonight and try to read my mind. I want to see how far you can reach, even if you will not be able to accomplish reading my thoughts. I will know how much energy it requires to resist you, be it a little, or a lot."

"Yes, Your Leadership," I say. My pulse races at the thought of practicing my mind reading powers. This is the first time I've gotten permission to use my Gift since classes started this summer.

"What about me?" Randon asks, then quickly adds, "Your Leadership." He bows slightly. "What's my test?"

"To do the same thing."

Randon frowns but doesn't challenge the command.

"Go and find out the secrets of others and bring the information to me," Grand Master continues. "You do not have to read minds to do that. You only need patience and observance."

"Yes, Your Leadership." Randon bows, then gives me a death glare before walking out, not waiting to be excused.

My stomach drops. He's going to try and find out something about me, I just know it, because I found out something private about him. I'm still disoriented by this unexpected discovery. He doesn't hate me the way I thought, but he hates the fact that he feels quite the opposite.

Target Practice

I RAISE MY BLASTER and shoot at the target near the wall of trees up ahead. The blaster ray misses the target and hits a tree.

Aurah laughs and my grip tightens on the blaster.

I shoot again. This time I hit the target. But that's only one out of four. Aurah hit all of her targets.

I step away from the start line and look at Commander Klein. He writes something on his clip board.

Aurah and I hand our blasters to the next two students in line, then take a seat at the on the long bench behind them. Randon is up next, after the two that are shooting. I stay as far from him on the bench as possible.

He's a lot less energetic than he usually is at target practice. He's very good at it, better than me. Maybe he'll finally stop harassing me now, because he's embarrassed about the mind reading thing.

He glances at me and I quickly look away.

It's his turn to go up.

"Aurah?" I say. "Can I read your mind?"

"Are you asking me if I think you can do it?" she says. "Or are you asking my permission?"

"Your permission." I watch Randon hit every target with hardly any effort at all.

"No," Aurah says. "And you're not allowed to use your powers, anyway."

I smile at her. "I am today."

Aurah shakes her head and sighs. "If you're going to read someone's mind at least don't ask them permission first. No one is going to say yes."

"But I have to be close to them to do it, and I think maybe they can feel it happening. At least if they agree, they'll resist less and it won't be so hard."

"You're probably supposed to try when it's hard."

Aurah watches Randon walk past us to take a seat at the end of the bench. "I wish I could do that," she says softly, her eyes still on Randon.

"You are. You hit every target."

"Reading minds."

"It's not as great you'd think," I say. "You find out stuff you didn't want to know."

"What really happened in the forest, with Randon?" Aura asks

I shift my position on the bench. Can *she* read minds?

"Nothing," I say, a bit too defensively. "Randon tried to scare me and jumped out at me."

"So then what are you hiding from Master Dukath?"

"What do you mean?"

"I don't have to be a mind reader to know you're hiding something. I've known you long enough that I can tell." Aurah smiles. "You've been different lately."

"How?"

"No talking!" Commander Klein says to us.

All heads turn our way and Randon gives us a glare.

He probably thinks we're talking about him.

* * *

The day's training exercises feel longer than usual. I'm surprised when I realize it's because I'd rather hang out with Rue, than be in classes all day. Something about her is peaceful and helps me get my mind off of my own problems. Being around her is like entering a different reality.

The last class of the day is equipment training, which is a lot of reading flight manuals and memorizing spacecraft layouts, since we won't go on an actual battle starship until the end of the course.

When General Dray finally dismisses the class, I notice that Randon lingers behind to talk to Aurah. I stop outside the door to listen.

"What did he say?" Randon asks her.

"Nothing," Aurah says, sounding irritated. "I asked him what he's hiding and then Commander Klein interrupted us."

"Can't you seduce him or something?"

"I thought he was like you—"

"He's not."

"Are you sure?"

"I would *know* if he was."

"Well then he's too self-disciplined to be seduced, apparently, like the great Masters."

"No, he's not," Randon scoffs. "He's just like the rest of the guys here."

"Except not as evil."

"Not yet. I'm sure Grand Master will help him with that."

"I'm not doing your dirty work for you. If you want to find out his secret then figure it out yourself."

Their voices come closer and I quickly move away from the door.

Suddenly Rue appears, standing at the end of the hall. She sees me and takes a deep breath as though to call to me. My flies up instantly and I put her in a hold with my Gift. I don't even have to try. The urgency makes the use of my powers instantaneous. I can't let Randon find out that I've broken the rules because of the girl.

Her eyes go wide with when she realizes she can't move. A rock falls from her hand and clatters to the stone floor.

Go to the Forest where the bird nest is and I'll meet you there, I say to her. I'm not sure why I even attempt it, since conversation only works between two Gifted people.

Rue's eyes are on me. Did she hear my thoughts?

I release her from the hold and she picks up her rock, then disappears around the corner just as Randon and Aurah come out of the classroom door.

"Bryn?" Randon says in an accusing tone. I turn, lowering my hand.

"Trying to read a child's mind?" Aurah asks.

Blasted, she saw me.

"No." I start to walk away but Aurah stops me.

"Wait." She grabs my arm.

"You can't touch me." I pull away.

Aurah frowns and lets go. She seems to regain her composure and gives me a sly smile. "Want to break the rules for once and come to my room?"

"No," I say, a little too sharply.

Aurah purses her lips and looks away.

"I would," I continue, "but the apprenticeship with Grand Master is really important to me and I don't want to mess it up."

"I guess I admire that," Aurah says.

"I admire the way you shoot a phaser blaster," I say, giving her a smile.

She laughs. "You'd better watch your back Bryn, I never miss."

I nod. She really is pretty when she smiles. I don't think she knows it though. Other than Rue, she's the only girl I've ever known who isn't scared of me. I've never had a girl ask me to her room before, so it's a compliment and I want her to know I appreciate that she finds me attractive enough to ask.

"Aura?"

"Yeah?"

I hesitate. I can't find the right words so I say, "call me Rynn. That's my new name."

Aurah rolls her eyes. "Alright, well go rip the head off a bird or whatever you guys do for Dukath," she says, dismissing me with a wave of her hand. She starts to walk away and I follow.

"You and Randon talk a lot, don't you?"

Aurah sighs. "Yeah, just talk, nothing more." She begins to walk faster. "I'll see you later, Bryn."

I stop.

"Bye." I wave, but she's already rounded the corner.

You're My Attachment

I RUB THE BACK of my neck, which is sweaty. I shouldn't have worn my cloak. The heat is slowing me down and even the shade between the trees doesn't help me cool off. At this rate, I'll miss supper, depending on how long I hang out with Rue.

Why did I tell her to meet me at the bird's tree in the forest? I could have picked someplace a lot closer to the school. But I couldn't think of any other place, in my rush to get rid of her. I don't have to go meet with her. I could just leave her out here waiting. And yet, I'm here.

My boots crunch the leaves on the ground. There's no wind and I can hear every sound in the forest. The leaves clapping together in the gentle breeze, the rustling of birds' wings. The buzz of insects. I look over my shoulder to make sure no one is following me.

Then I finally reach the place where I first met Rue, but she isn't here.

I look around. Did she decide not to come? Did she get lost?

She probably didn't get my communication to her. I'd never done it successfully with anyone other than my dad. But he doesn't use Gift powers, so I thought maybe it would work. But Rue isn't family, so we don't have any connection.

I sigh and head through an opening in the trees. "Rue?" I call out.

Why does she have to be so annoying? If she'd just leave me alone at the school then I wouldn't have to meet with her in private like this. She's going to get us both in trouble.

"Rue?" I call again. There's no response and I keep walking. Why should I even be concerned about her? She's just a kid and I'm a future Master. I'm never going to have kids, or a family.

I'll call one more time and if she doesn't respond I'll leave and go back for supper.

"Rynn!" Rue's high pitched voice sounds from somewhere far away. I head in that direction.

"Rynn... Rynn...!" She keeps calling. Then I see her running through the trees and I hold my breath. She's running too fast and she'll trip.

I run as well, to meet her half way. When I get closer, I see she's crying. She throws her arms me and buries her face in my cloak.

"I got lost," she mumbles. "I don't want to meet in the forest anymore."

"Okay." I pull her back and kneel down so I can give her a proper hug.

She sniffles. "The forest is scary."

"Yeah." A soft breeze blows over us. I rub Rue's back to comfort her, the way my mom used to when I was her age, and her heavy breathing slows.

"Now I can't play," she whimpers. "I have to go back for supper or I'll get in trouble."

She lets go of me and bows her head. She looks so sad that my chest physically hurts.

"I'll come and play with you after supper, okay?" I say, hoping to get rid of the heartbroken look on her face.

"That's what you said last time," she mumbles. "But you didn't come."

"I'll come this time."

She lifts her head. "Promise?"

I nod. "Yes. Now come on, let's walk back together before it gets too dark."

We walk in a companionable silence and Rue takes my hand. She holds only two of my fingers, her hand being too small to properly hold my hand. I help her keep her balance as we make our way over the tree roots on the uneven ground. Her grip is strong, crushing my fingers, but I don't mind.

We reach the edge of the forest where a large field of grass spreads out, before the school buildings on the other side. Rue lets me go and runs ahead.

I don't run after her. I can't return to the school with her, and be seen together. But now that the buildings are in view, I don't have to worry about her getting lost. I can keep an eye on her from a distance.

She stops and looks back, then spreads her arms out wide and falls into the tall grass, which is so tall that I don't see her anymore. I rush over to see what happened, and find her smiling up at me.

"What are you doing?"

"Sleeping in the grass."

I sit down beside her and look up at the clouds. Rue hums a tune and I close my eyes. I can't remember the last time I heard someone hum a tune, or sing.

"What are you singing?" I ask.

"A song my mom always sings. Want me to teach you?"

"No."

"When the sun shines in," Rue sings loudly. "Just lift up your chin. Frowners always lose, and smilers always win."

I laugh.

"What's funny?" Rue asks.

I open my eyes and find her looking at me with an angry pout on her face.

"Your song is funny."

"No it's not!"

I shrug.

"Why is it funny?" she demands.

"Because Dark Masters don't smile. And they always win."

"They smile." Rue sits up. "They have evil smiles, like this." She tries to give me an evil smile, tilting her chin down and looking up at me with a menacing glare.

I push her forehead playfully and she falls back onto the grass again.

"They smile!" She kicks my shoulder with her foot and I grab it. She squeals and tries to pull away, kicking and laughing when she can't get away. I lift her up by her ankle and she squeals even louder as I flip her upside down. She reaches her hands to the ground and does a hand stand.

"Look!" she shouts. "I did it!"

"Oh stars!" I set her back down.

"What?" Rue scrambles back into sitting position."

"I didn't do my test today and I have to go see Master after supper."

"What test?" Rue crosses her legs and looks at me wide eyed. "Is it hard?"

"Kind of. I'm supposed to practice reading someone's mind."

"Like a book?"

"No, like just hearing their thoughts."

"Oh. Is it loud?"

I look at Rue. "Can I try reading your mind?"

She pulls her knees up and hugs them. "Does it hurt?"

"Not if you don't resist."

"What does rees-is mean?"

"Just... if you try to stop me from doing it, then it might hurt more. But if you don't, then it's fine."

"Okay," Rue says, giving me a cautious look.

"Okay, what?"

"You can read my mind. I won't ress-is."

I shift my sitting position to face her, then hold out my hand near her head. She leans forward and lays her forehead into my palm like it's a pillow.

"Rue, you don't need to put your forehead on my hand. You can't..." I sigh. I'm always giving her rules and it's getting annoying. "Never mind. You ready?"

"Uh huh." She closes her eyes and scrunches up her face like she's about to get punched. I shift closer to her so she can lean her head against my shoulder, instead of my palm. Then I close my eyes and concentrate.

The first thing that hits me is how tired she is and I instantly want to make her comfortable, so she can rest.

I feel bad she's so tired. But she's also very alive and joyful.

I start with her surface feelings. She feels safe in my arms and content that I'm holding her. There's a lingering fear left over from being lost in the forest earlier. She doesn't resist the mind reading, so I search further, not having any trouble.

Her mind is unfocussed. She's thinking about Mr. Rock and how he's going to be lonely if she doesn't get back to her room soon. Her thoughts jump to her mom and dad. She feels abandoned by them.

I sense her greatest fear, that she'll never see them again, or that her mom will forget about her. She has bad dreams that they leave with Ungar, a big Ruleon alien who is a partner with her mom in her trading business. Her parents tell her Ungar is like her uncle, but he's not. Her images of him are scary and he makes her feel uncomfortable...

I pull my hand away, afraid of what else I might see.

"You love Mr. Rock a lot don't you?" I ask, trying to get her mind off of Ungar.

"Yes," she says softly.

"You shouldn't, because it's an attachment." She's unnaturally attached to that lifeless rock. If it goes missing one day it will break her heart.

"What's an attachment?"

"When you love something too much."

"Oh! Then you're my attachment."

"No."

Rue pauses, as though thinking about this a moment.

"Why shouldn't I love something very much?"

I look out across the tall grass to the fading sun. "Because, if you lose it you'll be too sad."

"But I want to keep Mr. Rock, forever."

I pull away from Rue. Supper is probably over by now. Her grandfather might be looking for her. But I don't want to go back just yet. I know that once I return to the Academy, I'll feel lonely again.

"Rue?"

She rests her head on my shoulder. She mumbles something in response.

"Why are you scared of Ungar?"

I hold my breath, waiting for her response. I don't know why I'm asking, but I'm worried about her returning to her planet. I don't think I really want to know the answer.

"He yells at me and makes me clean robot parts, in green water that makes my hands turn red and it hurts. And he..." Rue trails off.

"And he what?"

"I can't say."

My heart clenches. I move her hair away from her face and tuck it behind her ear.

Her cheeks are pink and there's a frown on her face. I lift my cloak off of her, worried that I might be overheating her.

I glance into her thoughts again.

I've made her sad by talking about Ungar and her parents. And she's thinking about night time coming and how she'll be alone in her room. She really is attached to me, which is surprising since we hardly know each other. Her child-like trust is humbling. But she also thinks she's not important enough for an older kid like me to go play with her. She sees me as some kind of hero.

I let go of her thoughts. "I really am going to come to your room tonight and play," I say. "With Mr. Rock, too."

Rue jumps up with an unexpected burst of energy and throws her arms around my neck.

"Okay!" She lets go and looks at me with her big hazel eyes. "Are you telling the truth this time?"

"Yes." I smile. "I have to go see my Master first, but then I'll come after."

"Okay." She pushes her palm to my forehead. "I can read your mind, too."

"You can? What am I thinking?"

"You are thinking..." she looks up and taps her chin with a finger. "That you will bring me a piece of chocolate square dessert when you come to my room, so I can eat it."

I take her hand and hold it. "You read my mind."

A MASTER IS NEVER SORRY

MY CLOAK WEIGHS HEAVY in my arms as I head to Master's office. The pockets are full of the rocks I got from the river, as a surprise for Rue. There's no time now to take them back to my room first.

"You're late," Master says as I step in front of his desk.

"And for that I know..." I start to say then stop.

I really don't want get punished again.

"And for that I know I should be sorry," I say instead.

Master's expression turns dark. "Sit down," he growls.

I quickly take a seat.

"I've told you before. A Master is *never* sorry." He eyes me with a suspicious look. "I don't have time for your lack of discipline today. Randon has brought something important to my attention, information I need to attend to."

My heart speeds up and I don't reply. Could he be talking about Rue?

"Tell me, Rynn," Master continues, leaning forward and interlacing his fingers on the large wooden desk. "Did you practice reading minds today?"

"Yes, Your Leadership."

"With whom?"

"Aurah," I say quickly.

"And, whom else?"

"Randon," I lie.

Master frowns and my muscles tense. A breeze enters the room from the hallway, rustling some papers on the desk. I wait as Master leans back in his chair.

"Tomorrow, I want you to try with someone outside of your friends." He slaps a large hand onto the table. "Now let's get on with it. I want to see how well you can force your way into my mind."

I sit up straighter in my chair. Should I actually try my hardest? Or just a little? The thought of seeing into Grand Master's mind is terrifying. But he's waiting, so I raise my hand to him.

I'll start with his surface level feelings, those are usually safe enough.

I close my eyes. A sick feeling crawls over me when I realize there are no surface feelings.

I try again. Maybe I just haven't found them yet. Grand Master can't be emotionless. And yet, I see nothing but a dark and empty void. I want to pull away now, but I know I haven't tried hard enough, to be convincing. I push a bit further, but all I find is more darkness and emptiness, as though he has no soul.

"You never did read Aurah's mind, did you?" Grand Master says.

I try to pull away, but can't. He's reading *my* thoughts, now that we're connected. Of course, for someone who is Gifted, the communication goes both ways. He tricked me.

I quickly think of Randon attacking me in the forest, and how uncomfortable he makes me feel when he's holding me down, or when he talks too close to my face. Grand Master won't want to see those thoughts for too long.

He releases my mind and I fall back into my seat. He knew I'd never be able to see into his thoughts, but it gave him access to mine. But I also tricked him, by showing him something he wouldn't like.

"I'll have a talk with Randon," Master says, slowly getting up. "That will be all for today."

I get up too. "Yes, Your Leadership."

"Tomorrow there will be no tests. I have some business I need to take care of." He moves slowly around his desk, like an old man. But his sluggish movements don't fool me. I know he's so much more powerful than he looks.

"Keep using your mind reading powers. You need to learn how to influence people to do your will, especially Randon. Make him stop when you want him to stop. I give you permission to use your Gift powers on him. Only, keep Randon alive. He's got potential."

"Yes, Your Leadership."

Master glances at me, as though trying to decide something. "Go now and take your rest. You will need it."

I nod and hurry out of the room.

* * *

By the time I reach the dining hall, all the food is put away, even the baskets of fruit which are usually left out all day for anyone to eat.

I walk to the kitchen area where the cooks spend most of their day. It is now abandoned and dark. My stomach growls. Rue must have missed supper too. Is she waiting for me in her room?

The lingering light of dusk outside the windows helps me see my way around the kitchen. I grab a slice of animal cheese and a bag of star grapes for myself, then look for chocolate squares for Rue. All I can find is baker's chocolate. She won't like that, it's too bitter.

I look in the Cold Room for milk. I could make Rue a hot drink, with the baker's chocolate and a sweetener, the way my mom used to make for me. I search the kitchen, looking for the pans. Then I finally spot them, hanging over the large wood burning stove, which still radiates heat when I go near it.

I set the food and milk down on a countertop and open the stove door to look inside. The black coals breathe red from the rush of air. I just need to throw some small pieces of wood on it to get it burning again.

I throw in an armload of kindling, then grab a pot for the milk. It seems to take forever before the milky froth finally rises up the sides of the pot. I throw in the chunks of chocolate and stir. The comforting smell of warm milk makes me smile. I put in more and more chunks of chocolate. Maybe I'll make myself a mug too, there's enough milk in the pot for two.

By the time I reach Rue's room it's already past bedtime. Her door is slightly ajar and I push it open with my foot, my arms full.

I look inside. She isn't there.

My stomach tightens. Did she get tired of waiting for me and go to *my* room? Or maybe she's just at the washroom down the hall.

I don't want to be seen waiting outside her door. It wouldn't take me long to get back to my room and check if she went there.

I walk fast, careful not to spill the two mugs of hot milk, which are still steaming.

When I enter the next building, through the tall archway passage, I see a little lump in front of my door like a sack of potatoes. It's Rue.

I hurry over.

She lifts her head and I kneel down in front of her. "Rue, you can't come here," I say.

She frowns and lowers her head again.

"I'm sorry I took so long," I whisper. "I made us hot milk."

"What?" Rue looks at the steaming mugs in my hand. "Why is it brown?"

There probably aren't many steaming deserts on a hot planet like the one she's from.

"It's melted chocolate squares, in milk," I say.

Rue's eyes light up. "Really?"

"Yeah. Come on, let's go to your room." I glance over my shoulder, half expecting to see Randon or Grand Master standing there.

"I was scared you weren't coming," Rue says.

"See, I came." I give her a smile. "I was just running late. I know I break my promises sometimes, but from now on when I make you a promise, I'll keep it, okay?"

"Okay."

"And if I break my promise, it's not because I..." I shift the food in my arms awkwardly. "It's not because I don't like you or forgot about you. It's just because something has happened, like I had to go see Grand Master or I got into trouble or something."

Rue nods. "Are we going to play with Mr. Rock, now?" she asks.

I get up. "Yes, and... I have a surprise for you."

A Surprise for You

I WALK AHEAD OF Rue, into her room, and set our mugs down on the bedside table. I glance around for candle holders and spot two on the window sill.

"Close the door behind you," I say. Rue does as I ask and the room darkens, shutting out the torch light from the hallway. "Are there any more candles?"

I set the food down as well and take out the extra sulfur sticks in my pocket, which I grabbed at the last moment from the kitchen.

Rue runs over and opens her side table drawer. A pile of candles roll around on the inside.

I take out a handful. "Let's light up this room, so it's not so dark and scary."

"Okay!" Rue claps her hands together and I get started on lighting the candles. The rocks in my pocket clatter together and I smile, thinking about how surprised she will be when I show her the rocks I brought.

Finally, when the candles are all lit, I hand Rue her mug of warm chocolate. It's cooled down enough now for her to hold it. She clasps it carefully in both hands, her fingers too tiny to reach around the mug.

"Stand here." I turn her around so she's facing the door. "And I'll tell you know when to turn around. Okay?"

"Okay," she gives me a sideways glance and starts to drink her milk. "It's hot!" she shouts.

"Shhh...Just sip it slowly." I go to the bed and unload my pockets, looking over my shoulder every two seconds to make sure Rue isn't peeking.

I set the rocks down gently so they don't clatter and so she doesn't guess the surprise. I spread them out over the entire bed, making it look like there are lots. I picked ones that were about the same size as Mr. Rock, but there are a handful of smaller ones and a few bigger ones that I thought were interesting.

When I'm done, I take my heavy cloak off, removing the stress of the day along with it. The room is already becoming warm from the row of candles lit on the windowsill. My shoulders relax and I turn to Rue.

"Okay, you can turn around now."

She turns slowly, her mug still up to her lips as she keeps sipping. She looks at me first, not noticing the rocks yet, and lowers her mug to smile at me.

I gesture towards the bed. "Look at your bed."

Her eyes move to the bed and she gasps. "Rocks!"

"Shhh…" I reach for her mug before she drops it. She shoves it at me, splashing milk on my shirt, and runs to her bed.

"Where did you find them?" she squeals, jumping onto the bed right in the middle of all the rocks. She looks at me expectantly and I shrug like it was no big deal. The walk to the creek was long and that's why I was late meeting Master Dukath, but Rue's excitement is worth it.

"I love them so much!" She begins organizing the rocks right away, separating the big ones from the small ones. "Those are the babies," she says, pointing to the small ones. "And these are the bigger kids, and these are the grown-ups and…"

She jumps up suddenly, upsetting the rocks she's only just organized. They all tumble towards her feet into a pile.

"I have to show Mr. Rock!"

"Shhh…" I shush her again. She's so easily excitable, like I was at her age, only she's less angry than me, and more hyper active.

Rue runs to her window sill, reaching up on her toes to get Mr. Rock. "He likes to look out the window when I'm not here," she explains.

I set her mug down and grab mine to taste the milk. It's warm and thick. I inhale the delicious scent of chocolate and take a seat on the edge of the bed. My feet hurt from all the walking in the forest I've been doing lately.

Rue returns to her bed and starts reorganizing the rocks. "Which one do you want to marry?" she asks Mr. Rock, holding him up to her face to talk to him, as though he's hard of hearing. She grabs a rock from the pile on the bed.

I look at Rue's organization. She's setting the largest rocks aside and seems less interested in them.

"This is Mrs. Rock," she says, showing me one of the rocks that looks a lot like Mr. Rock. I smile, wondering if she'll be able to tell them apart later.

"Why does Mr. Rock want to get married?" I ask.

"To have a best friend."

"Can't he just have a best friend and not get married?"

"No, because they have to be together forever. That's the only way."

I think of my mom and dad and how mom is never around, always out doing trades or traveling to other planets.

"Do you want to get married?" I ask Rue.

"Sure!" she beams at me.

"No," I shake my head. "Not to me. I mean, when you grow up."

She lowers back into her sitting position and shrugs. "When I grow up, I'll just get married to you."

I sigh and set my hot cocoa down on the bedside table. "I'm going to be really busy ruling the Galaxy," I say. "I'm not going to get married."

Rue ignores me and keeps organizing her rocks. I frown, watching her go about her work. I wish I could know for sure she'll be safe and end up happy when she grows up. "Don't you want to play with the big rocks?" I ask, pointing at the rocks she's set aside.

"No, those are mean rocks."

I smile. "Why are they mean?"

"Because they are big."

I hold back a laugh. "Can I play with them, then?"

"Yes." Rue gathers them into her arms and tries to hand them to me, but she can't hold them all at one time. I move over to help her.

"They'll be my army commanders," I say, taking them. "Since they're big and strong and mean. And I'll need some soldiers, too."

"You can have all the mean ones," Rue says, picking out some other rocks from the smaller pile; the ones with sharp edges.

I put mine onto the floor and grab my cloak to set it up as an army base. The hood will be the headquarters office, where they meet to discuss upcoming battles. I select the pointiest rock to be the leader.

"This is their leader." I lift it up to show Rue. She glances over.

"That's not the biggest one," she says.

"I know, but it's got the most sharp edges."

"Oh, okay." She climbs out of her bed, careful this time not to disrupt her organization. Then she kneels down and pats the bed. "I live on this planet," she says. "And you live down there on a different planet."

"Okay. But you probably shouldn't bring Mr. Rock to my planet," I say, noticing she's got Mr. Rock in her hand. "We're about to go to war soon."

"Mr. Rock can go to war too!" Rue says. "But he has to be back for supper so Mrs. Rock and the babies won't be worried."

I look up at the bed where twenty or so small rocks now surround Mrs. Rock.

"That's a lot of babies," I say. "Mrs. Rock should put them all in the military draft when they grow up, so they can join my army."

"Maybe," Rue says. "But this one…" she picks up the tiniest one, "is going to be a princess when she grows up, so she can't be a soldier."

"What's her name?"

"Rue."

"This is Master Rynn," I say, holding up my pointiest rock. "He rules the Galaxies."

Rue looks over. "Can Mrs. Rock visit your planet, for a peesh-full visit?"

"Peaceful?"

"Yes."

"What does she want?"

"She can trade fuel, like my dad does. We have a lot of fuel on my planet, so we can trade it. You can give me other things like…" She taps her finger to her chin. "Chocolate or sparkly clothes."

I nod. "That sounds like a good idea. We need lots of fuel for our fighter planes. But I don't think we have sparkly clothes on my planet."

I gather my leadership team together. "Master Rynn will send a shuttle to go pick up Mrs. Rock. That way we know she's not sneaking anything onto our base by bringing her own spacecraft, like bombs or spy equipment or some kind of surprise attack."

"She isn't going to do that!"

I stifle a grin. "Let me set up my chain of command first. I need to appoint a second in command, chief officer, to oversee the negotiations and all the other stuff that needs to get done. All the stuff that Master Rynn doesn't have time to do."

"What's the chief-offers name?"

I shrug. "Rand... Landon."

"Okay, but you have to hurry."

"Why?"

"Because Mrs. Rock will trade her fuel with another planet, if you don't hurry. The other aliens said they will give us more chocolate than you will. But you can buy first, if you hurry."

I nod and organize my rocks on my cloak into the sections of my base, according to their military positions.

"Your dad trades fuel?"

"Yeah." Rue busies herself with her rocks but seems to be waiting on me to finish setting up.

"Okay, the shuttle will be on its way soon to pick up Mrs. Rock. We just need to have the meeting room set up for her arrival."

I look around the room for some books or something to use as a conference table for my headquarters office.

"Rue, do you have any books?"

She doesn't reply and I glance over to see what she's doing. She's lying against the edge of her bed, her arms up on the mattress, holding rocks, but her eyes are closed and her head is resting on the bed.

"Rue?" I go over.

She's asleep.

I look at all the rocks on the bed. Should I move them? They're in some sort of order, groups that look like they must be families, each group with two larger rocks surrounded by smaller ones.

I pick Rue up and put her onto the bed, closer to the wall where she couldn't reach so there are no rocks. Hopefully she won't roll around too much in her sleep and end up on the rocks.

"Goodnight, Rue," I whisper, covering her with her blanket. Then I blow out all the candles except for one, and leave my cloak army base on the floor for tomorrow, locking the door behind me.

THE ELIMINATION GAMES

A GUST OF WIND whips the smell of rain and roots into my face. I clench my jaw to keep my teeth from chattering. A storm is coming and everything feels unsteady today.

I look up at the dark clouds overhead and shiver. Aurah and Randon walk quietly beside me as we head for the gathering hall with the other students.

"Where's your cloak?" Aurah asks me, as I rub my arms for warmth.

I shrug. "I don't know."

"Maybe you left it in Master Kra'an's granddaughter's room," Randon says.

I stop walking.

"Who?" Aurah asks, looking confused. She stops walking too and so does Randon.

I don't know a Master Kra'an, but Randon's mention of a granddaughter has my defenses up.

"One of the Masters that lives here," he replies, watching me with a grin on his face.

"What are you talking about?" I say, walking away. Did Randon see me go to Rita's room last night? Is this Master Kra'an her grandfather?

"Your little friend," Randon says, following me. "I know your secret—"

I turn and grab Randon in a Gift hold so tight he begins to choke.

Aurah takes a step back. The others have already gone into the school building and it's just the three of us outside. Randon's eyes go wide as he grabs at his neck, trying to loosen the invisible grip he can't find.

"Are you allowed to use your powers?" Aurah asks, sounding worried. "You'll get expelled."

I ignore her and force my way into Randon's mind. I'm a lot stronger when I'm mad. Master Dukath was right; anger and hate do make me stronger.

Randon's surface emotions are fear and anger, then I find what I'm looking for. He saw me with Rue last night and was jealous of the way I was paying special attention to her. I search further. He doesn't intend to tell Dukath about it, because he doesn't actually want me expelled.

I let him go and he falls to his knees, gasping for air. Was I keeping him from breathing this whole time?

Aurah curses and kneels down beside him, putting an arm around his shoulders as he tries to catch his breath. She gives me an angry glare.

"Get lost, Bryn," she says, glowering up at me.

I hesitate for a second, wanting to explain myself, but there's nothing to say. I step away from them and head into the next building.

* * *

"Quiet down!" Master Garionne says to the rowdy students gathered in Markin Hall. I glance around the theater-style room for a place to sit.

I can't remember the last time we had a gathering here, maybe when I was around ten earth-years old. The dark blue cushioned chairs and raised platform at the front make me nostalgic. Something about the formality of using the theater makes me think the announcement today won't be a happy one.

I take a seat at the back, away from everyone else.

Aurah and Randon walk in just as Master Garionne is about to start. He gives them a displeased glance then begins talking.

"Grand Master Dukath has called you all in here today to tell you about a new initiative for the Ruling Order Future Commanders Program," he says.

I spot Grand Master sitting in a chair beside three other commanders at the front. He was sitting so still I didn't even notice him. I can't see his face inside his hood, but I imagine his dark eyes staring back at me. I don't look away, the way I normally do. I'm not sure why. If he is looking at me, he'll have to look away first.

"As you know," Master Garionne continues. "Only twenty-five of you will graduate from this program and continue on to be leaders and commanders with the Ruling Order."

A hush falls over the room. Eighty students have been training this summer. Last summer it was one hundred and fifty. The summer before that it was two hundred and fifty.

I never thought about the selection process too much and how they decide who goes on to the next summer program. I always passed the program each year.

"To decide on the final twenty-five on this, our final year of training, we will be having a competition of sorts, a game, if you will." Master Garionne looks to Grand Master Dukath, who nods. "Starting tomorrow, there will be no more classes. Your final training will be a practical one, a competition... to the death."

Everyone is silent as we wait to hear more. Randon and Aurah look back at me and I suddenly wish I was sitting with them and not alone.

"You have a week to prepare, then we start the Elimination Games."

"Can we form teams?" Randon calls out, not bothering to raise his hand. His voice sounds raw and I feel a small pang of guilt for choking him.

"No," Master Garionne says. "Each man for himself."

"Or woman!" Aurah adds.

The guys laugh but she ignores them.

"What if someone has an advantage?" Aurah continues. "Like Gift powers?"

A few heads turn to me and I sink down in my seat.

"Everyone should use whatever advantage they have at their disposal, except for weapon's fire. There will be no weapons allowed. It is the only rule."

An outburst of disapproval breaks out and everyone starts talking at once.

"Quiet!" Master Garionne yells. "Effective immediately, all blasters and other weapons will be removed from the school grounds. Anyone caught trying to bring a weapon into the games will be automatically disqualified."

"What about just hiding, until the game is over?" someone asks. "Is that allowed?"

"You will be on a Capital Starship, with a system that can detect bio-signs on board. There's no place to hide. I recommend you familiarize yourselves with the ship's layout and operating systems."

I sit up in my seat. The thought of being on a Capital Starship is awesome; comfortable quarters, nice showers, carpeted flooring. Too bad we'll be there to kill each other.

"If someone is hurt and doesn't want to continue, can they ask to be disqualified?" Aurah asks.

"No," Master Dukath says before Master Garionne can answer. "Everyone remains on the ship until only twenty-five are left, no matter how long that takes."

I frown. With no blasters it will be more difficult for students to kill each other. Will they resort to using their bare hands?

I glance around the room. I do have an advantage, but I wouldn't want to use it to kill my fellow classmates. I've never purposefully used my Gift to kill anyone. And the one time I did kill someone by accident... I shake my head to dispel the memory.

What if Randon and Aurah get killed? I shiver unvoluntarily. No, Randon is smart, I can see him passing the Games and being one of the final twenty-five. He has a better chance than even I do. But if Aurah can't use her blaster skills then she'll be at a disadvantage. She's tall but not as physically strong as the guys.

I rub my face with my hands. This can't be the only way to decide who's going to be a future leader with the Ruling Order.

Master Garionne continues talking about the Game rules, but I can't concentrate. I keep thinking about Dad and Morlin and how they wouldn't like this at all. I do have powers that will give me an advantage, but they are strongest when I'm mad or irrational. And if I'm irrational in the Games then I could get myself killed. There are a lot of smart students in the summer program, like Randon, who could get the better of me with some machine or contraption. Or in my sleep.

I look over at Randon now. Would he kill me if it came down him getting into the Ruling Order or not? I know how he feels about me, but he feels even more strongly about ruling the Galaxy. And I almost just killed him just now, before this meeting. Maybe his feelings have changed.

Master Garionne dismisses us and everyone starts talking at the same time as they make their way out of the theater. I can already see the teams forming, despite the rule about no groups. They want to save each other and be the new future leaders of the Ruling Order.

They glance over at me and whisper to each other. They're plotting to take me down. I'll be the first target on everyone's list.

My stomach feels queasy with the food I ate at supper. Aurah and Randon walk out together, not looking back. I stay in my seat and wait until everyone leaves.

I've got one week. One week to figure out if I can kill my classmates to win a game, or if I should tell Dad or Morlin about all this, and just quit the Program.

One week left... with Rue.

Attachments are your weakness

My room is cold and dark when I walk in. I don't bother lighting any candles. I go to my bed and throw myself onto it, with my boots and clothes still on. My chest hurts as I take in a deep breath, as though I've been crying for hours, though I haven't.

I still need to get my cloak from Rue's room, but I can't play rocks tonight. I'm too on edge, with the Elimination Games being announced. I want to be part of the Ruling Order. It's what I've always wanted. I know this new Order will be the future of the Galaxy. But I don't want to risk my life for some competition.

I look up at the ceiling, wondering if Rue is feeling lonely and waiting for me to come play with her. I never promised

I would. Did I? A future ruler of the galaxy wouldn't waste time playing rocks with a child. And yet, our game last night reminded me of why I wanted to be part of the Ruling Order in the first place, to have commanders following my orders, to be a leader like Master Dukath said I will be, and to show my parents that I'm not just some freak with uncontrollable powers. I hate how they always pity me, like I have some kind of disability, instead of a strength. But Master Dukath understands me, and so do Randon and Aurah. We all want the same thing, to bring a true ruling force into the Galaxy that will keep order.

I close my eyes and start to drift off to sleep, the exhaustion from the day's events finally overcoming me. My mind wanders back to Rue. Hopefully she's already asleep and not too cold in her tiny, drafty room with no candles lit.

A light knock on my door startles me awake and I get up from my bed, my heart pounding.

"Rue?"

The knocking goes on and on.

"I'm coming!" I open the door to find Randon standing there.

"Something's happened," he says, his voice is so monotone it scares me.

"Happened?" I say. "What do you mean?"

He steps aside and I see a small coffin behind him. "I didn't actually mean to kill her."

The name carved on the lid says 'Rue.'

"No!" I yell.

I sit up in bed. My room is still dark and my heart pounds so hard that my chest aches.

It was just a dream.

Randon wouldn't kill a small child, would he. I shudder, remembering the bird he beheaded so easily. I push the thought away and jump out of bed. I'm still dressed and with my boots on. I don't know what time it is but I have to go check on Rue.

* * *

"Rue?" I say in a loud whisper, knocking on her door again, a little louder this time. Why isn't she opening the door?

I look down the hall at the other doors nearby. I can't call any louder or it will wake someone else up. I try the door handle. It's unlocked, which is good. Or maybe not.

Rue's room is dark and still. I make out the silhouette of a bundle of blankets on her bed. I walk over and gently move the blankets aside. She isn't there.

All the rocks are gone and my cloak is gone too. Where is she? Who can I ask? If I ask anyone they'll wonder why I'm asking.

I hurry out of the room and quietly close the door behind me. Randon mentioned her grandfather's name. What was it? Master Kryn? I lean my head against the door and close my eyes to think. What was his name?

Rue, where are you?

I sense someone watching me and open my eyes. In the corner of the hall is Master Dukath, hidden in the shadows, only his eyes gleam from beneath his hood. I jump away from Rue's door.

"Master," I say, my throat tightening.

"Rynn." He moves forward. "I didn't find you in your room. I sensed something was wrong."

I swallow hard. "I just thought I heard something coming from this room as I was passing by. I don't know whose room it is." My words sound guilty, even to my own ears.

"Perhaps you need to do a confession? It cleanses the mind."

My heart beats so strongly that I think I might faint.

"Yes, you're right," I say. "I will, Your Leadership. In the morning. I'm just so tired right now. I had a bad dream. I think I was sleepwalking. I don't even know how I got here." The lies keep piling up. I won't be able to hide them if I'm forced to do a confession. I need to just stop talking already.

Master watches me curiously. "Is it the Games that have you so troubled?"

"Yes," I nod. "I think so"

"You will pass," Master says. "I have foreseen it. You have my permission to use your Gift in any way you deem necessary. Even to kill."

"Thank you, Your Leadership."

"You should take your rest while you still can. You will not want to close your eyes, once you're in the Games."

"Yes, Master." I bow then quickly walk away.

* * *

Randon's door is partially open when I get there and I walk right in. The room is brightly lit, with candles set all around books and papers that are scattered on the floor; diagrams and instruction manuals on everything from weapons to spacecraft layouts.

I step on a page as I walk to Randon's bed. He's asleep with a book in his hand, but stirs at the crunch of paper beneath my boot. He blinks and sits up slowly.

"I need your help," I say. Randon simply blinks at me, looking confused.

"I can't find Rue," I continue.

"What?" He gets out of bed and stands up, still rubbing at his eyes. He's not wearing a shirt but thankfully he has his regular pants on. "It's the middle of the night." He runs his hands through his disheveled, bright-orange hair.

"Yes, and Rue's *missing*."

"What do you want me to do about it?"

"Come help me look for her in the forest. She might have gotten lost out there or something."

"She probably just went to your room."

"No, she isn't there. But you're right, we should check again in case she's there now. What did you say her grandfather's name was?"

Randon yawns. "You can't wake her grandfather up in the middle of the night. Grand Master will find out that you're spending time with her and you'll be expelled."

"I think he might already know."

"Then she's as good as dead."

"Don't say that!" I yell.

Randon jumps and looks startled for a second, then angry.

"Why'd you wake me up?" he yells back. "I don't *care* about Rue."

"Alright." I turn to leave.

"It's just like Master said," Randon calls after me. "Attachments are your weakness!"

FINDING RUE

"**R**ue!" I call into the trees. There's no answer.

After checking all the school buildings and the open field, the forest is the last place to look.

The cool light of dawn fills the sky and morning is already approaching. Now it's easier to see but harder for me to cling to the hope that I'll find Rue.

"Rue!" I call again. Randon's words won't leave my mind, *attachments are your weakness*. I push the thought away and keep going. Where could she be? Did she try to walk to the river to return the rocks to their home?

I walk further and further, but there is nothing but trees and ground and sky.

I stumble forward as a dizzy spell hits me, and grasp a nearby tree trunk to steady myself. For a moment I feel the energy inside the tree, something I've never felt before. But in my hazy tiredness I have less resistance to the Gift and I sense it's life force, a living entity that is as aware of me as I am of it.

I close my eyes and reach out to the rest of the forest through the tree. They're all connected. It's similar to reading someone's mind, only it's not human but the trees and grass and plants. They move as one, in the breeze. The wind travels from one side of the forest to the other and the animals wake with the dawn, to go looking for water. They answer me, one by one, as I speak to them. Not in words, but in another way that doesn't require words.

She isn't here.

Not in the grassy field which sways in the breeze, not among the plants with the small forest creatures, nor beneath the tall trees that look down from above. And not with the larger animals either. None have seen her.

My shoulders slump and I let go of the tree. There's no point in looking in the forest any further. No living thing has seen her. I have to go see Master for confession this morning. I can't escape it. Maybe it's better if he knows. Maybe he can take away this attachment I have to Rue, that is tearing me to pieces at not knowing what's happened to her.

I clench my fists. I should have gone to play rocks with her, like I said I would.

No, if I'm going to rule the Galaxy one day I can't have any attachments like this. I need to get rid of it.

* * *

Master Dukath is not in his study when I get there. I don't know what I would have done if he was. I can't go through with a confession. I just can't.

"Rynn?"

I jump at the sound of my name. Master Garionne stands at the door, watching me with suspicion.

"Grand Master isn't here," he says. "He was called away on an important matter. Whatever you're here to see him for, will have to wait."

I nod and Master Garionne continues on down the hall. I let out a sigh of relief and unclench both my fists. I can't take this constant feeling of being on edge. I walk out of the study and run right into Randon. I quickly wipe at the tears that I only now notice are in my eyes.

Randon looks like he hasn't slept either, with dark circles under his eyes.

"I found her," he says.

"What?" I hold my breath, hoping I heard him correctly.

"She was on a trip with her grandfather. She's fine."

"How did you find her?"

"She's in the chapel now with him," Randon blinks into the sunlight shining in front a nearby window. "And with some other Masters, doing the early morning chants."

I'm frozen for a moment as his words sink in.

Rue's okay.

"You're welcome," Randon calls after me, as I run off to the chapel.

***

The sound of chanting drifts down the garden path, reaching my ears before I reach the small chapel at the end of it. The front doors are open and I look inside.

Four Masters sit in meditation on the front bench. Rue is with them, seated beside an Elderly Master who is probably her grandfather. Her feet swing and she looks around while the others keep their eyes closed. She's wearing a dress today and looks perfectly fine. She's not hurt or lost or dead. I grip the stone of the archway, leaning against it for support. I was up all night searching for her.

Rue, you scared me.

Rue turns immediately and her face brightens when she sees me. She jumps down from the bench, getting her grandfather's attention and I back away from the entrance so I won't be seen.

Rue's footsteps clap against the stone floor as she hurries to the door. I get down on my knees to prepare for her arrival.

When she runs out from around the corner I scoop her up into my arms.

"Rynn!" she squeals, laughing. "Do you want to meet my grandpa?"

"The next time you go away, let me know first," I say, setting her back down. I set her wild hair behind both her ears. It would drive me crazy if I had hair in my face all the time, like Rue does.

"I did go, to tell you," Rue says. "But you were in the theater place, with all the other big kids."

I lift her chin. "Okay. But I was worried."

"Why?" she says, looking at me with her big eyes. "Because I am your attachment now?"

I smile. "You're a smart girl."

"I know."

"Can you write?"

"A little."

"You should write me a note, when you will be gone."

Rue shrugs, seeming bored of the conversation.

"Guess what?" I say.

"What?"

"I don't have classes all week!"

"You don't?" Rue gasps.

"No. And do you know what I want to do with all my free time?"

Rue narrows her eyes at me. "Sleep?"

"No." I lean in as though to tell her a secret. "I want to play rocks with you."

"Really?"

"Yes."

"Okay!" Rue squeals.

"But you should go back to your grandfather right now, okay?"

"Okay. But I want to play *now!*"

"I need to go sleep for a bit, while you're here at the chapel. I was up all night."

"Why were you up all night?"

"Rue, what happened to all your rocks, in your room?"

"I had to hide them and your cloak too, because grandpa was coming and then he would see them."

"Okay." I start to get up but she grabs my arm and pulls me back down.

"Don't forget," she says in a loud whisper. "You are going to play today."

"I won't forget."

Rue smacks my forehead with her palm and laughs, running back into the chapel before I can get her back.

YOUr HearTBeaT

I DREAM THAT I'M roaming the halls of the Capital Starship. There's no one left in the Elimination Games, because I've killed them all, except for Randon and Aurah. I can't remember how I killed them all, I just know I did.

The rules have changed and only one person can win. I can't decide if I want to live or die. If I live, that means Aurah and Randon will have to die, and I'd have to be the one to kill them. If I die, then Rue will never see me again.

I keep wandering and searching endlessly but all I find are more empty hallways humming with the sound of the ship's engine. The silence closes in around me and I want to scream.

I wake to a warm room and a stiff neck. I sit up slowly, my muscles aching.

Rue! I jump to my feet, panicked. Then remember that she's okay. I found her in the chapel.

Or Randon did.

I sit back down and look out the window. It's not morning anymore, but afternoon. Am I late for class? No, there aren't any classes anymore. I get to spend time with Rue, until the Elimination Games start. I should try and find out more about the Games and prepare somehow, but I don't even want to think about it.

My room is stuffy with the heat of mid-day. A familiar restlessness stirs inside of me, refusing to be dismissed. I thought I'd mastered these feelings, these desires, but maybe I've only been repressing them and now they're surfacing again out of the blue; a distraction from the stress of an upcoming challenge I don't know how to face.

I swallow hard. I can taste it, sweet and thick. I have to stop thinking about it. Future Masters don't get distracted by such desires. I just need to get out of my room and take a walk.

* * *

I stroll past the large tree in the middle of the cobblestone courtyard between the school buildings.

No one is around, in the school rooms or outside. The buildings are quiet and I feel abandoned, like I was in my dream.

The afternoon sun warms my back, reminding me of the first day of summer training this year. I was so excited to return for my fifth year with the Ruling Order training program. Even the fact that I had to deal with Randon all summer didn't get me down.

I frown now. I liked it better when I knew him as a bully. It was less complicated that way.

I head for the dining hall for some food. Maybe there will be some students in there and I won't feel so alone.

* * *

"You're so intense," Aurah says, sitting with me as I eat. She saw me heading into the dining hall and followed me in. "When you love someone, you love them to *death*, don't you?"

"No." I rip a thick slice of bread in half and shove it in my mouth. I don't even know why she's sitting with me, she's got no food with her. Maybe she's bored too. "Where's Randon?" I mumble, with bread in my mouth. "Why don't you go hang out with him?"

"Tell me about the little girl," Aurah replies.

I drink some water then shrug, not sure what to say.

"Well, you should really let her go, you know. She's an attachment."

I continue eating and don't reply. Aurah wouldn't know anything about attachments.

"She doesn't belong in our world," she continues. "The fighting and killing. You're going to be a leader in the Ruling Order someday."

I get up, leaving the rest of my food on the table. "I have to go."

***

"Do you have a sea monster?" Rue asks, holding her cards awkwardly in her small hands. She's sitting cross-legged on my bed and I'm leaned up against the cold stone wall, trying to cool off in the warm evening.

I look down at my cards, which I borrowed from Aurah, or rather, stole from her. I'll return them. She has a lot of weird stuff in her room, which she's traded for and collected throughout the years, like scarves and necklaces, and these playing cards. Useless stuff.

"Is this a sea monster?" I show Rue one of my cards that looks more like a snake than a sea creature.

She grabs it out of my hand. "Yes!"

"I have two more."

"Then you have to give them to me!"

"What if I didn't tell you I had the other two, and I just kept them? You wouldn't even know."

"You can't do that! You have to say that you have it, if I ask you."

I hand over my two other sea monster cards. "So this is a trust game?"

Rue sighs a big, exaggerated sigh and rolls her eyes. "No, it's a *card* game."

"Can we look at each other's cards then?"

"No!" Rue pushes her cards against her chest.

"Oh, okay. I think Randon would win at this game every time."

"It's your turn to ask me," Rue says.

"Okay, do you have three sea monster cards?"

"Gahhhh," Rue throws herself back onto my pillow and kicks her feet in the air.

"What?" I say. "I gave you three sea monster cards, so I know you have them."

"But they're *mine* now. You can't have them back. You're so bad at playing cards!"

"I am?"

"Yes."

"Okay, okay. I think I get it. But you should put your three sea monsters to the side then, because they're the points you won, right?"

Rue sits back up. She attempts to remove three cards from her hand and all her cards fall onto the bed. Now I know which cards to ask for. She scrambles to pick them back up, trying to hide them by leaning forward.

"Do you have a…" I look into her big hazel eyes. "A, um, bird card?"

"Nope! You have to pick up a card now."

I pick up a card then remember the chocolate squares I brought with me.

"Hey Rue, guess what I found in the kitchen?"

"What?"

I reach for my bag and take out a chocolate dessert square wrapped in wax paper. I open the paper and Rue's eyes light up. She drops her cards and reaches for the square.

"Can I have it?" she says.

"Okay, but can I have a bite first?"

She hesitates, biting her lip, her eyes still on the chocolate. "Um… okay."

The square is small and I have five more she doesn't know about, so I pop the whole thing into my mouth.

Rue gasps "Hey!" she blinks fast, her eyes tearing up almost instantly.

"I'm just joking with you. I have more," I say, grabbing the other pieces from the cloth bag. I hold them out to Rue but she turns her head away.

"Look." I try to show her but she continues to turn her back to me.

"I don't want one." She crosses her arms and refuses to look at me.

I set the pieces down and sigh. "I was just playing around. Do you want me to get one more from the kitchen, since I ate one of them? Then you can have six."

"No." Rue scoots away from me.

"Rue..." I reach for her but she slaps my hand away.

"Ouch!"

She smiles a little, but tries hard to keep her angry face in tact.

"Go away, you're mean and I don't want your dumb chocolate squares!" she says.

"Are you sure you don't want any? They're so good." I pick one up and unwrap it, then hold it out to her. "I know you love them."

Rue shakes her head and turns her shoulders away in a dramatic display of ignoring me. I put the square in front of her face and she pushes it away and turns all the way around, with her back to me again. I keep following her with the chocolate square and she keeps turning.

"It's really yummy." I squish the square to her cheeks and she squeals, scrambling off the bed and running away.

I chase after her. There isn't a lot of room for her to run and she jumps up onto my night table, then from there onto my bookcase.

"Rue, be careful." I reach for her and she takes the chocolate from my hand and shoves it in her mouth.

"Hey!" I say. "I want that back!"

Rue giggles as I squeeze her cheeks, pretending to try and get the square back out of her mouth. She jumps away from me and almost falls off the bookcase. I catch her and swing her up into my arms.

"Come on, let's finish our card game," I say, carrying her back to the bed. "And no cheating this time, okay?"

"I don't cheat!" she mumbles through her mouth full of chocolate. I put her down and sit beside her.

"I'm so tired." I lay back with a dramatic sigh and cover my face with my arm. My short sleep this morning didn't make up for being out all night. "I have to rest for a little bit first."

"No!" Rue smacks my arm. "You said we'd play."

"Yeah, but I thought you'd fall asleep by now. Why aren't you tired yet? It's already getting late."

"No, it's not." Rue tugs at my arm, trying to move it away from my face. "Wake up," she grunts.

I drop my arm and she smacks my cheeks with both her hands.

"Hey, I'm trying to sleep here," I laugh.

"No, you're not!"

"Okay, okay, no sleeping. But give me five minutes to just lay here okay?"

"How long is that?" Rue asks.

I close my eyes to think. How long is five minutes of earth time, where Rue's from? What time do they follow?

"How fast does your planet spin?" I ask her.

"My planet stays still."

I sigh. "Okay, well it's just a short time, five minutes."

Rue lays her head on my chest. "I can hear your heart beat," she says.

I take a breath, resting my hand on her hair.

"And I can hear you breathing too!" she says.

I laugh lightly.

"I can hear you laughing too!"

"I can hear you talking too much," I say.

Rue sighs and becomes quiet, her breathing getting deeper now. I move my hand away from her head and let it drop beside me.

"Rue?" I whisper, but she's already asleep. I close my eyes and let myself drift off to sleep, too.

Treemites

"**B**UT I DON'T LIKE it," Rue whines, swirling her spoon around in her treemeal.

I take another big spoonful from my bowl and eat it. "It tastes fine to me."

Rue sighs. It's been three days now of no school, and three days of the most fun I've had with anyone in my life, maybe the only fun I've ever had with anyone.

"Rue, I don't want to come back here and get you food later when you say you're starving, like you do every time you skip supper."

Rue frowns. "But it tastes bad." She blinks back tears and I can't tell if she really thinks it tastes that bad or if she's just upset that I'm not letting her have her way this time. She probably just wants chocolate instead.

"Eat some or I'm not going to play rocks with you," I say. She quickly gobbles up a spoonful then does a dramatic display of trying not to gag before swallowing it down.

"One more bite," I say, watching her to see if she'll listen.

Rue takes another spoonful and swallows it, shutting her eyes tight and shuddering.

"Now can we go play?" she says, wiping her mouth. A few heads turn in our direction but I don't care. Master Dukath is gone for the rest of the week until the Elimination Games begin, Randon isn't talking to me, and for all I know I may not even be alive a week from now, so I might as well spend all my time with Rue. Who cares what everyone thinks? They're all working in their teams on battle plans to take out other teams. My plan is simple; stay alive.

"Come on," Rue pulls on my arm with both her hands. I finish off the last bit of my treemeal then pull her bowl towards me so I can eat the rest of hers too. I stick my spoon into it and scoop some up. Something wiggles about at the bottom of her bowl. I look closer.

"What is that?" I say.

Rue looks down. "Ew... I don't know."

I stand up so fast my chair falls over behind me. "I'll be right back," I say, then run off.

***

"I don't know what you're talking about!" Randon yells at me. He's sitting on the floor in his room with Aurah, in front of a large map of the Capital Ship's layout.

Red x's are marked all over the map and pathways highlighted. Randon's hair is disheveled and looks shorter. Did Aurah give him a haircut? I frown. Would I have been included in their little meeting today if I hadn't choked Randon a few days ago?

"What did you put in Rue's food?" I repeat.

"I told you, nothing!" Randon glares at me from beneath his crop of orange hair.

"He was here with me all day," Aurah says.

I look back and forth between them. I don't know why I care that they're suddenly spending so much time together, but I do.

"What was in her food?" Aurah asks.

"I don't know, these little worms."

"In the treemeal they made today?"

"Yes."

"Those are treemites. They sometimes live in the tree grain and grow if they're left out in the sun."

"Are they bad to eat?" I ask.

Aurah gets up. "We should get her to a medic."

* * *

Randon stands with me outside Rue's door as I wait for the medic to come out. Rue's grandfather is in the room with her, along with two other Masters who are channeling the Gift for her recovery.

"I don't know why you'd even want an attachment like this," Randon mumbles, pacing back and forth. "Just ask Master to erase your memory of her, and move on."

My stomach clenches. It's the same thing Aurah said. Are they right?

The door to Rue's room opens suddenly and the medic steps out. He looks surprised to find us standing there, then tries to step around me. Randon blocks him.

"What's wrong with the girl?" he says.

The medic looks over his glasses at him. "She's having a difficult time fighting the parasites in her system. Now if you'll excuse me."

"Wait!" I grab his arm. If he doesn't give me the details I'm going to force it from his mind. "Will she be okay?"

"It's hard to tell," the medic says, pulling away from my grasp. "If she responds to the medication and her white blood cells are able to fight off the infection then, she'll make it through. But at her age, it may not turn out well."

I look to Rue's door. I want to go in and see her but her grandfather and the other Masters are still in there. A sick feeling stirs inside of me. She can't die.

The medic leaves and Randon stands there, no longer pacing but watching me.

I turn and walk away.

I can't deal with this. I need a distraction and I don't care if I get into trouble for it.

Back to Your Room

"CAN WE GO BACK to your room?" I say to Aurah.

She puts down the book that she's holding titled 'Capital Starship Engineering.' The library was the last place I thought to look for her, so it took me a while to find her. Now that I'm here, my palms are sweating as I wait for her answer.

"I think I've been reading for too long," Aurah says, narrowing her eyes at me. "Can you repeat what you just said?"

"Can we... go back to your room?" I ask again.

Aurah studies me for a moment. "You look terrible."

"Thanks."

"Is it the little girl? Are they having a hard time killing off the treemites?"

"I don't want to talk about it."

Aurah closes her book and starts to pack up her things. "Okay, let's go back to my room."

* * *

Aurah's room is the same size as mine and Randon's, and yet somehow it seems bigger and more open.

A red, sheer fabric is draped over the windows, making the room glow pink with the sunshine streaming through. There's also a red blanket on her bed and candles of all sizes set around the room. On her night stand sits a clear jar filled with water and stuffed with wild flowers. I touch one of the petals. I could bring Rue some flowers to brighten up her room while she's not feeling well. The image of her lying sick in bed assails me. I shut my eyes tight and rub my face with my hands.

"It's my fault she's sick," I say.

Aurah pulls me into a hug and I let her, grateful that she's not saying anything about attachments or why I'm stupid to have one.

I step back. "I'm fine," I say.

I don't need all this comforting. Rue will be fine. There's no reason to be so emotional about it. I came here so I wouldn't have to think about it.

Aurah's hands stay on my shoulders, her palms warming me through my shirt.

"What do you want, Bryn?" she asks, assessing me with her cool, green eyes.

"A distraction."

Aurah's hands slide down my arms to my belt.

She grabs the bottom of my shirt and pulls it up, untucking it from my pants. I help her remove the shirt, pulling it over my head. My heart pounds. She's knows why I'm here and what I need. I could get in so much trouble for this, but I just don't care anymore.

I realize I'm taller than her now, which is odd. I'd gotten used to her being taller than me each year at the Academy. I've only recently outgrown her and Randon, in height, but they still surpass me in age and courage. My heart races as Aurah tosses my shirt aside then rests her hands on my bare chest.

"Relax," she says, her palms cool against my skin. "I'm not going to lay with you. In that way. Come lie down. You look like you could use some rest."

I sit down on the edge of the bed and she climbs up, moving to sit behind me, then begins to massage my shoulders. It feels so amazing I sigh. She massages the muscles behind my neck, working her way down my back. I close my eyes. Why is this not allowed for Masters? It could take away so much built up stress. There would be peace in all the galaxy.

"Do you know why I don't follow Dukath's rules?" Aurah says.

I don't respond, too distracted by her skillful massage to speak. Her hands move down to my lower back and I sit up straighter.

"Because he wants us to break them," she says.

"Hmm?" I ask.

"I figured that out a long time ago."

"But," I clear my throat. "I always get punished if I break the rules."

Aurah slides her hands back up to my shoulders and I lean into her hands.

"Those aren't punishments," she says close to my ear. "They're just a test of your character. But you know what?"

"Hmm?"

"You can't be trained to become a heartless, ruthless leader."

"You don't think I can do it?" I sit up and look over my shoulder at her.

"No, I know you can do it. But it's not something you *train* for, it comes from inside of you. First, you have to stop being so..."

"So what?" I turn to face her and she lets go of me. She doesn't reply.

"So what?" I repeat. "So nice?"

Aurah smirks and a heat rises to my face. She doesn't know what she's talking about. She didn't know me when I was younger and had no control over my Power. When I killed my kindergarten classmate.

"You don't know me," I tell her.

"I know you," Aurah says under her breath, moving to get off the bed. Before she can climb down, I push her onto her back.

"Bryn, what are you—"

"What's wrong?" I say. "You've laid with all the other guys."

"No I haven't!" Aurah gives me an angry glare. She tries to get up but I push her back down, holding her wrists down against the bed.

A thrill rushes over me. Is this how Randon feels, when he holds me down and I can't push him off? Do I get the same fearful look in my eyes that are in Aurah's eyes now?

"What are you going to do now?" she asks, her expression changing from fear to a look of challenge.

I hesitate for a moment. She said to break the rules, didn't she?

I climb on top of her and the feeling inside of me grows; the one I feel when Randon does this to me. I never admitted it to myself, but for once I don't want to ignore my desires anymore. Or follow the rules. No one else around here does.

"Bryn!" Aurah turns her head to one side when I try to kiss her. "I know you don't want to do this!"

I lock her in an invisible hold and she stops moving.

"It's Rynn, not Bryn," I say between clenched teeth.

This is what I was meant for. Masters do whatever it takes to succeed. They make their enemies defenseless and take what they want.

Aurah does not look startled at being locked in a Gift hold, but instead, she looks sad.

I let her go of her and she sits up.

"I thought we were friends," she says, once she has her voice back.

I'm about to answer but then I stop. She's right, I shouldn't have done that. Even ruthless Master's have allies, and Aurah and I have been friends a long time.

"Will you lay with me?" I ask her.

"No," she snaps.

A sharp feeling of rejection washes over me. Is this the only way I'm ever going to be close to a girl in a romantic way, by forcing her? Am I really that repulsive to everyone?

An intense self-hatred grips me. Why is everything I need and crave, so wrong, and always just out of my reach?

"Were you really going to force me to?" Aurah asks.

"No," I say.

She sets her hand on my arm and I pull away. "It's not you," she says. "I just know you're not ready. And that's not the way to go about experiencing intimacy for the first time."

I don't say anything.

"Are you sure it's really me you want?" Aurah continues. "And that you're not just confused about Randon?"

"I know what I want." I get up to leave. Coming here was a mistake.

"Wait." Aurah climbs off the bed and grabs my shirt. She hands it to me and I snatch it away.

I know I need to apologize, but I can't seem to say the words.

Never apologize, Grand Master said.

I put my shirt back on, and leave.

MY TURN

"WHAT DO YOU WANT Bryn?" Randon says, not looking up from the starship layout he's marking lines on. His hair looks even more red than usual, in the sunlight that's coming in through the windows.

I close the door behind me, then lock it.

Randon looks up, his eyebrows raising as though I've not got his attention now.

There's a moment of silence as I hesitate.

"Why are you in my room?" Randon asks.

I lock him in a hold and force him to stand, with a simple wave of my hand. His eyes go wide with surprise as I slam him into the wall. He flinches, the back of his head hitting the stone.

"Bryn..." he struggles for air.

I loosen my grip to let him breathe, but don't let him go. For years he's been pinning me to the ground, attacking me by surprise, forcing himself on me. And I wasn't allowed to retaliate with the one strength I do have. But now I can. Now it's my turn.

"Don't," he hisses as I walk over to him.

"Don't what?" I ask. "Isn't this what you want?" I reach my hand up to his temple. "Let's find out."

Randon tries to turn his head away but can't.

I set my fingers to his forehead to read his mind. He's a mess of feelings that are hard to separate; excitement, anger, fear, worry. He shudders at the feel of my breath against his neck. His thoughts betray him.

"I can see what you're thinking." I rest my other hand on his chest.

"What are you doing?" He whispers, swallowing hard.

I clench his shirt in my fist. I shouldn't be doing this. These are his emotions, not mine. But they're so intoxicating. It's just the distraction I'd been looking for. I just want to get washed away in them.

"I can feel what you feel," I say close to his cheek. A heat that rushes through him, which then rushes through me too.

So this is what it's like to have romantic feelings for a person.

"Get out of my mind," Randon hisses. His initial excitement has now turned to embarrassment, something I'm not as interested in feeling.

I let go of him.

"I don't like you in the same way you like me," I say.

He doesn't answer. I've freed him from my hold. He could walk away, but he doesn't.

"I'm your weakness, aren't I?" I say, only realizing it now.

I lift my hand to his face and he flinches.

"This is the one thing you have no control over." I smile, running my thumb over his bottom lip. His breath catches. "I like seeing you like this, so undone, with nothing to say for once."

Randon turns his head away, his expression going from desire to anger, then back again.

I lower my hand to his chest. His heart beats, just like mine does; just like the little bird Rue found out in the forest. We're all the same, at the mercy of our own desires. He's trapped too, by emotions he has no outlet for.

Randon keeps his eyes on the opposite wall, in an effort not to look at me.

"Just because I feel this way about you," he says, "doesn't mean I don't *hate* you." His eyes flicker to mine, then away again. "Because I do.

I smile, my palm getting warm against his chest. His heart rate has slowed.

"And just because I don't have the same feelings for you," I say in return, "doesn't mean we can't Rule the Galaxy together."

Randon's shoulders relax slightly and I step away.

"I've never had a close friend," I say.

"And you never will." Randon shoves me and I stumble back.

"Do you always have to act angry?" I yell. "I've seen your thoughts. I already know how you feel about me."

"Get out of my room," Randon yells back.

I hesitate for a second then walk to the door and open it to leave.

"Bryn?" Randon says.

I stop. "What?"

He doesn't answer right away so I wait, expecting some sort of reprimand. I suddenly feel bad for invading his privacy. It's the same thing Grand Master did to me. Maybe I am becoming more like a Master after all.

"I hope Rue makes it through," he finally says.

"Me too," I say, then walk out, closing the door behind me.

* * *

I set my hands onto the stone floor of the chapel. There is nowhere left to go now, no one left to go to.

"Everything is falling apart," I whisper, kneeling before the altar. I lower my face to the cold floor. "Rue hasn't gotten any better. She might die. I don't know what to do. She can't die. Please, help."

I don't know who I'm invoking for help exactly, but I do know that there's more to the Galaxy than just those who are alive. And the Masters come here to reach out to that power.

A breeze blows in through the stone archway windows, triggering a memory from back home. Mom and Dad both at the park with me. We were having a picnic, back when Mom was still around every day. I see her smiling at a joke Dad makes. Then they become sad. 'Dr. Aravik was able to remove all the parasites but it was too late,' she says to Dad. They're talking about family friends; a kid who got sick.

Then the vision is gone.

I jump up from the cold floor.

Dr. Aravik! The microbiologist who once worked for the Opposition. He had the cure!

I run out of the chapel.

I have to contact Dad.

AS SHE SLEEPS

"You've grown," Dad says, giving me a nod.

I look away. Too many emotions rise up when I look at him.

I glance around the small space station instead. The stylish look of the terminal is refreshing to see. Everything here is modern and clean, a nice break from the dusty ruins of the old Academy buildings, on planet. The colored lights of the nearby control panel reminds me of the city. I miss the lights and sounds.

Dad and I are the only two at the station today, which orbits the planet below. Being up here makes the problems on planet feel distant, like a bad dream. I wait for Dad to say something. Why did he have to come, at the first sign of me needing something?

He moves closer, as though to give me a hug, and I back away. I don't want him to touch me, and it has nothing to do with Grand Master's rules.

"You didn't have to come all the way here," I say.

"Bryn..." Dad tries to give me a hug but I put my hand out to stop him. He hugs me anyway and I leave my hands hanging at my sides. As much as I don't want to admit it, I do miss Dad, and miss being home. Why can't I just hate him the way I hate Mom? It's so easy to hate Mom. But Dad just makes me feel like I'm breaking into a million pieces. Finally he lets go.

"You're getting so tall," he says, looking down at me. "How's your summer going? Why don't you come back home? Your mom's away again and it's been very quiet around the house."

"I want to stay here."

Dad nods and takes a seat on the cushioned bench along the wall. "Do you want to tell me about this little girl?"

"No."

"Well, considering that we're using up our entire life savings to have the only nano-parasitologist specialist in the Galaxy rush here to save her, I'd like to at least know her name."

"Rue," I say. Dad nods, watching me. I clench my jaw. He knows.

He could always sense everything about me. He obviously knows how much I care about Rue, and that I've never cared about anyone so strongly.

I turn to face him. I want to tell him everything; that it hurt when he sent me away, dumping me onto others to take care of me like I was some unwanted problem. That it hurts when he's always disappointed in me, and expects I'll fail at everything. But the words don't come out.

He waits for me to say something more about Rue. Should I tell him about the upcoming Games? Should I ask him to let Rue stay with our family for the rest of the summer? I could leave all of this behind; the Games, the Ruling Order, Master Dukath, everything. I could go home, and take Rita so she wouldn't have to be here alone, or return home to the horrible Ungar.

"You're too young for all of this intensive training," Dad says, giving me a look of concern. "If you don't feel you belong here—"

"I do belong here!" I yell.

It was a mistake to call him to help with my problem. Now he's just going to continue to think of me as incapable of everything.

"I'm not too *young* or too *sensitive* or too *out of control* with my powers to study here. I can end up doing something important one day. I'm not some sick child, so quit treating me that way." I turn and head for the door.

"Of course you're not," Dad says quickly. "Bryn, listen. I never said you're not capable. I just mean there's no rush in becoming part of an army or military group or growing up too fast."

I freeze. Does he know about Master Dukath's Leadership Program and what it's really about?

"In battle, people die," he continues. "Innocent villagers, teammates, captains and commanders. I just don't know if you're ready for all that, seeing as you're so concerned over one little girl—"

"She's not just some random little girl."

I clench my jaw. He's doing it again, implying I'm weak and can't handle anything.

"I have to go," I say, then leave.

* * *

I pace in front of Rue's bedroom as her grandfather and two other Masters whisper their healing chants.

Dr. Aravik has come and gone. Hours, maybe days have passed, I can't be sure, but he did complete the treatment. All that is left now is for us to wait and hope that it wasn't done too late.

The chanting stops suddenly and I hear a shuffling from inside the room. I stop pacing and step aside as the Masters walk out.

They take no notice of me, continuing down the hall with somber faces.

I look into Rue's room. Her small form lies beneath a clean white sheet. I should let her rest. But I can't wait until morning, I have to see her, even if she's asleep.

I go inside and notice that she's awake, her head is turned to one side and she's looking out the window. Her hands rest on the sheet, tiny and frail.

"Rue?"

She turns her head to look at me. "Rynn!" She smiles. Her voice sounds weak but she reaches her arms out to me anyway. I hurry over and kneel down beside her bed to give her a hug.

"They left me here in the dark," she says against my chest.

"I'll light some candles," I say, my throat tight with emotion. "And don't worry, you won't be alone. I'll stay here with you until morning, so you can sleep."

I open the night table drawer and take out some candles. There are still some matches in my pocket and a chocolate square, which I brought just in case Rue felt well enough to eat.

My fingers tremble slightly as I get up and set out each candle. Too much has happened. For now, everything is okay.

Rue made it through the surgery and she's going to be fine. But I can't protect her forever. What will happen next time things aren't okay?

When I'm done lighting the candles, I return to her bed and sit down beside her. "I told you that you should be scared of me," I say taking her hand. "That I might end up killing you someday."

Rue smiles. "You didn't kill me," she says.

"I'm sorry I made you eat the treemeal." My throat tightens even more and I can't swallow. "You told me it tastes bad and I didn't—"

I can't finish my sentence.

Rue shrugs. "I was only sick for a little bit. I'm okay now." She gives me another weak smile, her face far too pale. "The doctor said all the tree bugs are gone and I can do whatever I want tomorrow."

I nod. All the emotions of the last few days suddenly hit me at once. I don't want to cry in front of Rue, but it's hard to hold back the tears.

"Don't ever listen to me again, okay?" I say, wiping at my eyes. "Or anyone else. You do what you think is best. Listen to yourself."

"Okay," Rue says.

"We can play rocks tomorrow if you want."

Rue frowns. "I can't find Mr. Rock." Tears fill her eyes. "I tried to tell grandpa but no one was listening to me."

"I'm listening," I say. "I'll look all night until I find Mr. Rock. And Mrs. Rock too. And all their babies."

"They're not under the bed anymore." Rue's bottom lip quivers.

"Don't cry okay? I know they're all okay. I can feel it. I've got special powers, remember? If anything bad happened to Mr. Rock there would have been a big disturbance in the Universe and I would have felt it."

"Okay, but you told me not to listen to you," she says, smiling slightly. I smooth her hair back, away from her forehead which is damp.

"You know what? I do know where Mr. and Mrs. Rock are, and all their babies. I'll take you there tomorrow."

"Really?"

"Yes."

"Okay."

Rue closes her eyes, still smiling.

"Rue?"

"Yes?"

"Will you be my little sister?"

Rue smiles a bit bigger. "Okay. Can you teach me how to fight with a sword?"

"Sure. But we'll have to use sticks to practice, not real swords."

"Okay." Rue sighs and her breathing becomes deeper. She's exhausted.

"Rue?"

She doesn't reply this time and I watch her sleep for a moment. Then I carefully move over to the foot of her bed, to sit at her feet and lean against the wall.

I look at the moon outside her window and listen to her breathing as she sleeps.

"They're Taking Rue"

"Are you sure this is where Mr. Rock is?" Rue asks from behind me as I carry her on my back.

The trees of the forest sway in the breeze above us, making a rushing sound like a wave on a sandy beach.

"Yes, I'm sure," I say, lifting her higher so she doesn't slip down.

The air is crisp with the oncoming of fall, reminding me that summer training is coming to an end and so is my time with Rue. I push the thought away, listening instead for the sound of the river.

The wind stops rustling the trees for a moment and then I hear the water up ahead.

"We're almost there," I say to Rue. She bounces on my back and I hold her legs tighter, shifting her back into position. She's starting to feel like a sack of rocks on my back.

"Wow!" she yells in my ear as the rocky shore comes into view.

I kneel down to let her off my back and she runs to the river's edge.

"Rue!" I call after her. "Be careful."

She crouches down to look at the rocks on the bank and I join her.

"How are we going to find Mr. Rock?" she asks, glancing up at me with big, worried eyes.

"He's with his brothers and sisters and aunts and uncles and cousins," I say, pointing to the rocky shore.

Rue runs her hand over the stones. "Oh."

"And Mrs. Rock's babies are swimming in the river with all the other kids." I point to the shallow water filled with tiny rocks.

Rue smiles. "Yeah, they love to swim."

I pick up a random rock. "Do you want a new friend?"

"No." Rue's shoulders slump. Her skin is still ghostly pale. The enthusiasm of earlier has drained her.

"I'm sorry you got sick," I say, crouching down beside her.

"You already said that."

I nod. She's right. There's no reason for me to keep think-ing about it. She isn't mad at me. Yet I can't seem to let it go.

"I was happy when you made me eat the treemeal," Rue says.

I look at her, trying to see her face but her head is bowed. She doesn't sound like she's being sarcastic.

"Why?"

"Because that's what my mom always does. She makes me eat my food before I go play."

"Oh." I toss a rock into the river, thinking of my mom and how I can't remember the last time I saw her. And my dad, who came all this way to see me and I didn't even hug him back.

"My mom loves me," Rue says. "She said that's why she makes me eat my food. So that means you love me too."

There is a moment of silence as we listen to the trickling sounds of the river.

"I do," I say finally.

"What if my mom forgets me?" Rue says, hugging her knees, no longer interested in the rocks by her feet.

"She won't. You'll be home soon. The summer's almost over."

"No." Rue shakes her head. "She's still gone, after summer is over. Grandpa said."

I frown. "How long?"

"One moon cycle."

"Our moon cycle here or yours back home?"

Rue doesn't answer. But it's still a long time, whichever moon cycle it is.

"We still have time here together before I leave for my final training," I say, trying to lighten the mood. "Then there's only a short time after that, until you're home again."

Rue tilts her head up. "You're leaving?"

"It might only be for a few days. I don't know how long it will take."

"Then you're coming back after?"

"Sure." I smile, hoping she doesn't sense the worry I feel inside. "When I get back, I'll tell my dad that I want to stay here, at the school after training is over. I'll stay with you until your mom gets home, so you don't have to go back and stay with Ungar."

Rue jumps up, her energy suddenly renewed. "Can you teach me to fight with swords now?"

"Okay." I get up too. "Let's find some sticks."

She runs off into the forest and I follow after her.

The sun beats down from above as we step into a clearing. It feels good to be without a schedule. There are no classes this week. Master Dukath is off planet. Randon and Aurah, and the rest of the students, are busy plotting each other's deaths. And Rue and I are free to do whatever we want.

We search the ground for the right sized sticks for a sword fight.

"Look at this one!" I pick up a large stick that is perfectly straight. "It's perfect."

"Can I have it?" Rue yells, reaching for it. I pull it away.

"I found it first," I say. "And it's too heavy for you anyway."

"No, it's not!"

Her anger makes me realize I sound like Dad, telling her she can't do something because she's too weak. But she is weak right now, after being sick.

"What's wrong with that one?" I point to the stick she's holding.

She whips her stick through the air and slams it down onto the back of my hand.

"Ow!" I drop my stick and she jumps for it. I reach out my hand and use my Gift power. The stick flies to me before Rue can grab hold of it.

"Hey!" she yells. "No fair!"

I smile, grasping the stick tight. It feels good to use my Powers whenever I want. Drawing objects to myself is something I'm good at, something I practiced a lot with toys when I was little.

"Now, you will pay for trying to take my sword!" I say, raising my stick into the air.

Rue squeals and runs away. I chase after her. She's quick, moving between the trees faster than I can.

I scoop my stick in front of her to stop her from running away. She tries to dodge it but I grab her from behind.

"You shouldn't run so much," I say, catching my breath. "You're still getting better."

"I'm okay." Rue turns to face me, her breath coming out in fast gasps.

"How about we both use the same size sticks and I'll show you some blocking moves?"

Rue nods and I immediately begin to look for two equally sized sticks, that wouldn't be too heavy for Rue to hold.

"This one!" I pick up a good-sized stick and break off the extra branches on it.

Rue reaches for it.

"Say please," I taunt, pulling it away from her.

She stomps on my foot and I double over, pretending it hurt.

"Thanks!" Rue takes the stick out of my hand and begins to swing it around, almost knocking me in the eye with it.

"Careful." I grab the stick in the air.

"Hey! Let go."

"I need to find a stick for me first, then we'll fight."

"Okay." Rue begins practicing her moves against a tree, ignoring me as I search for my weapon. I finally find one and call her over.

"Watch me first, okay?" I say to her. She nods. "You need a good stance, feet solid on the ground so you don't fall over."

I show her a basic stance and a blocking move. She mimics me and my heart squeezes a little in my chest when I see her doing what I showed her. It's the first time I've ever taught anyone something and I like how it feels, like Rue looks up to me.

I show her a more complicated move and her eyes go wide with admiration. She tries to copy me but fumbles into the nook of a tree.

I rush over, but she's laughing when I get there.

"Let's stick with the simple blocking move for now," I say, holding out my hand to help her up. She takes it and bounces back up. "Ready?"

"Yes!"

I attack forward, careful not to put any force behind the swing.

"Good," I say as she blocks my attack with the counter move I showed her. I have the advantage, being taller and stronger, but she's hard to catch. She's small and quick.

I strike again but she does a back somersault to evade my blow.

"Quit rolling away," I say. "That's not the proper way to fight."

"But you're stronger," she says. "So it's better if I get away from you. Because I can't fight you."

I cross my arms. "Okay, but what if you're trapped and you can't get away?" I corner her against a tree and she smacks her stick down hard on my hand again. "Ouch! Stop it!" I drop my stick and rub my hand. "Strike to the chest, like I showed you, not my hand."

"But if I hurt your hand, you drop your sword."

"I can just pick it up again."

"Not if I chop your hand off!" Rue raises her stick and I grab it before she can hit me again.

"I'm hungry," she says, letting go of her stick. Her shoulders slump.

"Come on." I lift her up into my arms. "Let's go get some food."

"Without bugs please," Rue says.

"Good idea."

* * *

"Bryn!" Aurah barges into my room without knocking. I've just come back from the baths, having had free time in the afternoon while Rue was with her grandfather. I grab my shirt and quickly put it on.

"Don't you knock?"

"They're taking Rue," Aurah says.

"What?"

"Come on."

She runs out the door and I run after her.

* * *

"The girl has to go back," Master Dukath says. "She's been too sick and—"

"Her parents are still away," I interrupt. "She has no one to stay with on her home planet."

Master Dukath's face remains expressionless but I sense the irritation coming from him. He's returned early from his meetings, just to deal with Rue.

"She will be staying with a friend of the family, Ungar."

"Where is she?" I yell.

Master folds his hands onto his desk and leans forward. "It's not your place to decide where she stays and whom she stays with."

"Bryn..." A loud whisper from the door catches my attention. It's Aurah, waiting out in the hall for me. She's out of Master Dukath's line of sight and she nods her head, motioning for me to follow her. 'I know where she is,' she mouths silently.

I walk out of Dukath's office, not bothering to wait to be dismissed, nor bowing before leaving.

Broken

AURA HURRIES AHEAD OF me onto the cargo spacecraft, which has its bay doors open.

The workers unloading supplies ignore us as we briskly walk past into the open cargo area. The place is dirty and smells of fuel fumes.

Aurah points up to a balcony on the upper level, where the offices are. I nod, and we head up the metal stairs. I still feel awkward around her, for not even apologizing. Yet she's still helping me.

The stairs rattle as we run up. A guard stands at the office door where Aurah said Rue would be.

"No admittance," he barks.

"Dukath sent us." Aurah steps up to the guard.

He looks us over, crossing his large arms over his chest. "No one's allowed in. I have strict orders."

"You have permission to let us in," I say, trying out my Gift of influence on him. The guard blinks but doesn't say anything. I swallow hard. I should have practiced mind manipulation more, like Master Dukath told me to.

I try again. "Master Dukath just gave you permission to let us in. You were just talking to him on the comm system."

The guard nods and steps aside.

Aurah gives me a thumbs up and I let out the breath I was holding in. She opens the door and we both walk in.

The room seems empty and my heart drops. Did they take Rue away already?

"Rynn!" Rue scrambles out from under a large desk where she's hiding.

I drop to my knees and she comes running into my arms.

"I don't want to go back! I want to stay here with you!" she cries.

I want to tell her that she can stay here with me and be my sister forever, but I can't. Aurah is right. Rue doesn't belong in our world. I could be dead in a few days in the Elimination Games. And even if I survive, I'm not old enough to take care of Rue. She needs parents.

"I'll convince them to let you stay here with your grandfather, okay?" I manage to say.

"He's gone too, he had to go." Rue begins to sob. I hold her tight.

Aurah clears her throat and I look up.

"Dukath is coming," she says, poking her head out the door to look. "With Commander Garionne and Commander Klein."

I pull Rue out of our hug and grasp her tiny shoulders. I have to let go of her, like Aurah said. I look into her big, hazel eyes.

The sound of Dukath and the commanders' footsteps move closer and I know I have to say this now.

I swallow the lump in my throat. "Rue, I love you."

Rue shakes her head no, tears streaming down her cheeks. She seems to know that my words are a goodbye.

"When you see the stars at night," I continue, pushing through the pain in my throat. "Remember that I'm on one of those planets."

Rue shuts her eyes tight, her bottom lip quivering.

"And when I'm ruler over the Galaxies," I continue, "I'll come find you and we'll rule together. I promise. And you'll be my little sister forever. Or we can get married when you're older like you said, whatever you want. Okay? Just don't forget about me."

"You'll forget... about me," she says scattered hiccups.

"No, I won't. Ever. I promise."

Rue nods, looking defeated.

"Don't be scared—"

"The time for goodbyes are over," Master Dukath says behind me.

"No!" Rue screams. The sound pierces my soul.

She throws her arms around me again and I lift her up into my arms, then turn to face Dukath.

"She doesn't want to go," I say, even though I know I'm not going to win this fight.

"There is no one here to watch after her," Dukath says calmly. "Her parents have asked for her to be returned to Kahnju to stay with her uncle Ungar. We can't hold her here against her parents' will."

"He's not her uncle. She can't stay with him," I say, clutching Rue against me. Her little heart hammers against my chest and she grasps my shirt tight in her fists.

"Her parents are the ones to make that decision. This ship is scheduled to leave now and they are waiting for her arrival on Kahnju."

"Then I'll go with her," I say, tempted to use my Powers on Dukath, but knowing it won't work.

"Her grandfather has given specific instructions to have you kept away from her." Master Dukath turns to the commanders at his side and nods to them. They walk forward and reach for Rue.

"Stop!" I put out my hand and the guards fly back.

"Bryn," Aurah says. "Just let her go. The longer you drag this out, the harder it will be on her."

I shake my head no, but lower my hand. Commander Klein steps forward and pulls Rue from my arms. I let her go, but she clings to my shirt, refusing to be removed.

"No!" Her screams pierce my chest like a knife, but I let Commander Garionne unclasp her fists from my shirt and they take her away.

Rue's sobbing turns to whimpering as she gives up the fight.

I can't move. Aurah grabs my arm and pulls me along.

"Come on Bryn, we need to get out of here."

A moment later we're outside the room and I hear the office door shut. Rue's muffled cries fade off behind the closed door.

* * *

I hug my knees to my chest, staring down at the stone floor. The chapel is cold and drafty. The scent of rain blows in through the unshuttered windows. Raindrops patter against the stone walls and shower the trees outside, yet in my mind all I hear are Rue's screams.

I'd hoped coming to the chapel would help bring me some peace, but it hasn't. The pain won't let me breathe. It throbs on and on, like the rain outside.

Master Dukath was right, attachments break you down.

I should have done something more to keep her from being taken away. I shouldn't have let her go. Now she's officially gone. She'll be back on her home planet with that alien she's so scared of.

I get up off the floor.

I can't take this anymore.

* * *

"Please, Your Leadership," I say, on my knees before Grand Master. "Please erase all my memories of Rue." I swallow down my pride. "I don't want to feel this way anymore."

"You're very passionate, Bryn," Master Dukath says, using my old name. "It gives you access to immense power. But it must be directed in the correct way. Not like this."

With one flick of his finger he has me standing up straight again.

I don't respond. If I say anything now, it will be something I'll regret later.

"Now you know how much attachments hurt. It was your grandfather's weakness as well, but I believe it does not have to be yours. You are not the only one disappointing me with your attachments. Randon must let go of his attachment to you, if he wishes to rule as one of the Leaders."

Master Dukath shuffles back to his chair. "You will both come to me to have your memories of these attachments erased, and I will keep a closer eye on you both from now on."

I frown. I came here for myself, not Randon. It should be his choice if he wants his memory erased.

"Eventually, one must become broken, my young apprentice," Dukath continues. "In order to be put back together as a stronger, more powerful force. One that is unbreakable."

I nod.

"Go, tell Randon what I've told you. Then come back to me when you're both ready to leave all of this childishness behind you, and then you will be ready to face your final challenge in the Elimination Games."

I nod again, unable to speak. Every muscle in my body aches. The pain isn't just in my heart, it has consumed every part of me.

I bow to Grand Master before walking out of his office, broken.

STAY THE NIGHT

R ANDON AND AURA STOP talking when I walk into the room.

I can tell they've been talking about me by their sudden silence.

"Aurah, I need to talk to Randon, alone," I say, not looking at her. My eyes stay on Randon. He stares back, a flash of curiosity in his bright blue eyes.

Aurah gets up without a word and leaves. I close the door after her, then lock it.

Randon stands up from the bed, on alert now. Does he know I lost Rue? Does he think I'm going lash out at him in anger?

He doesn't say anything, waiting for me to say what I came here to say.

A memory, long buried, flashes through my mind; me throwing a classmate across the playground with my Gift power, because he laughed at me.

I'm not that kid anymore.

"Relax," I say. "I'm not going to hurt you."

Randon studies me with a cautious look.

"Tell me what you want," I say softly, my hand still resting on the door handle. My stomach still feels tight with the pain of losing Rue. If Randon's attachment to me is anything like how I feel about Rue, then he's not going to be happy about what I came here to tell him.

"What I want?" he asks after a moment, sitting back down on the bed. "Want with what?"

"With me."

I walk over to the bed and sit beside him.

"Nothing." Randon shifts over, putting some distance between us.

"Grand Master wants to erase your memory," I say.

"What? Why?"

"He wants to take away the memories that have made you attached to me."

Randon presses his lips together, his hand clenching into a fist.

"He's going to erase all my memories of Rue, too," I continue. "So I won't have to feel like this anymore." I swallow hard. I could never have properly loved Rue anyway. I'm too impulsive, and selfish. I don't have any way to care for her. I can only hope that someday, someone will make her happier than I ever could.

Randon's shoulders slump and he bows his head.

I sigh. Master Dukath was right. Randon needs to forget how he feels about me, if we're going to be leaders together in the Ruling Order. Master Dukath is wise. I should have listened to him in the first place. He said no touching anyone, but I held Rue in my arms, many times. He said no attachments, but I let Rue into my emotions.

The sound of her screams in the cargo ship office haunt me. I clench my fists. I have to stop thinking about it, but I can't. I need to feel something else, anything.

"I got to say goodbye to Rue," I say, turning to Randon. "I got to hug her and... tell her how much I will miss her."

I hesitate for a second before continuing, my heart racing with the unease of what I'm about to say next. "I know how you feel about me."

Randon gives me an angry glare. "I feel nothing but hate towards you."

I nod, taking a deep breath as I sort out my thoughts. "I hate Rue too, for making me love her this much."

Randon looks away, scowling. "Can you tell Dukath to have your memories erased, too?"

"He already said he would."

"No, I mean memories of me, not Rue."

"Of you? Why?"

"Because... Just..." Randon lets out a breath. He tries again, then stops. I've never seen him emotional before, other than his anger. He's the least sensitive person I know, yet now he seems unable to say what he wants to say, as though he's nervous.

"Can I read your thoughts?" I ask, raising my hand. "Would it help?"

"No." Randon swipes at my hand. It reminds me of Rue, and my the pain in my chest is unbearable.

"You asked me what I want..." Randon says.

I nod, bracing myself for his answer.

"I just want to lay down. I'm really tired." He looks at his hands in his lap.

"Oh." I get up from the bed so he can have room to lay down. "I'll go."

Randon doesn't move to lie down and I suddenly realize what he's actually saying, but can't seem to ask for.

I sit back down. "Do you want me to stay here with you, for the night?" I ask for him.

Randon nods, ever so slightly. He avoids looking at me, keeping his eyes hidden beneath his mop of orange hair. I'd always thought he was quite easy on the eyes, truth be told, but I would never have admitted it.

I glance at the bed. It's barely big enough for the both of us. The thought of laying down together makes me feel weird, but it's not so unreasonable of a request that I can't bear with it.

As painful as it was, I got a chance to say goodbye to Rue, before she was taken away. I can give Randon that chance too, in his way.

I pull my feet up and lay down against the wall, giving Randon as much room as I can. I leave my boots on. The bed is still made, which makes me feel better because it seems less intimate.

I pull the pillow out from under the blankets and lay my head on it. A sigh escapes me. I'm more tired than I realized. I close my eyes for a moment, enjoying finally lying down.

The bed shifts and Randon joins me, lying onto his back beside me. I bring the pillow closer to him, so we can share it. He moves closer until our shoulders touch.

"Sometimes I don't understand you," I say, fighting against the tiredness now threatening to overtake me. I don't want to fall asleep yet. I want to give Randon his chance to say whatever he needs to say to me, before tomorrow.

The bed is too small for my height so I have to keep my knees bent. Randon's knees are also bent and bump against mine.

"Do you promise you'll ask Dukath, to make you forget everything too?" he asks.

"All my memories of you?"

"Yes. From the day you read my mind, in his study, until now. I mean, until tomorrow morning."

"I don't think Master Dukath will be taking requests," I say, jokingly.

"You're right." Randon rests his arm across his forehead. "He'll probably just erase everything, since we were kids."

I nod. It makes sense.

Randon's arm drops to his side and his hand brushes against mine. I resist the urge to move my hand away. He'll just feel rejected.

After a moment, he takes my hand in his, grasping it tight in a nervous sort of way. His hand is smaller than mine, his palm warm and clammy.

"I'm scared of the Games," he says, gripping my hand tighter.

I turn my head to look at him and he quickly looks away.

I stare at the ceiling instead.

"I think everyone is scared of the Games," I offer.

"And I'm scared of how I feel about you." He lets go of my hand. "Never mind."

"I understand," I say, taking his hand back.

Randon stiffens, as though trying to decide whether or not he should pull away.

After a moment, he gives in and we rest in silence.

The rain has started up again outside and the stone wall against my shoulder is sucking the heat from me. I shift away from it, moving closer to Randon's side.

"Dukath is the only one who didn't mind that I am the way I am," he says after a moment. "He said my struggles would help me become more powerful because they made me angry, and anger makes a person strong."

I wait a moment in case he wants to say more.

He doesn't continue so I say, "he said something like that to me too. I was uncontrollable as a kid. I was different. And I had a lot of anger."

"Yes, you did." Randon smiles.

"Anger, and my power, is a bad combination." I squeeze Randon's hand.

How many times did I unintentionally hurt someone because of my anger? And yet, I never hurt Randon, even when he was a bully to me.

I always thought it was because Dukath had a strict rule about me not using my powers. But I realize now, that if I was truly angry at Randon, I could have hurt him. Did I willingly let him use me as an outlet for his anger, and affection? Because I knew how much he needed it?

I glance at him again and see that he's still got a smile on his face; a genuine one that I rarely ever see. It makes him look younger.

"Remember the Star Destroyer we learned about in class?" Randon says.

I nod.

"If this is the Super Destroyer..." he raises our clasped hands up towards the ceiling, then holds his other hand up too, showing the size of about a shoe length. "Then this, is how big *my* Destroyer is going to be."

Randon spreads his arms out wide, smacking me in the face with my own arm, then lowers our hands again. "*Our* Super Destroyer," he adds.

I turn onto my side to face him. I can see the freckles on his face, this close up. "Are you going to call it that, the Super Destroyer?"

"No." Randon turns onto his side too. "I'm not sure what I'll call it yet, maybe 'Planet Destroyer,' because it will destroy planets, or "Destroyer Planet," because it will be as big as a whole planet, and we will have a huge military base on it. I'll build one that can destroy five or six planets at the same time." His eyes flash.

"You're going to destroy all these planets for fun?" I ask.

"Maybe," Randon shrugs.

"You could just threaten to destroy them, if the residents don't give you what you ask for," I offer. "Instead of destroying everything they have on their planet. You know you could use their planet's resources—"

"Ask?"

"I mean take."

Randon studies me. "We could make a good team," he says. His smile fades. "Can you go back to hating me, after your memory is erased?"

"Probably," I say.

"It would be easier for me, if you did. I don't like it when you're nice. It makes me weak."

"I won't be nice. You've been bullying me since I was ten. So it shouldn't be too hard to go back to hating you."

"Getting bullied makes a person tough."

"That's what bullies always say."

"Because it's true."

"How did you turn out to be such a mean kid?"

Randon shrugs. "I'm just naturally evil."

"That's true," I say.

"I don't want my memories erased." Randon says, sitting up. "I don't want to go back to how we were before. I want to just focus on leading the Ruling Order together." He lies onto his back again and looks up at the ceiling.

We listen to the rain clink against the windows for a moment. I can smell the dirt and roots of the nearby forest, drinking in the rain.

"Once we're out there, in battle," I say, "blowing up starships and conquering planets, all of this…" I look down at our clasped hands. "All this emotional stuff won't matter anymore. We'll be doing what we were born to do."

Randon nods, and I can't help but think of Rue. She will always matter. I promised her I'd never forget her, right before she was taken away. And now I'll be heading into Dukath's office in the morning to do just that.

I don't want to forget her, even if remembering kills me inside. It was my fault she got sick and almost died and that she has to return to Kahnju, to Ungar, to clean robot parts and who knows what else.

I squeeze Randon's hand.

"Ouch." Randon pulls away and I drape my arms across my face, to cover my eyes, unable to hold back the tears.

"I'm sorry you lost her," Randon says, knowing immediately what's wrong. I pull the pillow over my face and Randon doesn't say anything else.

The sound of the rain continues, reminding me of being in the chapel earlier, when it felt like this pain would suffocate me. It eased only for a moment, while I was talking to Randon and distracted, but now it's back, stronger than ever. If I don't have my memory erased, this will tear me apart and I'll lose the Games for sure, and my life.

I take the pillow off my head and get up to go wash my face. "I'll be right back," I say.

"Okay." Randon's voice sounds different and I look over. He quickly covers his face with his arm and turns away, but not before I see that his eyes are red from crying.

I sigh. Now I understand why attachments are forbidden.

MY THOUGHTS ARE PRIVATE

I WAKE TO THE sun shining on my face and lift my hand to block out its bright glare. The air is thick with moisture and I feel too warm in my bed.

I look around and see a star chart on the wall and papers all over the floor. This isn't my room.

I turn to see Randon lying beside me.

Then I remember. He wanted me to stay with him before Master Dukath erased his memory. But now he doesn't want it erased. I wonder what Master Dukath will say.

Randon continues to sleep, looking peaceful. I turn on my back again and stifle a sigh. My body feels heavy and my chest aches.

Rue...

The pain comes flooding back and I clench my fists.

Randon stirs, then wakes, rubbing his eyes and stretching. I didn't want to wake him. I'm not doing well right now. I still don't know what to do. Should I let Master Dukath erase my memories of her, or not?

If I continue feeling this way then I know I won't make it through the Games. But I promised her I'd never forget her and that's literally Master Dukath will do.

Randon turns to me and looks confused for a second. I lift my hand to his temple to read his mind, without asking, desperate for the distraction of feeling something other than my own emotions. I close my eyes and concentrate.

"Bryn?" he says, but I ignore him and lock in to his mind.

He's easy to read, having just woken and without his guard up yet. He's surprised to find me in his bed. He thought I would leave for sure after he fell asleep.

His pain is strong too, but different than mine, not raw and fresh but an old and heavy wound that pulls him into despair frequently. He knows that I'll never like him in the same way he likes me. He feels different than the other students.

There's something else too, something that isn't pain or sadness. I focus in on that. It's joy, at having me here, and the relief of finally letting himself just feel whatever he wants, even if just for now.

His emotions shift to something a lot more enticing; his desire for me.

"Bryn..." Randon pushes my hand away. "My thoughts are private."

I open my eyes to find that Randon's gaze is on my lips.

"Go ahead," I say, knowing what he wants to do. "I'll forget it soon anyway."

He doesn't hesitate, but lifts his hand up to the back of my neck, shifting closer to me until our knees collide. I hold my breath as he leans in to close the distance between us, his fingers curling into my hair.

A loud banging on the door makes us jump apart.

I sit up quickly. Randon grumbles and covers his face with the pillow. I have to climb over him to get out of the bed and answer the door, but he doesn't get up.

Aurah is standing on the other side when I get there, with her arms crossed and a frown on her face.

"Thought I'd find you here," she says. "Dukath's looking for you and he's mad that you weren't in your room this morning."

She glances past me to the bed. "You'd better put your cloak on and pretend you were wandering the forest all night. He's mad at Randon, too."

GOODBYE RUE...

"I HAVE TO DO one more thing before I get my memory erased," I say to Aurah, as we run down the hall to Dukath's study.

Randon gives me a concerned look. "Bryn—"

"Just tell Master that I was at the baths and I'm still getting dressed."

Aurah nods and I hesitate, wondering what I should say to Randon before he goes in.

I set my hand on his shoulder briefly, then walk away.

* * *

I kneel onto the cold stone floor of the chapel, the smell of the stone and wood around me bringing me peace.

"Grandfather," I whisper, my breath puffing out into the cold morning air. "I'm not doing very well in my training. I let myself have an attachment." I think of Rue and my chest tightens. "I'm not strong like the others, like Randon…"

I stop, remembering the insecurities I saw in Randon's thoughts. He has doubts like everyone else, but doesn't let them hold him back. And I also saw his strong desires. He never let them get in his way, or break him down, the way I have.

I feel a stirring of the Power inside of me; the energy that's in everything; in the forest and the animals, in the Masters and the students, in Aurah and Randon. I've upset the balance, in so many ways.

"I'm sorry I forced myself on Aurah," I whisper, not to Grandfather this time, but to the greater Power out there, the one that gives me my special abilities and is alive inside of me.

I swallow hard. I need to do this confession, for myself, not for Dukath. He'll invade my thoughts soon enough, but for now they're still my own, they're my mistakes, my pain, my regrets.

"I treated her the way all the other guys do, but worse. And I went into Randon's thoughts, when he told me not to. I don't know why I did it." I bow my head. "He's the only one who was never afraid to be close to me. I… I don't want to feel anything at all. It's just better that way. I don't want to love anyone or need anything from them. All I want is to know Rue will be safe and not left with Ungar."

I shut my eyes tight and tears roll down my cheeks. "Please, I just need to know she won't be left with the alien, and that she'll be safe."

A fluttering of wings makes me jump and I look up at the window. A forest bird settles onto the stone window sill, letting out a coarse *caw*. It turns its head to the side to look at me, then drops something to the ground from it's claw. It clatters over the stone floor and comes to a stop in front of me.

It's a rock. I reach down and pick it up.

It's not just any rock, it's *Mr. Rock*. Rue's markings are still on it. She put two dots for the eyes and a line for the mouth. I grasp it tightly in my hand. A peace washes over me. I know she'll be okay.

All things will work out for good, to those who walk in the Gift of the Universe. The Mantra comes to my mind. I'll see Rue again, no matter what happens.

I don't want to forget her, ever, no matter how much pain it causes me. And I don't want to forget my night with Randon either, even though I promised him I would. I want to keep all my memories.

"Thank you," I whisper to the bird. Then I get up and leave.

* * *

I run into Dukath's office to find Randon standing very still in front of Dukath's desk.

"Sorry I'm late," I say, catching my breath. Randon doesn't move and I realize that Master has him locked in a hold.

"So nice of you to grace us with your presence," he says to me, keeping his eyes on Randon.

My heart pounds. "I don't want to forget," I say, getting right to the point. "I want to remember everything, so that I'll never forget how much pain attachments can cause, and I'll be more careful in the future not to have them. I want to remember Rue and..." I glance over at Randon again, but I can't tell if he can hear me. "I want to remember this entire summer with Randon."

"That's not for you to decide," Master Dukath says calmly. "And you will address me as Master."

I glare at him. "These memories, *Master*, are my own and I want to keep them. I've changed my mind about having them erased."

"Are you challenging me, Bryn?"

"No..."

Suddenly, a stabbing pain pierces my head and I shut my eyes tight, falling to my knees.

"Grand Master, stop," Randon says beside me.

Then I hear him cry out in pain too.

"This pain," Dukath says, "you *will never* forget. Your attachments, however, you will forget. I can make you mighty, a great force in the Universe, to be feared by all, but I can also make you into nothing and destroy you. You will learn to respect your *Master*."

I fight to hold on to my memories of Rue, even as they begin to slip away; her hazel eyes, so excited when I surprised her with all the rocks from the river. Her death-grip hugs. How relieved I was when I found her in the chapel, after she'd disappeared.

They fade away from my mind, one by one. Only the emotions remain; the worry that gripped my chest when I thought she was missing, the pain that pierced my heart at the sound of her cries when she was taken away, the joy I felt whenever we spent time together. Her smile, her laugh, her spirit.

No...

I promised her I would never forget her. But it's too late.

Goodbye Rue...

GOODBYE RANDON

I BLINK AND MY vision clears. The pain in my head slowly eases and I look up.

I'm in Master Dukath's office. His desk looms in front of me.

Why am I on my knees? I don't even remember coming here.

I turn slowly, my head aching when I move it. Randon is beside me, his hands covering his face. He's crying. It scares me. I've never seen Randon cry before. Is it really him?

"Randon?"

I look up and see Grand Master with his hand outstretched. What's he doing to Randon?

I put my hand on Randon's shoulder and concentrate. I want to see what's happening. Grand Master is tormenting him.

"Stop it," I say softly. I want to yell it but I don't have enough energy. I'm emotionally drained but don't know why.

Let him go!

I stretch my arm out to Grand Master and his hold on Randon wavers for a moment. Randon takes a few quick breaths.

He's being punished, Master says to my mind, *for his unclean thoughts.*

They're his thoughts, I reply. *He has a right to his own thoughts.*

Not under my rule, he doesn't.

Randon's memories surface as the three of us are locked together in thought. All the moments that built to his attachment to me; they're slipping away, one at a time. The first time he met me, when he learned about my powers and it made him angry. That's when his attachment to me started. He wanted to be like me, but didn't want me to know that he admired my abilities. I see my younger self, smiling at him, so open and naïve. Then Randon shoves me, just to have a reason to touch me. He's mad that I don't retaliate when he's mean.

The memories begin slipping away faster now. All the times he threatened me, pinned me to the ground, spilled my food at meal times, startled me in my sleep, played tricks on me. Then more private moments; sleepless nights when he fought not to give in to intimate thoughts about me. And then I see myself sitting with a little girl at the lunch table and Randon's immense jealousy of our friendship. His memories of the girl are recent, but I have no idea who she is.

Dukath leaves only the jealousy, anger, rivalry and hate Randon felt towards me, without the actual memories that accompany them.

There is one last memory that isn't fully stolen yet, a recent one. I take hold of it with all my strength so Dukath can't snatch that too; it's Randon and I lying together on his bed, talking about his plans to make the largest Super Destroyer weapon of all time. I won't let Dukath have that one.

He tries to remove it, but I fight him and Randon collapses to the ground, unconscious, his mind out of reach now.

Dukath turns his attention to me and I freeze.

Does he know that Randon still has one memory unerased?

I can tell by his expression that he's going to take away everything I just saw.

He grips me in a hold and I fall to the ground beside Randon. Then, everything turns dark.

* * *

"I hope this headache goes away by tomorrow," I say to Aurah. She's visiting me in my room, something I don't think she's ever done before. I'm not exactly sure why she's here and it's a bit awkward to have her sitting on my bed. She looks sad; also something I'm not used to seeing.

"Aurah?"

"Yes?"

"Am I dying?" That would explain all her sad looks and melancholy.

"No." She smiles, finally.

"But you'd tell me if I was, right?"

"Yes, I'd tell you."

A new thought occurs to me. "Did I lose my Powers?"

"No, I don't think you've lost them. You're just a little weak from..." she trails off.

I sit up, the movement making my head throb. "I still don't understand what I'm sick with."

"You're not sick with anything."

"Easy for you to say," I groan. I look around the room. It's different than I last remember it being. But whenever I try to think back to what I did yesterday, my head hurts more. I *do* remember being worried about the Elimination Games, and Aurah and Randon being mad at me during the announcement assembly. Why were they mad?

"So are you and Randon ready for the Elimination Games?" I ask, glad that at least Aurah is no longer mad at me, like she was yesterday.

"He's not feeling well either."

"Oh." Good. He's the first person who will try to kill me in the Games, and he's smart, so I have to watch out for him. Although, I do have my Powers and I could choke hold him until he runs out of air...

"Aurah?"

"Yeah?"

"Before the Elimination Games announcement in Markin Hall, did I choke Randon?"

She sighs. "Yes. Why?"

"I don't remember why I did that. What was I mad about?"

Aurah hesitates. "You were just trying out your powers. Dukath said you could use them again and so you tried choking Randon."

That doesn't seem like me. I hate Randon, but I can't imagine trying something like that on him, knowing he'd kill me in my sleep later, if I did. And when did Grand Master give me permission to use my powers? I definitely don't recall that.

"Grand Master never gave me permission to use my powers," I say, running a hand through my hair. "He just said I could read minds, for one of his tests."

I try to remember what happened that day, or the day before that, but it only makes my head hurt more. My only clear memories are of being in classes during the day, and an anxious feeling of wanting classes to be over so I could go do something else, something I was really looking forward to doing, but now I don't know what it was.

"Stop," Aurah says, interrupting my thoughts.

"Stop what?"

"Stop trying to remember. They're all gone. All the memories from this summer, you won't find them."

"What do you mean? I remember this summer."

"What do you remember?"

I frown. "Uh... target practice. You got every shot. And I had to wander the forest as a punishment one night. Randon jumped me..."

Aurah doesn't say anything. She's right though, I hardly remember a thing. It's as though my summer went from the first day of classes, to the Elimination Games announcement in a flash.

"Dukath erased your memory of most of the stuff that happened over the summer."

"He did? Why?"

"Because he believed it was affecting your training."

I lay back down. What did I do that was so bad? It's probably a good thing I don't remember.

"I'm sure he had a good reason," I say to Aurah. But now I'm curious and really want to know. "Do *you* know what memories he erased?"

Aurah shrugs. She either doesn't know or she doesn't want to tell me.

Or isn't allowed to.

Another thought occurs to me, Master Dukath's number one rule. "Did I have an *attachment?*"

Aurah stares out the window above my bed. I've always thought she was pretty, but I've never felt any affection that was more than friendship, towards her. She intimidates me too much.

Everyone else in the program is male, so it couldn't have been an attachment to them, unless friendship attachments are also forbidden. Though, in truth, I never felt a close friendship to any of my other classmates.

"Did Master say how long I'll be sick for?" I ask.

"You're not sick," Aurah replies. "Just get up and find some headache elixir."

"But I can feel it in my chest and stomach, too. I'm nauseous and I feel like I do after..." I stop. I finally recognize the sick feeling. It's how I feel after crying for a long time. Like when I killed that kid in school. I cried a lot.

Did I kill someone?

"Aurah, you have to tell me. Did something *bad* happen?"

"You've had some emotional trauma, that's all. It's probably a good thing that you don't know why it's there."

Emotional trauma? Now I'm worried.

"Did my dad die?"

"No." Aurah gets up from the side of my bed. "I'm going to check on Randon, now. Believe it or not, he's doing worse than you. I think he completely passed out."

"From what?"

Aurah hesitates at my bedside, but doesn't answer.

"It doesn't matter. I'm glad he's suffering for once."

"Don't say that," Aurah snaps.

I give he a questioning look. "Why not? He hates me and enjoys making my life miserable."

She shakes her head and sighs. "Just try and be friends in the Elimination Games, okay?"

"Are you serious?"

"Let's keep all three of us alive."

"He'll kill me if I don't kill him first."

"He'll never kill you, Bryn."

I look away, frustrated by her comments. "It's *Rynn*." I don't feel like talking to her anymore. Her cryptic answers are annoying. But she's right about the memory thing. My headache gets worse whenever I try to remember anything.

Now that I know the memories were taken for a reason, I can just leave them alone and not try to remember. Grand

Master knows what's best for me, so there's no point in trying to undo what he's done for my benefit.

Aurah leaves and I get up to go close door. A clanking sound catches my attention and I look down. A smooth stone rolls to a stop at my feet. It fell out of my pocket.

I pick it up to get a closer look. There are some markings on it. A pain grips my chest and I recognize it right away. *Attachment.*

I drop the rock like it burned me.

It must have some sort of spell over it. Who put it into my pocket?

My head hurts again. It's one of the things I'm supposed to forget.

I pick up the rock and put it back into my pocket. I won't get rid of it just yet.

If Randon is feeling worse than I am, then I might just have a chance at winning in the Games.

I'm going to win, but it won't be easy. Grand Master himself said I'll be the leader someday, and I think that the day is coming soon. I don't care if Randon lives or dies. No one will miss me if I die. I've got nothing to lose and everything to gain.

I go to my dresser and take out a change of clothes.

Tomorrow night, the Games begin. I have a lot to do to get ready.

enemies again

MY EYES PINCH FROM the glare off the dark blue pendant around Randon's neck. I take a step back. The crystal makes my chest hurt and my head pound.

I came looking for Master Garionne, who usually writes in the library in the afternoon, but Randon found me first.

"What is that?" I ask, glancing at the crystal again. It seems to drain me of energy just being near it. Maybe I'm still sick from before.

The library is empty and there is no sign of Master Garionne. It's so quiet I can hear the rain outside, tapping against the stained glass windows above us. Randon moves closer and I back away from him.

"It's something that came at a high price," he says. "But totally worth it."

I keep backing away until I hit a desk behind me, and stop.

Randon grins. Did Dukath give him that crystal? To level out the playing field for the Games, since I've got powers and the others don't?

Suddenly Randon lunges at me and grabs my neck. I try to pull his hands away, but the crystal is up against me now and I've got no strength.

"Not so tough now, are you?" Randon says.

I try to swallow but can't. "Please..."

Randon's grip is so tight I can't speak.

"How does it feel, Bryn? To be choked? Not so fun is it?"

"Stop it!" Aurah's voice echoes through the empty library.

Randon's grip loosens as he looks over his shoulder. He lets go and I collapse to the ground.

"We have to stick *together*," Aurah scolds, walking up to Randon and pointing a finger in his face. "Or we'll die in the Games."

"Isn't that the point?" Randon smirks. "To kill each other and be the last one standing?"

I glance up at them, still on the floor at Randon's feet. It's not just the crystal that's draining my energy, it's a feeling of betrayal. But why would I expect anything less from him? It's not a betrayal if he's always been like this—hating me his entire life.

There's a strange emotional inside of me, like I feel differently about him than before, but I don't know why. I just know I won't kill him in the Games, even though I have an advantage with my Powers. And even though I know he'll try and kill me. But if he brings that crystal with him to the Games, then I might have to kill him, in self defense.

"The point is to be one of the last *twenty-five* left standing," Aurah says to Randon. "We need each other. We can all win."

Her words bring back a memory from the beginning of the summer. Randon said the same thing to me in the forest, when he attacked me and held me down. *We need each other.*

"I don't need anyone," Randon snaps, walking away.

I get up and stand beside Aurah, still lightheaded from my exposure to the crystal.

"Do you really want to lead the Future Command with those other useless classmates?" Aurah continues. "Wouldn't you rather it be us?"

Randon stops. He turns and glances at us. Then leaves the library.

Aurah looks me over. "Are ryou okay?" Her angry expression has been replaced by a sadness, that I've never seen on her until today.

I nod.

"I'll make sure Randon gets rid of that thing," she says.

"It cost me a lot," Randon says. He's at the library entrance and hasn't actually left.

"I don't care how much it cost you," Aurah shouts at him. "We're getting rid of it!"

"Why, so Bryn can kill me in my sleep?"

"He's *not* going to do that, and you know it."

The spacious hall goes silent. I'm too emotional to say anything, which is the worst thing I could be feeling right now, before a match to the death in the Games.

* * *

"You have one day to familiarize yourselves with the layout of the ship," Commander Klein announces as we all shuffle together into a lineup. We've been brought out to a clearing in the woods, under the night sky.

"Once on board," Commander Klein continues, "you will be assigned your quarters for the night, and in twenty-four hours, Master Dukath will make the opening announcements for the Elimination Games to begin."

I shift my bag on my shoulder, anxious to move forward in line and get onto the ship. It's chilly this late at night, away from the protection of the school buildings. But the cold makes me feel alert and ready to fight. The 'emotion sickness," as Aurah put it, that I was feeling all day has finally settled down. Since I don't remember what happened, it's easier to ignore the left over, dull ache in my chest.

I glance at Aurah. She's wearing a dark green sleeveless shirt, despite the chill, and stands tall and determined, amidst the others, her backpack slung lazily over one shoulder. I'm glad she wants us to be a team, even if she wants Randon to also be with us.

He stands next to her, looking deep in thought and staring ahead. He apologized to me, in his own way, for threatening me with the crystal. But I'm not ready to trust him just yet, even if we've agreed to be a team. At least if we're working together, we'll stand a good chance against the rest.

Commander Klein continues his speech and I glance around at the others. A sick feeling settles in my stomach when I think that I will have to kill some of them.

I grasp straps of my backpack and look up at the starry sky. The Capital Starship hovers above us, a small dot of red amidst the stars, waiting for us to be taken up by shuttle. It looks small from down here, but I know it's as large as a small city on my planet.

"Line up over here," Commander Klein shouts. "In single file."

Aurah grabs my arm. "You ready for this?" she whispers.

I nod and we get into position, Aurah first, then Randon, then me.

"Once you cross these gates," Commander Klein continues, "there's no turning back. So if you want out, now is the time to walk away."

The students look at each other. No one moves to leave.

"Anyone?" Commander Klein asks one final time.

A hush falls over the crowd.

For a moment I have a crazy thought. I could go home and leave this all behind. I've had this thought before, but it's part of the memories that have been erased. But it's more than just wanting to escape such a horrible game. I had something else I wanted to live for. Something that didn't have to do with becoming part of the Command team of the Ruling Order, which has always been my one goal in life.

"Good." Commander Klein's voice cuts through the silence. "Now, get moving."

The line begins to move ahead and my pulse speeds up. Each student is patted down and checked for weapons, then made to walk through a scanner. Randon glances back at me over his shoulder.

"I'm fine," I hiss, and he faces forward again. I wipe my sweaty palms on my shirt. My Powers haven't been the same since Randon brought out that crystal, but I'm sure I can handle lifting a small phaser blaster off the ground. I'll find out soon enough.

It's Aurah's turn to go up. She raises her hands for the pat down, and her bag is taken by two officers to be checked. I watch as she is sent through the scanner, then stops on the other side to wait for us. Randon is up next. They take his bag and my heart beats faster.

"Don't touch that!" Randon yells at one of the officers, startling me, even though I already know it's part of the plan. It's the distraction he's making so I can sneak Aurah's blaster in.

The officer checking Randon's bag holds up the small knife placed there, to be discovered. It has a carefully crafted wooden handle in the shape of a sea creature. It's actually Aurah's, a gift from a guy she met on one of her trips.

All eyes turn to Randon and the guards move in to surround him.

"My grandfather gave that to me," Randon continues. "I'm not leaving it behind!"

I reach under my cloak for the small blaster I have hidden there, then lower it to the ground using my Powers. It hovers awkwardly for a moment and a drop of sweat drips down my temple as I concentrate.

No body is looking at me, they're all focused on Randon. I move the blaster forward, just slightly above the ground and away from the lights and the crowd. Randon continues to argue with the guards, making a scene to keep their attention.

"It's not a weapon. It's a gift," he shouts. "It brings me luck."

I move the phaser away from the scanners and around, then back towards Aurah who's on the other side. She quickly grabs for it when it bumps her ankle.

"It will be in your room at the school, when you return," Commander Klein says, stepping in and taking the knife from the officers. He seems more resigned than angry, maybe even tired.

Randon gets shoved through the sensors, his bag thrown at him. He joins Aurah, who gives him a small nod. She has the weapon.

They head to the shuttle together and my shoulders relax. Now It's my turn to go through.

I step forward.

There's no turning back now.

SLeep aT YOUR OWN RISK

THE DOOR TO MY new bedroom quarters swishes open to reveal a clean and neat interior.

I smile at the wonderful smell of new furniture and metal. I wouldn't mind dying here. At least I'll go out in luxury.

The Capital starship is a first class vessel with a modern design. It makes me more eager to win the Games, if only to live in one of these starships my entire life. A narrow window above the bed runs halfway around the circular room, showcasing the stars and multi-colored gasses of outer space, on the outside of the ship.

I step inside and take a deep breath. The windows are spotless, the carpets clean. There is not a speck of dust in sight. I stretch, admiring the rounded ceiling above.

Despite the nice surroundings, I can't completely forget why we're here. Five students walked away before going through the weapons detectors, and now we're down to seventy-five—five less students that I may have to kill.

The door makes a gentle hissing sound and I turn, ready to defend myself, but it is just closing.

I sigh, wishing I had a way to contact Aurah.

The bed is a lot larger than the ones we get at the school. The blankets look brand new, tucked neatly under the mattress on all sides.

I throw my backpack onto the bed, and take a seat. Opposite the bed are two cushioned chairs with a small table between them and a reading lamp on it. I don't see any drawers to put things in. They must be built into the walls.

I get up and walk around, running my fingers over the detailing along the walls. There might be a button to push or something to trigger hidden drawers to open, which I'm sure are here somewhere.

There is no decor, other than one artist piece on the wall; a painting of a fighter plane zooming into a black hole.

I jump as a hidden door hisses open. It's so perfectly concealed in the wall that I didn't notice anything was there.

I step inside.

It's a washroom with a walk-in shower and a long countertop that has a sink and a mirror above it.

I step in front of the mirror and look at myself. Mirrors are not allowed at the Academy and I haven't seen myself reflected clearly like this, in a long time.

I stand up straighter. Dad was right. I have grown. My jet black hair and white skin make me stand out at the Academy. Randon stands out too, with his fiery red hair and bright blue eyes. He's even whiter than I am, with his aversion to the sun. I always admired him for being unaffected by human emotions. Attachments will never be a problem for him.

For a guy with no special powers, he sure knows how to be ruthless. It's a good thing he agreed to be on my team.

I run my fingers through my hair. It's longer than I remember it being. I definitely need a shower.

As far as I know, we have free time on the ship until tomorrow evening. The room temperature is perfectly regulated and it's strange not to feel a draft over my skin when I take my shirt off.

I remove my shoes and socks as well. The ship's engines vibrate the floor beneath my feet.

My Gift feels stronger now that I'm on board.

Maybe this is where I've always been meant to be. Not in the rustic buildings of an ancient school where dust covers everything. I like order and cleanliness.

I step into the shower and turn the water on. No more bathhouses with muddy water in them for me!

The settings on the small console beneath the shower head are confusing, with symbols that don't make sense. I push a couple buttons and suddenly warm water cascades over me. I sigh, resigned to my fate. I will either die here on this ship, or continue on. Either way, I will never have to see the Academy again.

I look for bars of soap but find only small liquid gel capsules, which I assume are soap. I break one open and rub the gel on my palms. It lathers and I rub it into my hair. My mind wanders to the speech given by Commander Garionne in the theater hall. Only twenty-Five of us will survive the Games. Those who win, will go to the Ruling Order Military Base, where Master Dukath is building his new super weapon. It's an undisclosed star system. No one knows were the Base is. Randon wants to be Leader, but I know he won't get to, because Master Dukath promised it to me. It's one of the few memories I do still have, of the summer.

After my long shower, the bathroom is full of steam, covering the mirror in a haze. I find a towel on a high shelf and wrap it around my waist, then head back into my bedroom, where the air is cooler.

I pull out the official Elimination Games uniform from my bag; black pants and fitted long sleeved shirt with a Ruling Order symbol on the shoulder.

It feels good to be cleaned up and dressed in uniform. It hugs my body in a way that will allow me to run more freely, than I could in the shapeless garments worn at the Academy. I pull on new socks and the shiny black boots provided, then take a seat in a lounging chair to look at my Comm Unit.

I scroll through the details of the Games. There aren't any specifications on how to actually play the game or rules on killing other opponents, other than the no weapons allowed rule, so it must be up to us how we do it.

I continue reading. During sleep hours, the Game is on pause. The doors to our quarters open for exactly two minutes between 01:00 hours and 01:02 so we can get inside for sleep hours. Before and after that time, the doors are locked and unavailable, except for the other two minutes in the morning, between 07:00 to 07:02.

That's six hours of sleep. Hardly enough time to rest and regroup and strategize before the Game starts again. Maybe that's the point. We aren't supposed to work in groups anyway. It's every man for himself.

I sigh when I see the next rule on the list. If you miss your door times you get locked out in the Game for the entire night. Does that mean we could also stay locked in our room all day, if we miss the morning door opening times? Is it a loophole in the rules; a cheap way to win?

I get up and try unlocking the bedroom door, unsettled now by the idea of being locked in a room. It slides open to reveal the dimly lit hallway. My shoulders relax. Not locked in yet. I don't even know what time it is.

My stomach rumbles, reminding me that I didn't eat supper before the shuttle came to get us. I was too nervous to eat.

I check the time on my Comm Unit. Just after the 11:00 hour. I still have two hours before door closing time, if that rule is already in effect. The Games don't officially start until after the opening ceremonies tomorrow. I should be fine.

I head out into the hallway in search of food.

* * *

I follow the path of the soft lighting, running down the hallways along the carpeted floor. It feels safer to walk in the dim light of off-hours, than in the blaring glare of day hours, which were turned on when we first arrived.

I hurry past the silent rooms on either side of the hallway. They remind me of my dream, of being alone on a starship and everyone else being dead, except for Randon and Aurah. I wish I knew where their rooms were. Everyone was placed in different sections all over the ship, a whip built for thousands. We're likely all far apart, in an attempt to discourage teams. Aurah promised to regroup tomorrow once the Games start, and share a room then; strength in numbers and all that.

I walk faster. The mess hall is farther than I thought it would be, when I searched the map on my Comm Unit.

After three more hallways, I round the corner and see the low purple lights of the Mess Hall come into view.

I made it.

Even though the Games haven't started, I still feel like a walking target. I need to be alert for anyone wanting to get me out of the Games before they even start. Randon used to make me feel like this, on edge, when I was a kid. But this is way worse.

The tables and chairs loom empty in the shadows. The only sound is the snack machines along the wall, humming softly. My stomach growls again.

"Bryn?"

I jump at the sound of my name and turn to see Randon balancing an armload of food containers.

"Randon? What are you doing here?"

"Getting food."

"That's a lot of food for one night."

"It's not for one night. Go grab three bags of bread and follow me."

I nod and go look for the bread.

* * *

"They don't have meal breaks during the day," Randon explains, setting the containers onto the floor in his room.

He pushes a spot on the wall and a small door slide opens, revealing a refrigerated meal storage compartment. I hand him the bread I brought.

"The Red Group is planning to siege the mess hall, so no one can eat," he says.

"The Red Group?"

"That's what I call them. They're the largest group. There's twenty of them and they all want to survive."

Randon piles the containers neatly into the refrigerator. "I heard them talking," he continues. "They're planning on attacking the smaller groups and anyone who is playing solo, when they go looking for food in the mess hall."

Randon finishes stacking the containers then gets up. "I'm going to poison the food that's left in the mess hall, then break all the food synthesizers so they have to eat only what's physically there."

"What? Why?" I say.

He gives me a weary look. "Do you want to kill each classmate one by one, with your bare hands?"

"No..."

He's right, we'll be here until the Games are over and we can't just wait and hope for others to die. We have to do it ourselves.

"They'll figure it out soon enough," Randon says. "I brought some contaminated treemeal with me."

"What's that?" The mention of treemeal triggers a feeling like a memory from my childhood, but it feels more recent.

"It's got live treemites. I found it in the treemeal that…" He stops suddenly.

"What?"

His eyes search mine, looking at me in a way that he's never looked at me before.

"What?" I say again, stepping back.

"You don't remember her, do you?"

Before I can ask him what he's talking about, Randon walks to the door.

"I'm going back to get containers of water. Come and help me carry them."

"We have water in our rooms and in all the washrooms around the ship."

"They'll all be contaminated by tomorrow night," Randon says.

"There are supposed to be twenty-five survivors, remember? What if your plan kills everyone and we're the only ones left?"

Randon grins. "Then we're the only ones left."

* * *

I set the water container down beside the others with a grunt. It's our third round for water and we have enough to last us quite a while.

"I think it's enough water," I say, stretching.

I glance at the clock near Randon's bed. It's halfway through sleep time and if I went to bed now I'd get about three hours of sleep.

"Tomorrow night, you and Aurah can stay here," Randon says.

I nod, my muscles aching. The thought of walking back to my room alone makes me nervous. Passing by the other sleeping quarters is like walking past tombs. They will be tombs, soon enough.

"I need to sit down for a bit," I say, rubbing my face with my hands. Maybe I can fall asleep here and not have to walk back to my room tonight. "I'll just rest for a bit in one of the chairs—"

"Take the bed," Randon says.

I lower my hands from my face. "What?"

He drops into one of the lounging chairs and sighs. "I'm going to stay up."

I look to the bed. It's still perfectly made and untouched. "Are you planning to kill me in my sleep?"

Randon smiles and I smile too, despite myself.

"Sleep at your own risk, Bryn," he says, wiggling his eyebrows.

I'm not sure how to respond. Is he being *friendly?* Can I really trust him and just go to sleep on his bed?

"Stop being so paranoid,"" Randon says yawning.

"Do you want me to leave my own room, so you can sleep?"

"No…" I say. That would defeat the purpose, which is to not be alone on this death ship while I sleep. But I don't tell Randon that.

"Go ahead." Randon nods to the bed, his eyes already hazy with tiredness. The words reminds me of something, another one of those memories just out of reach, but strong enough to bring up confusing emotions. I had said the same thing to him I think, 'go ahead…'

Suddenly a memory surfaces; us in his room. I was lying on his bed.

That makes no sense.

Randon watches me silently and I turn away.

My head hurts with that familiar stabbing pain I've been getting in the last few days.

I climb onto the bed and kick my boots off, then pull the blanket over my head and fall instantly to sleep.

you and Randon?

I DREAM OF A dark planet, made entirely of burning lava and black mountains. The heat from the lava is warm on my face and the air is bitter with the smell of burning.

A flash of blue catches my eye and I look over to see two Masters fighting on the dark coals of a mountain side.

One of them is a Dark Lord. He's suddenly overtaken by the other Master and he falls, landing onto the hot coals and igniting into flames. I look away.

"Bryn," someone says from behind me. I turn to see the Master who just won the fight on the lava. He has light colored hair and a long beard. His eyes are a striking blue, just like Randon's.

"Don't let him turn to the evil way," he says to me.

"Who?"

"My grandson, Randon."

"But…" I start to say, then stop. Randon is already evil. He's not a Dark Lord and can never become one, because he doesn't have the same powers as me, but he's not a very nice person either.

"He doesn't have the Gift," I say instead.

"He must never find out, that he does." The Master's blue eyes remind me of Randon's. "Protect him, Bryn."

I wake with a headache and it takes me a minute to get my bearings. I'm not at the Academy, but in a really nice room. Randon is in a lounge chair, his eyes closed. Then I remember. We're starting the Games today.

I sit up. What time is it?

The unsettled feeling left behind from my dream makes me even more anxious about the first day of the Games.

I grab Randon's Comm Unit, sitting on the desk by the bed and it lights up. It's already an hour past wake time. Are we supposed to report somewhere this morning? The Opening Ceremony isn't until evening but I still wouldn't want to miss anything. Did everyone eat in the mess hall together?

The poison!

I scramble out of bed and go to Randon.

"Randon?" I push on his shoulder. "Randon, wake up."

He blinks, his eyes glazed over with sleep. I remember my dream again; Randon's grandfather telling me to protect him and not let him turn evil. I shake my head. It was just a silly dream.

"It's morning," I say.

"Ouch…" Randon rubs the back of his neck. I suddenly feel bad I took the bed all to myself.

"Did you poison the mess hall food?"

Randon gets up and walks over to his bed, then falls down into it.

"I'm going to sleep for a bit longer," he mumbles.

I leave to go find Aurah, deciding it's better that Randon gets more sleep and is at the top of his game tonight.

* * *

The mess hall is alive with activity when I get there. I guess I'm not the only one who slept in this morning.

Food is laid out on tables that are set against the far wall, in a buffet style. I head for the food synthesizer instead. I don't know if Randon poisoned all this food last night, while I was sleeping, or if it was just synthesized this morning. I won't risk it.

Our meals at the Academy were always laid out in this way, by the cooks. But here there are food synthesizers. I head to one, to get a simple dessert bread. I also have a craving for warm milk with melted chocolate in it.

"Where's Randon?" Aurah grabs my arm as I walk by. I hadn't even noticed her.

"Hi."

"Where's Randon?" she repeats.

"In his room."

"You were in his room?"

"Yeah—"

"And you left him there, asleep?" Aurah gives me a look of disbelief.

"Uh, yeah?"

"Did you lock the door behind you?"

"I don't know...?"

"Five students were killed last night in the mess hall."

"What? When?"

"You saw Randon this morning, right?"

"Yes, when I got up. He was fine. Why?"

Aurah nods and lets go of my arm. We start walking towards the food synthesizer together.

"It happened around 04:30," Aurah continues.

A chill runs down my spine. Could it have been Randon who killed those students?

The food synthesizer stations have no line-ups, as everyone is crowding around the buffet.

"People are saying it was you and Randon," Aurah whispers. "That you two were seen here around that time. And now some of them want revenge."

"It wasn't us," I say, suddenly becoming worried. "I don't think the door locked behind me when I left Randon's room."

"Let's go." Aurah grabs my dessert bread, that has just materialized, and hurries off.

* * *

The door to Randon's quarters swishes open and Aurah and I rush in. Randon is still in his bed sleeping. We both breathe a sigh of relief and exchange a glance.

"We should check if he's okay." Aurah walks over to the bed.

"Don't wake him," I say.

I look down at Randon. Anyone could have walked in here and killed him, he's such a heavy sleeper.

"The Game wasn't supposed to start until tonight," I whisper to Aurah.

She shrugs. "Well, those who are dead, are dead. So I guess they won't be in the Games." She looks around the room at all the water containers. "You two were busy last night!"

"I have to protect Randon," I say.

Aurah raises her eyebrows at me.

"I just mean, we all have to look out for each other," I quickly add, my cheeks flushing for some reason. "Like you said.

She nods. "Let's go out in the hall and let him sleep for a few hours. I get the feeling he was pretty busy all night."

* * *

"The Red Team?" Aurah asks, once we're out in the hall, leaning back against Randon's door.

I take the last bite of my bread, before answering.

"Yeah, that's what Randon calls them. They're the biggest group," I tell her.

"I think I know who they are, then." Aurah fidgets with her phaser in her hand.

"I'd put that away, before someone sees it," I mumble through the last of my bread.

Aurah clips the gun back to her belt and sets her shirt over it. "I can't believe you two missed the death match in the mess hall last night. It sounds like you missed it by only a few minutes." She stretches her hands above her head. "Why didn't you guys invite me to help, with the food thing. It's a great plan. I'm glad we've got our own food and water locked away."

"We didn't know where you were." I grab my drink.

"So now we're down to seventy players," Aurah says. "The rules are 'no hiding,' but I really think we should hide out this first night. It will be a bloodbath before sleep hours."

"That's in the rules?"

"Apparently," Aurah shrugs, lowering her arms. "Did you read them?"

"Some of it."

"Doesn't matter. You know I don't like following rules. I just like knowing them so I can plan how to break them."

"Aurah..."

"Yeah?"

I set my drink aside, not sure how to say this. "Me and Randon..." I clear my throat. "Did we become friends or something? Is that part of what Master Dukath erased in my memory?"

Aurah doesn't answer right away and it's all the answer I need. So something did happen. But what? I don't know how to ask her what I really want to ask, but I think she knows anyway.

"You spent the night in his room last night," she says to me.

"Is that a question?"

"Did you sleep in his bed?"

"Last night?"

"Yes."

"Yeah, why?"

Aurah's eyebrows shoot up. "With him?"

"No! He slept in the chair. You know Randon hates me."

Aurah rolls her eyes. "He doesn't hate you. He's just competitive."

"He's stronger than me."

"In a way, but you have powers that he doesn't."

"Yeah, but I don't know how to use them very well."

"You just have to focus."

"It's not that easy."

"I'd be perfecting those powers every second of every day, if I had them."

"Master Dukath said I couldn't use them—"

"Again, me and rules don't mix."

"Did anything happen between me and Randon?" I blurt out. "Like, romantically, on planet this summer? Is that why I had my memory erased?"

Attachments are strictly forbidden but friendships are okay. So it had to be that. Aurah and I have been friends a long time and that has never been an issue.

When Aurah doesn't reply my palms become sweaty.

"It couldn't have been like that," I say, wiping my hands on my pants. "I like girls, not guys. I don't understand—"

"Nothing happened between you two," Aurah says.

"Oh," I sigh. "Good. I didn't actually think so, but I was just getting this weird connection or something, like we were friends maybe."

Aurah nods.

"Can I ask you something?" I say, rubbing the back of my neck.

"Yep," she says, looking ahead and not at me.

"I just have these...feelings that weren't there before."

"Of what?" Aurah looks at me now and I start fidgeting with the laces of my boots.

"Feelings of what?" Aurah asks again, looking genuinely curious.

"I don't know, towards Randon," I say, keeping my eyes on my books. "It's confusing. It's like I want his attention and I feel better when he's with me." I shake my head. "I've always avoided him, and now I'm sitting at his door to make sure no one harms him while he's sleeping."

"Don't over think it," Aurah says. "You'd guard my room too, if I were asleep and there was danger."

"Yeah," I say, but it isn't the same and I don't think she understands.

"He's very charismatic," Aurah adds. "It will help him to be a leader someday. He doesn't let anyone close to him. We're the only ones he tolerates." Aurah smiles at me. "I can see why you'd feel confused though. He is the prettiest guy I've ever seen."

I laugh at her choice of words.

"I think he might even be prettier than me," Aurah adjusts her short hair and I laugh again. "I should have cut his hair really short," she says. "I only ended up making him look all stylish and alluring. I'm such a good hair stylist, I should start charging for my services."

I groan. "Let's stop talking about Randon, please. It's weird."

Aurah nudges my shoulder. "Don't take yourself so seriously. It's just stress, making you desperate for affection in anyone within arm's reach. You're just looking for security and you know he's strong, mentally at least. This whole blasted game is really scary."

I nod. She's right. "Randon never feels desperate for affection though," I say. "I think he's a robot."

"You'd be surprised."

I look at Aurah. "You and Randon...?"

"No!" She scrunches up her face. "He doesn't like me in that way. Obviously since he likes you."

"What?"

"Oh, nothing." She shakes her head. "Never mind."

"Do you think the others in the Program struggle with this too?"

"The need for affection?"

"I guess."

"I know they do. I'm the only girl here, trust me, they struggle with hormones too."

"Oh." My shoulders slump. "Aurah, back when we were at the school and I came to your room..." I look down at the ground. "I shouldn't have—"

"Wow, I'm surprised you remember that! Dukath saw fit to leave that memory in place?"

I don't reply.

"You don't need to keep apologizing for that, okay?"

"Okay."

Suddenly the door we're leaning against swishes open and we both fall onto our backs at Randon's feet.

He looks down at us.

"What the hell?"

"Hi Randon," Aurah says. "We were just talking about you."

THe OPenInG ceremonIes

"I WENT AROUND AND changed the default passcodes on a bunch of important rooms last night. I'll change it for Randon's room too," Aurah says, walking into the Command Center ahead of us. "Now we're the only ones who can get into rooms like these."

Randon and I follow her in and the door slides closed behind us. Randon takes a seat at the head of the table and I sit to his right. Aurah sits across from me.

"Couldn't someone just change the codes back?" Randon asks, clasping his hands in front of him on the desk. The glass touch-screen surface turns on, illuminating our faces from below.

"They can't. They'd need our passcodes first," Aurah says. "I also got into the ship's computer last night and changed the admin access to recognize my voice only. I don't know if anyone has noticed yet, but today we can set both of your voices as admin too."

"That goes against one of the rules." I say.

Randon smiles. "Good job."

"What if we get disqualified?" I continue.

"The codes will probably get reset before the Games start anyway," Randon says, studying the touch screen options on the table's surface.

Aurah crosses her arms and leans back in her chair. "Well we have them until then."

"Here's what I know about the teams that have formed." Randon moves his hand over the table and begins to draw circles. He writes 'Red Team' on the screen with his finger and the number 15 beside it. "Aurah, pull up a map and mark the rooms you've changed the passcodes for."

"I thought there were twenty on the Red Team," I say.

"There were, yesterday."

"The students who were killed last night, were all from the Red Team?" I ask.

"Yes."

"But they're such a big group. How did they get attacked?"

"They weren't all together at the same time. And they were unprepared." Randon continues writing.

Aurah spins her map on the table screen, trying to get it to face the right way. "Was it you?"

Randon winks at her. "And now they're down to fifteen."

A shiver runs down my spine. "You killed them?"

"They were dumb enough to drink the juice I left out on the tables," Randon shrugs.

"Did you use the treemeal?" I ask.

"You remember the treemeal?" Aurah looks at me.

"What do you mean, remember it?"

"No," Randon says. "The treemites take time to work. It was something else I was trying."

"What do you mean, Aurah?" I say, ignoring Randon. "Do I remember what, about the treemeal?"

She doesn't reply and Randon keeps his eyes down on the table, also avoiding my gaze. Does he know what Aurah's talking about?

"What about you, Bryn?" Randon asks. "Any ideas on how to kill off the rest?"

I sit back in my chair. I don't want to play this game the way Master Dukath wants us to. It feels like a defeat, even if we win.

"How about we make explosives and trap them in a room and blow them up?" I say casually. "Or carry around thin bags made of plastic to put over their heads and suffocate them?"

Aurah gives me a questioning look.

"I like the explosives idea," Randon says, ignoring my attempt at sarcasm. "Maybe we can take out the entire Red Team at one time."

"For an explosion big enough to kill them," Aurah says, "you'd compromise the ship's hull—"

"Or, you could just blow up the meeting tonight and kill everyone, even the Masters," I say.

Randon laughs unexpectedly and my stomach does a little flip of surprise. The sound of his laughter fills me with joy for some reason, despite how annoyed I am at him right now.

"I like the way you think," Randon smiles at me.

"You'd be willing to blow up Grand Master?"

"We don't need Masters," Aurah mumbles. "We can lead ourselves." She starts marking her map with angry swipes of her finger.

"I don't think it's that simple," I say. "Master Dukath is the one who set up the Ruling Order and—"

"I don't know why you two are so scared of him," Aurah snaps.

"I do," Randon says. "But he would foresee it anyway. You can't trap a Grand Master that easily."

"Then we'll just trap the others, some other way," Aurah adds, a bit aggressively.

I sit up in my seat. "I thought you wanted us to just observe on the first night, instead of jumping right into mass murder."

Aurah crosses her arms. "Hiding out is against the rules."

"It's not hiding out, it's observing," I say. "And you don't care about the rules anyway."

Randon watches me and doesn't say anything. I slouch back down in my seat, beneath his gaze, then begin to fidget with my sleeves.

"I think that's a good idea," Randon says after a moment.

"What is?" I look up.

"Pulling back and observing on the first night." Randon gives me a smile and I sink down further in my seat. Why does he keep smiling at me? The only look he's every given me in the past was a disgusted look. I think about what Aurah said, that stress makes people needy for each other.

I look at her then. She's grinning down at the table screen now, having closed the map she was looking at and opened a message box instead. A second later a notification window pops up in front of me. I open it.

I think he likes you... it says. I quickly close it, then kick Aurah under the table. "Stop it," I hiss.

"Ouch." She laughs and Randon looks at us.

"Let's focus," he says. "We need to figure out a way to get everything needed to make small explosives."

"Okay," Aurah and I say at the same time.

* * *

"There are no heroes here," Commander Klein declares. "Only survivors."

I glance around the gathering space. Only about half the students have shown up for the Opening Ceremonies, even though it was mandatory.

Randon and Aurah stand on either side of me. I lean towards Randon to get a better look at the stage and our shoulders touch. He steps away and I step away too, bumping into Aurah on the other side.

"Sorry," I whisper.

She puts her arm around me and squeezes my shoulders. "He's just a little shy," she whispers.

"Be quiet," I hiss back, not wanting Randon to hear her. I try to push her away but she grips my shoulders even tighter.

"Shush Bryn," she whispers. "Pay attention." She nods to the front, a smile on her face. Randon gives us both an annoyed look, as though to warn us to shut up.

"Contamination of the food and water is now against the rules," Commander Klein continues and Randon grins.

I look up to where Master Dukath is seated. He's in a secured area behind glass, looking down at us from an upper balcony, alongside two other Masters who are both dressed in dark cloaks. They're Dark Lords. I can sense their powers. Seeing the three of them together, looming above us, is unsettling.

"Coward," Aurah whispers looking up at them as well.

"I don't think you're supposed to put your arm around me," I say to her.

She gives my shoulders one final squeeze, then lets me go.

"We could have bombed the place after all," Randon whispers, leaning in. "Grand Master is protected and we could have gotten rid of half the students in one shot." He stays close for a moment, as though waiting for my response, but I just nod, thinking about what Aurah said, that Randon doesn't let anyone close to him, except us.

The room goes dark and a projection of a planet lights up in front of us.

"The Ruling Order, will be the greatest force in all the Galaxies," Dukath's voice comes from all directions, through hidden speakers. It isn't him speaking from behind the glass, but part of a projection show, prerecorded like some sort of propaganda advertisement. "Keeping order and ruling over all."

The hologram of the planet zooms in to show a large military base stationed there, then moves through the various sections, including what appears to be a massive army training camp.

I suddenly feel really small. The Ruling Order army is larger than I ever imagined. Could I really *lead* the them all? Was my dad right, that I'm not capable of something like this?

I glance at Randon. His eyes shine in the reflection of the hologram.

"Bigger than I thought," I whisper to him. He doesn't move away from me this time, when our shoulders touch.

"Yes." His glance turns to me for a second then back at the hologram. "Don't worry, I'll be there to help you. I can oversee the army and do the speeches and stuff." He moves away again and my shoulders relax.

Then I remember my dream about Randon's grandfather, saying Randon has powers too, like me. Could it be true? That kind of power would be really dangerous in his hands. But wouldn't he know he had it, if he did? And wouldn't I have sensed it by now? Maybe that's why I've felt so drawn to him lately.

"Only twenty-five of you will rule the Galaxy as Commanders of the Ruling Order," Dukath's voice continues.

A group of students cheer, raising their fists into the air. Suddenly I have a vision of their raised fists burning, then their entire bodies bursting into flames. The vision lasts only a second. I don't get them often, but it's part of my Gift, a part that I know very little about.

I can't just ignore it.

"We need to get out of here," I whisper to Randon, grabbing his arm.

He pulls away, looking annoyed.

"Randon, I'm serious," I continue. "I had a vision. Something bad is going to happen."

He nods and reaches in front of me to grab Aurah's arm.

"What are you doing?" Aurah hisses as Randon drags her with him.

"We have to go," he says.

We hurry to the door. It doesn't open when we approach it.

"Bryn," Randon turns to me. "Use your powers." His expression is serious, as though the locked door has confirmed for him that we're in danger.

My palms begin to sweat. I need to understand how something works, in order to use my Gift to manipulate it. I'm not familiar with how the mechanism works, inside the door. I don't know which gears to activate or which wires to send energy through.

I close my eyes and try to concentrate over the sound of my pounding heart. Maybe I can just force it open with a mental feat of strength, and not have to figure out the inner workings. I shake my head, unable to focus with Dukath's words echoing all around the room through the speakers.

"What is that?" Aurah says. I open my eyes and see that she's pointing to the other corner of the room. A light colored gas seeps in from down below a door. Everyone is faced forward and watching the presentation, unaware.

"Hurry," Randon says to me.

"I can't do it," my voice cracks and sweat drips down my brow.

Aurah fumbles with a pack on her belt and pulls out a small screwdriver. "Unscrew the door control panel," she says, handing me the screwdriver. The smoke begins to make its way across the floor towards us, still low to the ground. I start unscrewing the panel as fast as I can. The gas reaches our feet and my ankles begin to itch but I ignore it.

"What the hell?" someone says from the seating area. Everyone starts to look down at their feet. I remove a screw then start on the next one.

"Found them," Aurah pulls out a small pair of scissors and I get another screw off.

"Give me that." Randon snatches the screwdriver out of my hand and wedges it under the panel, then pops the entire thing off. The last two screws go flying. Aurah pulls out a handful of colorful wires and begins to cut some of them. They spark and she curses under her breath.

"Be careful," I tell her as the smoke around us lifts higher. "I think the gas is flammable."

She connects two wires and the red light at the top of the door panel beeps, then turns green. The door slides open.

A scream from behind us startles me. I look back and see flames igniting on a student's body, then leaping onto the person beside him.

Randon shoves me out the door before the others come running towards it. They try to push their way to the doors, but they close again. I look up to see a grin on Master Dukath's face from the enclosed balcony above. A few of the students make it through before the door shuts with a definite crunch, breaking off the arm of a student who was still trying to get out. My stomach heaves.

"Don't watch!" Aurah yells at me, but I'm frozen in place. I can't look away. How did the door close again after Aurah rewired it? Is Dukath doing this?

"We need to wash this stuff off. Now!" Aurah yells.

"Bryn!" Randon grabs me by the shoulders. "Snap out of it. We need to get back to our room."

Harvoth's Fever

R ANDON CURSES AS HE passes me the shower head. "Come on Bryn, isn't your skin burning?"

He pulls his shirt over his head. Aurah grabs the shower head from me and begins to rinse herself off. She's already undressed and not shy at all, but I don't watch. Randon doesn't either. I can't clear my mind of the image of the students who were burning and their scared expressions when they couldn't get out in time before the door closed.

"Here." Aurah hands Randon the shower head and leaves the shower, closing the door behind her.

"Bryn," Randon says, waving his hand in front of my face. "Do you want your skin to get eaten away by this chemical?"

"It was Master Dukath."

"What?"

"Him and the Dark Lords with him. They started the fires."

"This gas is burning through my skin." He begins to undo his belt then stops. "Here," he reaches past me and opens the shower door. "Wait out there if you're not in a hurry to rinse off. I think I'm about to burst into flames." He shoves me out and closes the door behind me.

I look at my reflection in the washroom mirror. A rash has formed on my neck, all the way around the collar of my shirt where I didn't rinse off yet. Suddenly it feels like I'm on fire, an acid burning my skin away and stealing the breath from my lungs.

"Randon!" I bang on the shower door. "Hurry up."

"Pass me a towel!" he calls back. I grab one and open the shower door to toss it in. Little bursts of flames suddenly pop up on my shirt, melting the fabric to my skin.

"What the?" I smack at the flames with my hand, burning my fingers in the process. "Ouch." I pull frantically on my sleeves, trying to get my shirt off but the fabric is already stuck to my skin.

Randon hurries out of the shower with a towel around his waist. "What the hell?" he says when he sees me. He grabs the bottom of my shirt and pulls it up over my head, yanking it off along with the patches of burnt skin stuck to it.

I yelp and Randon throws the shirt into the sink.

It bursts into flames.

"Your back's on fire!" Randon shoves me into the shower stall. He turns the water on and rinses me off with the shower head. The cold water cools the skin on my back.

I fumble with my belt, my legs already searing with pain, but my scorched fingers hurt too much to be useful, I can't feel anything with my fingertips. Randon pushes my hands aside and unsnaps the clip on my belt in one quick move, then hands me the shower head.

"You're on your own now," he says and steps out of the shower.

* * *

Aurah restores the door keypad to the panel on the wall. "This should keep the door locked, even if someone overrides the computer system. It's controlled only locally now, with this panel."

Randon and I look up from our sitting position on the floor, where we're eating a cold pasta dish from the food stash Randon put away. The Games have officially begun and we've locked ourselves in our room.

My skin still hurts from the burns but feels a lot better after Aurah helped me put on a fast working ointment, from the room's first aid kit. I burned my back, arms and fingers, but nowhere else, thankfully. Now my fingers are numb with the healing cream. I used all of it, so hopefully we won't be needing any more anytime soon.

"You were smart to bring food to the room," I say to Randon.

He looks deep in thought. Aurah walks over and sits down on the other side of Randon.

"Do you think they'll enforce the no hiding rule?" she asks.

"Probably," I say. "But night time hours start in like ten minutes anyway."

Randon takes a breath as though to respond but a bleep sound interrupts him. It's the call button for the door.

"Don't answer it," Aurah says, getting up.

We stop eating. The ringing goes on and on.

Randon gets up too.

"Don't open it!" Aurah pushes him back.

"I won't." Randon goes to the door console and turns on the small screen. "Who is it?" he says, pushing the comm button.

"Please, help me!" a voice calls from the small speakers. Randon leans down to get a closer look at the screen. I get up and join him.

"I just need clean water," the voice says. "Please." I look at the screen. It's one of the boys from the school. His eyes are wide with fear, staring into the camera outside the door.

"How does he know we have clean water?" Randon says.

"It could be a trap." Aurah looks to me. "Can you tell if it is?"

"Me?" I say.

"Yes," Aurah hisses. "Use your powers."

"Oh." I close my eyes and concentrate, setting my hand onto the door and reaching through it to the boy on the other side. Human's are easier for me to connect with, through my Gift. They give off an energy that I'm used to.

The boy's mind is not hard to read. "It's not a trap."

I pull my hand away from the door and shudder. "He's actually sick. I think it's Harvoth's fever."

"Then we could catch it too," Aura says. "Don't open the door."

"Please," the boy on the other side of the door pleads. "I have white blood cell pills. I just need clean water to take them."

Randon punches the numbers into the keypad.

"Randon!" Aurah yells, pushing him aside, but it's too late, the door opens.

A dark-haired boy topples forward into the room. A bottle of pills falls out of his hand and they spill onto the carpet.

"What happened to you?" Randon asks the boy.

"I just need water—"

"First tell us what happened."

"My group contaminated the water with Harvoth's fever."

"All of the water on the ship?"

"Yes, but Master Dukath is aware of it now."

"Then how did you get sick? Didn't you know?"

"Randon…" I say, feeling bad for the boy. "He needs to take the pills right away if he's going to survive."

When Randon doesn't respond the boy quickly continues.

"The fruit…" he says, coughing. "It was washed in the water and I ate some. My team gave me the pills, but they only work dissolved in water and they wouldn't let me back into the team room after I got sick."

I head to the back of the room where we have our water.

"Aurah, grab a towel," Randon commands.

I hurry to open a bottle, then turn to see Randon standing behind the boy, his knees on either side of his shoulders. He takes the towel from Aurah.

"Don't watch," he says to me then drops the towel on the boy's head. The boy starts to protest but Randon grabs him in a headlock and snaps his neck in one quick move.

The boy drops to the ground, dead.

* * *

"It was a mercy killing," Aurah says, taking a seat beside me on the floor. I know she thinks I'm being quiet because Randon killed the sick kid, but it's not what's bothering me. It was only one death, our first killing as a team, and the Games have just started. The reality of it all is just now dawning on me and I'm scared, not for myself but for Aurah and Randon. I don't want them to die.

"The two Masters that were with Dukath tonight, at the opening ceremonies, they're Dark Lords. They're the ones that were starting the fires. It was all planned," I say, not wanting to talk about the boy Randon killed.

"I figured as much."

"How did you know?"

"I know Dukath."

"I think he's going to let me win." I look down at my hands in my lap. "But I'm worried about you two."

"Bryn, you were in that room when the gas was released too, weren't you? And you got more hurt than either of us. Plus you weren't able to get out without my help. So I don't think they're favoring anyone, let alone you."

I nod. "You're right, I wouldn't have gotten out without you two."

"But it was your powers that warned us. We had a head start."

I take a deep breath and let it out slowly. The clock on the night stand says 01:20. It's officially off-hours for the Games, but I can't seem to relax. "I don't know if I can kill people, like Randon can," I say. "He's stronger—"

"No, he's not. Quit saying that. This upset him too, you know. He's just better at hiding it. That's why he's locked himself in the washroom for the last hour."

"You're right. I shouldn't make him do all the killing. I would have tried to save that guy, if Randon hadn't killed him."

"I already told you. Jared wouldn't have gotten better fast enough to make it through the Games, even if the pills worked, he'd need weeks to fully recover and he would have been an easy target for anyone else anyway."

My chest tightens at the mention of the boy's name. "You knew him?"

Aurah doesn't look at me. "And now we have the white blood cell Immune Booster pills he brought with him, which will help us heal from just about any virus," she says.

The washroom door opens and Randon steps out, his hair dripping wet. "Did you know the shower is also a decontamination chamber?" he says, walking past us. "It wouldn't hurt for both of you to use it. Since that boy was in our room."

His lack of concern for the boy is oddly reassuring. At least we don't need to worry about him having an emotional breakdown.

I turn to Aurah. "Do you want to go first?" Aurah gets up and heads for the washroom.

I watch Randon as he rummages through the refrigerator silently. I don't know how he can eat after dragging a dead body down the hallway. But Aurah's right. It was a mercy killing and I wouldn't have wanted to watch Jared suffer for days only to end up being killed anyway before the games were through.

I close my eyes and lean my head back against the wall. I've never been more tired in all my life.

YOU BY MY SIDE

"**B**RYN." I HEAR RANDON'S voice in my mind and wake from an uncomfortable sleep on the floor. "Get up. It's your turn for decontamination."

I glance at the clock. I fell asleep for half an hour.

"I really don't feel like it," I say, sitting up.

"Just go." Randon walks over to the bed and sits down.

I sigh and head to the washroom.

The decontamination process is slow and boring, and the air is hard to breathe in the enclosed shower stall once it's started.

I almost fall asleep a few times but when it's finally over I feel better, safer.

I get dressed, feeling slow and sluggish.

When I step out from the washroom the room is all dark. It takes a moment for my eyes to adjust.

Aurah is curled up on the lounge chairs, which are now facing each other and pushed together to form a little bed. She must not have wanted to share the bed with Randon.

I look over to the bed. It's empty.

Then I spot Randon, sitting on the floor and reading a small tablet in his lap. I guess he's staying up tonight.

I walk over to the bed and remove the blanket, then take it to Aurah and drape it over her, tucking it in around her so it doesn't just drape down to the ground. She mumbles something but doesn't wake up.

"Hey," Randon says softly from the corner of the room. "What about us?"

"What do you mean?"

Randon doesn't answer and I'm way too tired to figure him out right now. The decontamination process has drained all my energy.

I head back to the bed and throw myself down onto it, groaning into the clean smelling pillow. All my muscles ache and it feels amazing to be laying down.

The light from Randon's tablet goes out but I can still see him in the dim glow from the stars shining in through the windows. He doesn't move from his spot on the floor. I really should just let him have the bed, he slept in the chair last night.

He gets up and walks away. I close my eyes. I'll just rest for ten minutes, then I'll let Randon take the bed and I can sleep on the floor.

A minute later I feel a blanket land on my back and I open my eyes. Did Randon just bring me a blanket? I roll onto my back to make room for him. He looks down at the spot beside me for a moment then finally sits down and lays onto his back too, keeping as much distance between us as possible. He has a light jacket on, which he doesn't remove, despite it probably not being too comfortable to sleep in.

"This game isn't right," I say softly. "Killing off other classmates that are training on the same side. We're not enemies. They're not a threat to the galaxy or to the Ruling Order."

"They're a threat to my personal galaxy," Randon says.

I almost laugh but don't have the energy. "It's not the Master's Way."

"Existence is both good and evil," Randon whispers.

"Existence is a desire for life, not death."

"You sound more like a Temple Master, than a Dark Lord. You'll end up losing your life, thinking that way."

"What do you mean?"

"Would you two shut up," Aurah mumbles from the other side of the room. "I'm trying to sleep here."

Randon and I stop talking. He closes his eyes.

I'm exhausted, but I can tell I won't be able to sleep. Too many thoughts are running around in my head. Thoughts I don't want to think about.

I won't make it through the end of the Games. But even if I do, I'm not ready to just throw away everything Morlin taught me about the Way of the Masters.

I sit up.

"Bryn?" Randon says. "You okay?"

I remove my boots, throwing them to the ground, then lay back down, closer to Randon this time, so our shoulders touch.

"Don't you already have enough room?" Randon says.

I shift away, in opposite direction, as far as I can go. Of course Randon wouldn't want me so close. Why am I acting like this, like I want to be close to Randon all of a sudden?

My throat feels tight and I drape my arm over my eyes. I hate this yearning, desperately longing for something but I don't really know what I want.

The pain in my throat intensifies and I blink back tears. What's my problem anyway? Randon is right here, beside me, even in the same bed. Aurah's not that far away either. I'm not *alone*. I'm part of their group. So then why do I feel *so alone*?

I think back to the battle and survival techniques we learned in Leadership Training. There was nothing in the psychological training about this part, the part where you stop all the fighting to rest for the night and realize that you're empty, and can't remember why you're even fighting in the first place.

I take my arm away from my face and lay it beside me onto the bed, accidentally bumping Randon's arm. I look over and see that his eyes are closed. Has he fallen asleep?

I watch him for a moment then slip my hand into his palm and interlace our fingers. He doesn't open his eyes but he clasps my hand in return. My shoulders relax and I let out a slow breath. It comes out staggered, like I've been crying. I squeeze Randon's hand back.

"Go to sleep, Bryn." He turns his head away from me, but continues to hold my hand. I close my eyes, too, my body relaxing, finally. The warmth of Randon's hand calms every part of me, and I fall fast asleep.

Jealous

I WAKE, SURROUNDED BY warmth, not the usual cold of my drafty stone room at the Academy. No sun shines in through the windows. There's no breeze. I open my eyes to the dim lighting of our quarters and the black of space outside the windows.

I turn my head to see Randon sleeping on his side now, his hand on his pillow also resting against my shoulder. That explains why I'm so warm. His heat and his breath.

I close my eyes. I don't want to kill anybody today.

The door call-button bleeps and my heart leaps in my chest. I sit up and Randon wakes. The clock shows that it's after 08:00 hours. We slept past the door-open time.

"Someone's at the door," I say to Randon.

"What?" He sits up too, his clear blue eyes hazy with sleep. He blinks and looks around. We slept right through the night, the best sleep I've had in as long as I can remember.

The banging on the door starts up again.

"Who's at the door?" Aurah says in a groggy voice from across the room. She throws her blanket aside and fights her way out of the chairs she was lying on, cursing the whole time until she's finally up.

"Wait!" I say.

"Don't open it," Randon says at the same time.

"I'm not *going to*." Aurah dismisses us with a wave and goes to the door console.

Randon and I both start to get out of bed, when there is a loud bang from the door and sparks go flying. Aurah screams and jumps back.

The door opens and two armed guards storm into the room, another two following behind them. Randon and I quickly get to our feet and I step in front of him, to shield him from the guards. His grandfather entrusted me to keep him safe.

"Sleep hours are over," one of the guards says. He grabs Aurah by the arm and drags her towards the door.

"Hey!" she yells, trying to pull away, but the guard is stronger.

"This door is not working," another guard says. "Assign them new quarters."

"No!" Aurah yells from outside the door.

"Bryn, grab water!" Randon shouts as two guards come towards us. I dodge the one coming for me, and grab two bottles of water before he snatches me by arm and forces me out of the room. Randon lunges for the chairs, grabbing Aurah's jacket, which has the phaser in it, before he's also forcefully removed.

"Next time you resist, we will open fire," the guard says to him. We're shoved out of the room and into the hall. "No hiding during day-hours. It's the rules."

"We weren't *hiding*," Aurah snarls. "There was no alarm or anything to wake us up."

"Have this room permanently sealed," one of them says to the others. They nod and get to work. "Keep moving," he says to us, pushing Randon with his gun. I give him a shove with my Gift, into the wall. He looks confused for a moment and Aurah grabs my hand to lower it.

"Don't," she says, pulling me along. "Just follow them."

* * *

"Maybe you could distract some of the guys and help us win," I say to Aurah, teasing her. She gives me a death glare in return.

"I probably could," she says, leaning back and sticking her chest out in her white tank top. I roll my eyes and look away.

It's hot on board today, too hot. I'd always hated the cool stone buildings at the Academy but now I'm starting to think that being too hot is worse.

Randon shakes his head slowly, seeming deep in thought.

"I got us in here," Aurah says, waving her hand to indicate the Weapon's Room we're in.

"Yeah, but there are no weapons, so a lot of good that did us."

Aurah glares at Randon, her lips set in a tight line. She lowers her hands and I glance at her white tank top again. She didn't have the time to put on a bra before we were thrown out of our room this morning, and my eyes keep wandering back to the thin fabric that hugs her chest.

"I was hoping we'd at least find some armor or something," she mumbles.

"Why is it so hot everywhere?" I say, forcing my eyes away from Aurah and down to our last water bottle, sitting on the bench between us. It's half empty now. We all took one drink from it earlier, but I'm still thirsty. And hungry.

"Do you think the food synthesizers are fixed yet?" I ask.

"I think Dukath turned them off," Aurah replies. "And no one's said anything about the water contamination being dealt with yet. So for now, this bottle is all we have." She picks it up and sets it on the other side of her. "And we're saving it."

My eyes wandering to her chest again.

"My face is up here, Bryn," Aurah says. "They're probably messing with the environmental controls to make us too hot and even more thirsty, since there's no water."

"Dukath's taking control of the Games," Randon says. "With the armed guards being everywhere."

I nod, my eyes drifting to Aurah's tank top again.

Randon grabs her jacket from the bench beside him and tosses it at her.

"Put this on," he commands.

"Why?" Aurah asks, taken by surprise.

Randon glowers at her. "It's got your gun in it, so you should wear it."

She smiles a little, looking between Randon and me. "Oh," she says, then puts it on.

"We need to get to the Captain's office, on the bridge," Randon says, wiping sweat form his brow. He's leaned back against the wall and seems to be taking the heat the worst. "That's where the main controls are. You said that's where you reset the admin codes from, right?"

"It might not be that easy," Aurah sighs. She seems drained from the heat too.

The sound of the door sliding open makes us all jump up to our feet. Aurah reaches for her blaster but doesn't pull it out.

A blonde-haired boy, who I recognize from the Academy, runs in. He looks about as young as me but I know he can't be, because I'm the youngest. How he managed to pass the First Order training course, with such a small figure, I will never understand.

He doesn't seem surprised to find us in the room, as though he knew we'd be here.

"Master Randon, I'd like to join your team," he says, falling down on one knee in front of Randon.

Randon's lips curl into a satisfied grin.

"Master, huh?" he says.

"Yes, Sir," the boy says. "I mean, yes Master."

Randon looks down at the boy.

"What's your name?"

"My name's Cole." The blonde boy looks at Randon in a way that makes me want to punch the kid.

"How did you survive this long, Cole?" Randon asks him.

"By being smart, and invisible, Sir. And pretending to be on different teams at once. I'm the spy for Aiden's team."

"Is that the largest team?" Aurah asks.

"Used to be," the boy turns to her.

"You just admitted to being a spy," I say.

Randon holds up a hand, as though to shush me.

"Why would we consider letting you join the winning side?" he asks Cole.

"Because, Sir, I have lots of inside information about the other teams and I have access to the ship's main computer."

"How?" Aurah asks.

"Let's not waste our time," Randon says. He turns to me. "I need to know if he's telling us the truth, before we believe him."

I nod. "If this is not a trick," I say to Cole, "then you won't mind if I read your mind."

He frowns but doesn't protest. Randon nods to me and I step forward, setting my hand on top of Cole's head. I close my eyes and concentrate. His surface emotions are pretty straight forward, excitement and fear, and something else, like hero worship for Randon. I force myself to ignore that part, which goes a bit deeper than hero worship.

I move on to see his memories of the Games so far. I see the face of Aiden. He's the big guy that always won the physical combat training challenges, I recognize him now. He's a new student this year.

Then I see the faces of his team members. They don't sleep in their individual quarters but have set up a base where they all stay together, hidden somewhere in the maintenance wing.

Cole's memory of the ship's layout is fuzzy. They've already made explosives which they plan to use on the others.

I focus harder, wanting to find Cole's true motivation for helping us and turning on the others. But motivations are hard; even the person who I'm reading might not know their own motivations. He did admit to pretending to be on everyone else's team, so he could be doing the same to us.

I find something Cole is trying to hide. He does believe he can win by joining us, but that's not the only reason he wants to be on our team. He's been watching Randon for years and is scared of him, but also admires him. He saw him drag Jared's body out of our room last night, when he was out spying for Aiden. He's not scared of me, even though he knows I have powers that others don't.

I'm done searching his mind. If he had bad intentions it would have been obvious. I'm about to let him go when I see a memory with me in it, holding a little girl in my arms. He was spying on me at the Academy too, always jealous that Randon paid so much attention to me. But I don't remember this little girl.

I search all his memories of the summer, looking for anything that has me in them. Every one he has, is filled with images of the girl. I see myself smiling, walking hand in hand with her. She looks at me like I'm her hero. Then I'm kneeling before her in front of the chapel doors and hugging her. I look so happy, and then...

Cole cries out in pain and I know I'm taking too long, searching his mind too much, but I have to know. Another memory—hushed voices of a conversation, something about the little girl being sick, and her name was...

"Bryn!" Randon pulls my hand off of Cole's head, breaking my concentration and snapping me out of my connection.

Cole collapses to the floor and Randon kneels down beside him. "Did you at least get information out of him, before you killed him?"

"He's not dead, he's just weak," I say, stepping away from them.

"Is he telling the truth? Does he really want to help us?" Aurah asks.

"Yes."

"Why?"

I don't respond.

"Are you okay?" Aurah asks, looking at me more closely.

"Tell me about the girl."

"What girl?" Aurah looks away but I grab her by her jacket collar.

"The *girl* that everyone saw me with, all summer, but I know nothing about," I hiss.

Aurah shoves me away from her. "It's not for me to tell. Dukath erased your memories of her."

Cole groans on the ground and Randon helps him sit up, putting his arm around his shoulders in a protective sort of way. I clench my fists.

Randon helps him over to the bench, sitting down close beside him. Cole holds his gaze for longer than necessary and Randon seems intrigued.

"Cole," I say, interrupting their staring contest.

He looks at me. "What's Aiden's next plan of attack?"

He rubs his forehead. "Um... killing you guys, I guess. That's why I came, to warn you. But they don't tell me everything and I..." he cringes. "My head hurts."

Randon sets his hand on Cole's back, rubbing it lightly as though to comfort him. I put my hand out and push them apart with a blast of my Gift. It happens so fast that I don't even remember deciding to do it.

They slide to opposite sides and Randon blinks in surprise, looking around as though not sure what happened.

I pull Cole forward with my Gift and he flies to me. A second later my hand is around his throat. "I've read your mind," I whisper to him, so Randon and Aurah don't hear. "Keep away from Randon or I'll show you exactly why you should be scared of me."

I pull back and see that his face is turned red. I quickly let go of his throat and he coughs, falling to his knees and clutching his neck.

"Bryn!" Randon says. "Can we keep him alive for a bit at least?" His eyes search mine. "What is it? Did you see something in his thoughts?"

"No."

"Is he lying to us? Does he want to kill me or something?"

"No. That's not what he wants to do with you."

Randon's confused expression changes and he grins. "Oh…" He looks down at Cole, his smile growing. I clench my fists.

"Well, we need him," Aurah says, crossing her arms. "I want to get into the ship's system and turn off this blasted heat!"

"Good idea," Randon replies. "Let's keep this one alive."

WHY'D YOU KILL THEM?

"T his isn't going to work," I say, tapping my foot as we wait for the elevator to go up.

"Focus, Bryn," Aurah snaps. The elevator stops and Randon and Cole step out first. Aurah and I follow after them.

Cole's plan is to get the armor and guns from the guards, which involves me using my Gift of Influence over them. Then, we'll get into Aiden's base, armed, and detonate their bombs against them.

I can see a lot of problems with this plan, but whenever I bring it up, Randon ignores me.

"No one will be at your base when we get there?" Randon says to Cole as they walk side by side, ahead of Aurah and me.

"Just the two guarding the doors for the day. The rest are out killing all the single players today, those who aren't part of groups," Cole responds.

"How are they killing all the single players?" Aurah asks.

Cole doesn't turn around to acknowledge her, but he answers. "They're surrounding them and beating them to death. Tomorrow they'll use the bombs on the groups."

"Why can't I just use my Gift on the two guys guarding the doors?" I ask. "Instead of on the ship's guards."

"We need the armor and guns," Randon says. "For the rest of us who don't have powers."

I don't know if my dream about Randon's Grandfather meant anything, or if it was just a dream, but if Randon really does have powers that he doesn't know about, wouldn't this be the time to tell him? So he can defend himself?

Cole stops walking and I almost run into him. Two armed guards come around the corner at the end of the hall and head towards us. Randon and Cole step out of the way, making way for me. It's my turn.

"No groups allowed," one of the guards says.

I stretch out my hand towards them, my heart pounding. This has to work.

"You're tired," I say. "So tired that you're going to fall asleep, right now." Sweat drips down my brow. "And you'll stay asleep, for hours."

No one moves, except for Cole, who bites his nails as we wait to see what will happen. If I don't succeed, I could get us all killed.

The guards reach for their guns and Randon pulls me back. But their guns drop from their hands, even as they lift them, and the guards collapse to the floor in a clatter of armor.

There is a moment of silence as we all seem to hold our breath, waiting to see if they are actually asleep. Then Aurah grabs one of the guns on the floor.

"Nice!" Randon pats me on the back and I let out a sigh of relief. "Bryn, you be lookout on one end of the hall and Aurah, you on the other."

Aurah and I exchange a glance. Cole is already disassembling one of the guard's armor. I crouch down to take the blaster.

"Hey!" Cole says. "I was going to take that one!"

I ignore him and head to the end of the hall to keep watch.

* * *

"Why are we always the backup?" I whisper to Aurah. We stop at the end of the hall as Randon and Cole march ahead in their full armor, carrying the blasters. Randon made me give Cole the one I took, and now I'm defenseless.

Aurah sighs. "I don't like this."

"Me neither."

"A weapon isn't always a good thing to display," she says. "It can get used against you, if it gets into the enemy's hands."

"They won't even need to use the blasters," I say. "The guys guarding Aiden's base will have to let them pass, if they say they're doing security checks."

"Maybe, but doesn't Cole look a little small to be a guard?"

Cole turns. "Stay here," he says, then walks ahead with Randon. I don't want to leave Randon alone with Cole, even if they have armor on.

Aurah grabs my shoulder to hold me back. "Don't worry, they know what they're doing."

Cole and Randon cover their heads with their helmets and round the corner.

A second later, the sound of blaster shots fill the halls, and loud cries.

"Randon!" I run ahead. Aurah is right behind me.

When we turn the corner, Randon and Cole are standing by two boys who are lying on the floor at their feet. Cole continues shooting one of the boys on the ground, even though he is clearly dead.

Randon grabs Cole's arm and Cole stops.

"Why'd you kill them?" I ask, looking at Randon.

"Why not?" Cole replies. "They would have been blown up later, with the rest, anyway."

"I wasn't talking to you," I snap. I turn to Randon. "You were supposed to tell them it was a security check and go in."

"The doors only open for the two minutes before sleep hours," Randon says. He still has the guard helmet on and I can't see his face.

"I forgot," I say. "But now the others will know we were here, and might figure out our plan with the bombs." I look down at all the blood on the carpet. "We'll have to hide the bodies."

"Go detonate the bombs," Randon says to Cole, ignoring me. "And hurry."

Cole punches the passcode into the keypad and the door opens. He gives Randon a salute then runs inside.

Randon removes his helmet and wipes at his face.

"I thought you said the doors don't—"

"Hey!" The yell comes from our left and we all turn. Two guards appear at the end of the hall and raise their blasters. Randon raises his.

"Stop!" I yell, hitting the guards with a blast of energy. They go flying back. I hold them both down and walk over. I'm getting better at this, I knocked them right out. Now Aurah and I can use their armor.

* * *

The heat inside the armored suit is unbearable. It's hard to see out of the helmet too, but I feel more powerful this way. Aurah doesn't complain but I know her suit must be even more uncomfortable than mine, because it has a guy's breastplate not a girl's.

Randon leads the way with Cole ahead of us and I'm not exactly sure what the plan is anymore, other than shooting anyone we see.

The first guy we come across ignores us completely. He continues his work of stringing a wire trap of some sort to an opening in the ceiling above. He's not doing anything against the rules and doesn't pay any attention to us in our guard armor.

Randon shifts his blaster in his arms but doesn't raise it. My insides dance around. This doesn't feel right. We're cheating and the others don't stand a chance. I know I shouldn't care, like Randon and Cole don't, but I do.

I watch as the boy sets his trap.

He stops and looks up, when we don't leave.

"Am I in trouble for something?" he asks.

Suddenly Cole opens fire and the boy cries out. His cries are stifled by the loud sound of the blaster firing, as Cole continues to shoot.

"Stop!" Aurah yells, grabbing his arm. I can't see her expression inside her helmet but I imagine it's just as alarmed as I feel.

"Save your blaster's power," Randon adds. "It only takes one shot to kill someone."

A group of boys come running around the corner then stop when they see us. They look confused. They're unarmed.

"Jason!" one of them shouts, rushing over to the boy on the ground. Cole fires at the boy who spoke and the others look startled.

They turn to run but then Randon begins to shoot and Cole joins in. The boys are dead in a matter of seconds.

I try not to look down at the dead players all around us. If we go around as guards like this, none of the other players stand a chance.

"Randon, Aurah, Bryn and Cole," a voice booms into my headset. "This is Commander Klein."

No one moves.

"Dukath wants to see you all in the gathering space," the Commander yells. "Now!"

I remove my helmet and so do Randon and Aurah. Randon curses and Aurah throws her helmet down. Cole removes his last, and I see that he's smiling. I resist the urge to choke that smile off his face.

"We should store these blasters somewhere, before going to see Dukath," he says. "Where are we all sleeping tonight? We can store them there."

Is he stupid?

"We're not going to need blasters, after seeing Dukath," I say.

"Why not?"

I sigh. He is stupid.

"We should hand them over to Dukath," I say. "He'll ask for them anyway."

"Bryn's right," Aurah says, starting to remove her armor. I do the same, pulling the arm pieces off.

"Maybe he won't think to ask," Cole says.

"Cole's right," Randon says. "We should store the blasters for later."

"Are you kidding, we're probably already disqualified."

"Maybe you should be," Randon says, stepping closer to me. "Because you have such a losing attitude."

I stop removing my armor and step up to Randon so we're face to fact. "I think someone who can't play the game properly, is the loser."

Aurah steps between us and gives us a gentle push in opposite directions. "Come on, Dukath's waiting and he doesn't like to wait."

Aurah kicks at her armor on the floor and an arm piece goes flying into the wall. "This was a dumb idea." She picks up a blaster. "We can't just leave these here for others to take. We'll take them with us."

Randon runs his hand through his hair. He's acting like he doesn't care we got caught, but I can tell he's worried. Joining the Ruling Order is all he's ever wanted. Now, we might get disqualified and lose that chance.

"I'll take the blame," I say. "Dukath won't disqualify me. He wants me to win because of my powers."

Randon's mind seems elsewhere and he doesn't respond, ignoring me, again.

Betrayed

"I MADE THE RULES very clear," Dukath says. He frowns down at us from behind the glass viewing window high above. We're back in the gathering space where almost have the students lost their lives during the opening ceremonies. Their bodies are still on the ground, scorched to black cinders.

My pulse pounds in my ears as we wait for Dukath to tell us our punishment. If we're disqualified, I'll kill Cole myself, right here and now, in this very room.

I glance at him. His Ruling Order uniform fits too big and he his face is flushed with the heat. He looks like a spoiled brat, glaring back at Dukath in defiance.

Randon and Aurah stand at attention, smart enough not to make any wrong moves. Their expressions give nothing away. I look back to Dukath, wishing we still had our armor on, so I wouldn't feel so exposed. What if he sets us all aflame?

"There are twenty-four players left," Cole says. "So technically, we've won."

We all turn to him. This is news to us.

Dukath reaches out his hand and Cole makes a choking sound.

"Quiet," he says. "I've changed the rules." He lowers his hand and Cole starts breathing again. "I don't know you well, boy. Who might you be?"

"My name's Cole... Master."

Dukath narrows his eyes at him. "Cole, is it. I've decided not to disqualify all of you, just one. Tell me, who do you think I should disqualify?"

"Bryn," Cole replies immediately. I clench my jaw.

"And you, Bryn?" Dukath turns his eyes to me. "Who do you think we should disqualify?"

"Cole," I say without hesitation.

Dukath nods slowly then sits back in his seat. "Aurah, what about you? Tell me who I should

disqualify."

Aurah hesitates. Does she really have to think about this, even for a second?

"Randon," she finally says.

Randon and I turn to her. She keeps her gaze forward, an angry expression on her face.

"I see." Dukath smiles. "Randon? Who do you say I should disqualify?"

"Any of these three, just not me, Your Leadership," Randon says.

Dukath clasps his hands together, watching us. "Very well," he says after a moment. "Go and finish the Game. If you're so eager to kill, then I'll change the rules once again. Only fifteen can remain, for the Game to end. If there are more than fifteen alive before the end of this day, then the count goes down to five."

"*Five?*" Aurah says.

"Yes," Dukath says, with a hint of irritation in his voice. "If you can't bring the number of players down to fifteen by the end of the day, then the rules change and only five can be left standing. Understand?"

Nobody replies. Five would not be enough to lead the entire Ruling Order. He can't really mean to follow through with this threat.

"Go on," Dukath says, waving his hand at us like we're his pets being shooed away.

Randon bows briskly. "Yes, Your Leadership."

He marches out of the room, not looking at us.

Aurah bows so low that I know she's being sarcastic, then she runs after Randon, not addressing Dukath with any parting words.

Cole and I bow at the same time. "Thank you, Your Leader—" I start to say.

"You are ever wise, Grand Master," Cole speaks over me. "Thank you for sparing us our lives."

I look to Dukath. Surely he can tell that Cole is mocking him and deserves a punishment. But he says nothing and I finish my bow, then hurry after Randon and Aurah.

* * *

"Randon, would you just wait!" Aurah calls down the hallway as I hurry after them. Randon is in the elevator at the end of the hall. The doors close before Aurah can reach him, and I'm even farther down the hall. I reach out my hand and stop the elevator doors from shutting completely, forcing them open again.

Randon crosses his arms, not looking pleased. "Leave me alone, Bryn," he says.

I can understand why he's mad at Aurah, but is he mad at me, too?

"Dukath was playing games with us," Aurah says, catching her breath once she reaches the elevator. She steps in and Randon backs up. Cole shows up and I quickly get into the elevator and hit the close button before he can get in.

"Hey!" I hear him yell from the other side of the doors, but I hold the doors shut.

"Aurah, what were you doing?" I say. "Why did you turn against us? Why didn't you vote out Cole?"

"Dukath was just testing us," she growls. "If we all voted out Cole, he'd know we were working as a team; you, me and Randon. And working as a team is against the rules, remember? Then he would have kicked all three of us out. Randon was the only one who hadn't gotten a vote yet, you voted for Cole and he voted for you. So that left Randon."

"Why didn't you vote yourself out then?" I say.

"If there's one thing Dukath hates more than attachments, it's self-sacrifice for others."

Randon doesn't say anything but he seems to have calmed down.

"We're all still here, aren't we?" Aurah continues. "So let's just get over it."

She steps in front of Randon so he will look at her. "I'm sorry, okay?"

He turns his head away.

"You know what?" Aurah throws up her hands. "I don't care if you're mad at me. You can just team up with your little worshiper Cole. I'll win this game on my own." She turns to me. "Let me out of this elevator, Bryn. It's too stuffy in here."

I open the doors and Cole is still standing there, wide-eyed. Aurah pushes him aside and storms off. He loses his balance and topples into the wall.

"Aurah!" I call after her. "You can't go out on your own. Aiden's team is hunting singles today, remember?"

"They're all dead!" She yells back. "*Remember?*"

I want to go after her but I'm torn between following her, or staying with Randon. I don't want her wandering around on her own, but I also don't want to leave Randon alone with Cole.

I step out of the elevator and Cole steps in. Randon holds the door open for me.

"Bryn—"

"See you later," Cole says, pushing the close button, but Randon keeps his hand on the doors. I look to Aurah's retreating back, then back to Randon. I don't know what to do.

Randon gives me a resigned look, then lets go of the doors. "See you, Bryn," he says, and the doors slide closed.

* * *

I wander the halls, my nerves on edge. I didn't find Aurah after I left Randon and now I'm lost too.

It feels like I've been wondering for a long time, yet the hallway lights are still at full brightness, which means it's still wake-hours.

I come up to another console. None of them seem to be working but I try anyway. It doesn't respond. Aurah would know how to get access to it. She's amazing with technology. And Randon would come up with a good plan. He's good with strategy. Now I've lost both of them.

The ship hums as I walk down the empty halls. I keep a brisk stride to show confidence, in case I come across someone unexpectedly. Wandering alone in the Game has been my worst fear since I had that horrible dream, and now I'm doing just that.

I quicken my pace. I need to get back to our room. I don't want to miss the two minutes we have to get into a room before night hours. Then I remember; the guards said the room would be permanently sealed. Did that actually happen?

Each hallway I walk down is empty. I shudder despite the heat, which has gradually grown hotter. At least I'm no longer wearing the heavy guard boots anymore. Being barefoot helps with the heat.

The keypads outside each door are turned off too. None of the ship's comm systems are working. I glance at the wide doors on either side of the hall. They don't look like sleeping quarters, which means they may not open before night hours. I can't just wander the halls all night. I'll need to get back to the sleeping quarters section of the ship.

Why didn't I just get in the elevator with Randon? He held the door open for me. How much more of an invitation did I need? But if I'd gone with them, I'd still be following Cole around, watching him kill anyone he comes across.

I clench my jaw. That's what *I* should be doing, playing the Game. If we don't get the count down to fifteen before the night is over, there will be more that have to be killed tomorrow.

The image of Cole shooting the boy when he was already dead, gives me the chills.

I stop walking. I made a mistake leaving Randon alone with him.

"Are you alone?"

The voice startles me. I turn.

It's Aiden, looking satisfied with himself, a grin on his face. He is larger than I remembered. Behind him stand six other guys.

"Where's Randon?" This time the voice comes from the other end of the hall. I turn to see five more guys walking towards me from the other side, the two groups closing in on me.

"How many people can you choke with your powers, at one time?" another one says, as they continue to move in. My pulse races, making it harder to think clearly. How can I fight them from both sides?

Aiden stops a few feet in front of me and crosses his arms, looking down his nose at me.

"Give Randon a message for us," he says. "Tell him we didn't kill you because we wanted him to watch you suffer and die in person." He takes out an injection device from his pocket and holds it up for me to see. It's one of the devices used by the medics at the Academy.

The boys grab hold of me from all sides.

I try to break away, but there are too many of them.

"You can't all win," I say, craning my neck to pull back from the needle Aiden is holding near me. "Master Dukath has changed the rules. He's only allowing fifteen to win."

I look down at the injection device. I want to hate Aiden, that would help me be stronger, but all I can think of is what he's about to inject me with. The fear makes it impossible to focus on my Gift. I try again to pull free but the hands holding me are too strong.

Randon...

I close my eyes and call out with my Gift. If Randon is Gifted too, he might hear me.

"Stop chanting!" Aiden yells, startling me. I open my eyes. Was I chanting?

Aiden's hand trembles and sweat drips down his brow. I don't have to read his mind to know he's scared too. His fear is obvious. Is he scared of me *chanting* things?

I start chanting a mantra my brother once taught me, to distract Aiden long enough for me to read his mind.

"When I am afraid, I put my trust in the energy inside of me, the power stronger than fear," I whisper.

I see his thoughts. He thinks my powers are some sort of magic, rather than a natural force working with its surroundings. His biggest fear is of being cursed, with something called the Blind Man's Curse, a tale his brother told him about the Dark Lords, when he was little.

I stop chanting and look at Aiden. "Every hand that is laid upon me right now, will be cursed..." I say. Aiden freezes and a look of uncertainty crosses his face. "Cursed with Blind Man's Curse," I add.

Aiden steps back. If I can stall him long enough, Randon might come. A wave of dizziness hits me. The heat and the smell of the boys sweating, closed in all around me, is too much and I need to get away.

Randon. Can you hear me?

It's no use. I need to do something else.

I look up at the blaring lights above. I need to act fast, before Aiden guesses that I have no power to curse him but I simply read his mind.

I focus on the glass tubes above. They pop and explode in a shower of bright, liquid light, blinding me and the others for a moment. Aiden cries out and the boys shout all around me in confusion, releasing me.

I blow out all the lights down the entire hall, including the emergency lights that run along the bottom, so there is only darkness.

Glass shatters everywhere and I cover my head with my arms, waiting for the commotion to stop.

I hear the shouts of the boys retreating down the hall. Their boots crunch glass and they're bodies bang against the walls a they scramble for the nearest elevator.

It opens with a flash of light in the distance, then they're all gone and it's silent again. I lower my hands and open my eyes.

I'm engulfed in darkness and stand barefoot, surrounded by glass, unable to walk any which way.

on the outside

I SET MY PALM against the warm metal of the wall nearest to me and focus my energies on the ship. It isn't alive like the forest, but I reach out to it anyway, searching for the life within it.

I sense the warp core at the center of the ship, its energy strong and powerful. But there is something unbalanced about it, like the core is unstable somehow. The ship feels like a massive tomb, mostly empty of life, except for a few scattered life forms.

I search for Randon and Aurah, but I can't sense where they are, only that they're still alive.

I pick up some movement; patrol guards in the hallway directly above me. They move closer and I lock onto them. Maybe I can use their headset audio.

I clear my throat, then give it a try. "This is Commander Klein," I say, directing my voice into their headsets. I've never done mind manipulation from a distance. But the guards are so accustomed to receiving orders that they're easily fooled.

"Go ahead, Commander," one of them replies.

"There has been a disturbance in the area directly below you. All the lights are out. Go down and report back to me what's happened."

They start to move again, going back the way they came.

I wait in the darkness, bracing myself for something unseen jumping out at me. My muscles tense, as though at any moment something will reach out of the dark and grab me.

I shake my head. My mind is starting to play tricks on me.

A moment later, I hear the elevator doors open and see two guards step out. Their boots crunch over the glass as they come down the hall in my direction. They take in their surroundings, shining their target lights from their blasters upward to the ceiling.

"Hey!" I yell.

They stop and raise their blasters, the light blinding me. "Lower your blasters and come here."

They start to walk again. I'm getting better at this. But then again, guards are easy, they are used to not questioning orders.

"Clear the glass away from around your feet," I say to them once they reach me.

They do as I say and I wait for them to finish, before I speak again.

"Give me your boots," I say to the nearest guard. He sets his blaster down and takes off his boots,

then hands them to me.

I quickly put them on. "Stay here and don't move until someone comes to get you. Do not respond to anyone on your headsets."

I take a step forward, glass crunching under my boot. The guards remain still. I grab one of their blasters and run to the elevator.

* * *

My boots thump loudly down the dark hallway, lit only with the night hours lighting. The sound reverberates, as though someone else is making the footsteps behind me, and not me. I glance over my shoulder for the hundredth time. No one is there.

I continue on. No one answered the call button back at our room, which I finally found my way back to. It showed no signs of being permanently sealed, but I wasn't able to get it open, and no one answered on the other side. Now I'm headed for Aurah's quarters, which she pointed out on the maps we were looking at when in the Command Center. Her and Randon's assigned rooms weren't actually that far apart.

When I reach the door I hit the call button.

Come on, be inside. There is no answer.

I hit the call button again, imagining them all inside, safe and resting, but ignoring the ringing. It's impossible to tell if anyone is actually inside or not. I wait for a moment longer, then walk away.

I feel like I'm wandering the forest at night again. Only, this is worse.

There's one more place left to check for my team, then I'll have no choice but to wander for the night and try not to fall asleep, so I don't get killed.

I head for my assigned quarters, which is in a completely different sector. There's no reason why they would have chosen to go to my room, but I can't think of anywhere else to try. I don't dare knock on a random door.

The halls are empty and my muscles tense at every small sound. I don't have the energy to fight off an unexpected attack. Hopefully Randon and Aurah found a safe place to rest for the night.

I step into the elevator to go to the eighth level. The heat inside the elevator is unbearable, worse than in the hallways.

When the elevator opens on the eighth level, I hear voices.

I brace myself for a possible attack, then I recognize Aurah's white tank top and Randon's orange mop of hair. They're sitting in front of my door, halfway down the hall.

They talk quietly together and I see Cole is with them too. He leans forward, having been hidden behind Randon, and makes dramatic hand gestures as he talks. Aurah and Randon nod their heads as they listen.

A pang of jealousy grips me. Have I been replaced? But they're sitting in front of *my* door, so they must be waiting for me.

Aurah sees me first. She jumps to her feet, then Randon turns around. When he sees me he gets up and runs down to meet me. Aurah stays at the room door with her arms crossed, but a smile on her face.

I walk forward to meet Randon, then stop, unsure of what kind of welcome I'll receive. He could still be upset with me and is coming to tell me to get lost.

Randon doesn't slow his stride as he approaches, colliding with me in a hug. I stumble a few steps back, stunned.

"Bryn." He tightens the arms around me, his voice muffled in my shoulder. I hug him back. He smells like soap and the Academy halls somehow, making me nostalgic all of a sudden. I cling to him a bit too long.

The night hours lights at our feet suddenly pop and turn out, leaving us in the dark.

Randon pulls back, looking down at the lights. I can't see his face now, just his outline. Aurah and Cole look over.

"We're fine," I call to them. "The lights just went out."

Randon is still holding onto my arms. "When we found Aurah and she said you never joined her, I thought you were..." He stops and I wait. "I heard you call to me," he says. "I thought maybe you died and I was hearing a ghost."

"You heard me?"

"Yes, like you were right there beside me."

Should I tell him about my dream? That he might also have Gift powers?

Aurah watches us from the end of the hall. After a moment, she seems satisfied that no harm has come to us and sits back down beside Cole, who ignores us.

I take Randon's hand. He heard me call to him. He's like me. But if the dream was a real vision, then I can't tell him about his Gift ability. His grandfather told me and not tell him.

"Well, if you're not dead," he says, pulling his hand away. "Then give us the passcode for your room, so we can sleep there for the night instead of out in the hall."

"Hasn't door time passed already?" I say.

"Yeah, but Aurah can take care of that. She just needs your passcode."

Randon grabs my wrist and yanks me towards him.

"Bryn?" he says.

"Hmm?" I manage. His grip on my wrist tightens. I wait.

"Never mind." He lets go of my wrist and steps away. "We have some food and water if you want some."

I clear my throat. "Okay."

We head back to join Aurah and Cole.

POSSESSIVE

"TELL ME ABOUT THE little girl," I whisper to Aurah.

She turns her head to look at me, lying on the floor beside me. I'm relieved she's not asleep. Cole is somewhere on the other side of the room, also sleeping on the floor. Randon won the toss-up for the bed.

"I'll tell you someday," Aurah whispers back. "But not tonight. We need our sleep time so we can be alert in the morning."

"I can't sleep because of the heat."

"I can't sleep because I know the bombs we set in Aiden's base will go off soon."

I'd forgotten about the bombs. "Do you think we'll feel it?" I ask. "Or hear it?"

"I hope not. But then at least the games will be over and it won't go down to five left standing."

"What if it causes a breach in the hull?"

"We're far enough away that the area would be contained—"

"I'm trying to sleep," Randon says from the bed.

We lay in silence for a while and I look out the windows to the stars. Cole shuffles around in his spot on the floor, then gets up. I watch him in the shadows. I hate that he is on our team now, but Randon seems to think he'll come in handy.

Cole doesn't move but just stands there. Goosebumps break out on my arms. Does he think we're asleep? Is he going to try to kill me?

He starts to move again, heading in my direction. I tense, ready for a fight. But he passes by me and walks over to the bed.

I sit up. If he tries to hurt Randon, I'll kill him. I wait to see what he will do next. The longer I wait, the harder my heart pounds.

Aurah nudges my shoulder. "Don't start a fight tonight, okay?" she whispers.

"Me?" Why does she think I'll start a fight?

She nods her head towards the bed and I turn to look. Cole is climbing in. I clench my fist, ready to pound him, but Aurah gently pulls me back by my shoulder.

I lay back down onto the floor. The hum of the ship drones on. I don't bother to try and keep an eye on what Cole is doing. I don't want to know.

Why am I jealous anyway? It's not like Randon and I... I push the idea away as soon as it surfaces. It's not that. I just don't want someone with no conscience like Cole, to get close to him.

I rub my face with my hands, knowing that the truth is something I don't want to admit.

"What the hell are you doing?" Randon yells suddenly, startling both me and Aurah. She squeals as Cole comes tumbling off the bed and rolls across the floor right into her. Randon jumps up and slams his fist against the wall, turning the lights on. The sudden blast of light pierces my eyes and Aurah groans in protest.

"Get off of me." She shoves Cole and he runs off into the bathroom. The door slides closed behind him.

"I'm going to kill him," Randon says, his face red.

"Just shut off the lights already," Aurah says, sounding impatient. She covers her eyes with her arm.

Randon turns off the lights and the room is bathed in darkness once again. "Bryn?" he says.

"Yeah?"

"Do you want the bed? I don't want it anymore."

"Uh... no thanks. I'm fine on the floor."

My eyes adjust to the darkness again and I get up.

I want to ask Randon about Cole, so I'm not left with this feeling eating away at me. He's still standing by the bed, as though unsure where to go next. I go over and blurt out my next words before I can change my mind. "Why did you let Cole climb into bed with you?"

Randon's eyes flash. "I thought it was *you*," he hisses. The starlight from the window reflects in his eyes as they study mine. His expression changes. "Would that bother you, if I let him?"

I don't respond.

"You couldn't stop looking at Aurah's tank top today," he says.

"You guys know I can hear you, right?" Aurah says from the floor.

Randon pulls me aside, to the other end of the room.

"When did you get taller than me?" he asks. He lets go of his grip on my arm and stands in front of me. "What do you want, Bryn?"

"Want?" I run my hands through my hair. It has gotten even warmer now.

Randon waits for me to answer his question.

"I don't know. I think I just want your attention," I answer honestly.

"Well, you've got it."

I look away. "Maybe I don't want to share it."

"That's kind of selfish, don't you think?"

"I'm a selfish person."

"And possessive."

I look at Randon then, and see that he has a grin on his face.

"Maybe a bit of that too," I say. My cheeks heat up. Soon we'll all die from heat exposure and none of this will matter anymore. "Do you like Cole?" I've already said too much so I might as well keep going.

"What's not to like?"

I step back and Randon steps forward.

"Wait. Bryn, I'm not interested in Cole," he says. "You'd enjoy being worshiped too—"

I push him away. "Don't let me stop you from having whatever you want."

"Okay." Randon closes the distance between us and I set my hand against his chest to hold him back.

"That's not what I meant," I say.

His heart races beneath my palm. Am I'm playing with his feelings? Why do I want to keep him all for myself, when I know I'm not the same as him?

He runs a hand through is hair. "I don't really know what I want either," he whispers.

I relax my hand to let him forward. When he doesn't, I grasp the fabric of his shirt and ball it up in my fist, not sure if I want to shove him away or pull him to me. I hate that I need him, but I do. He's *mine* and no one else's.

He's right, I *am* very possessive.

"Would you guys stop it already," Aurah barks and we quickly move apart. "Cole's watching you from the bathroom door and it's weirding me out."

We both turn and the bathroom door slides closed with a swish.

"Can we lock him in there somehow?" I say to Randon. I'm still holding onto his shirt. I can't seem to let go. He's the only person who's ever shown this kind of interest in me and I crave it. I yank him towards me but he pushes me away.

"We should get some sleep." He unlatches my fist from his shirt and glances towards Aurah. Then he leans in to talk to me quietly. "I like to keep my personal life private, Bryn."

"I'd like that too," Aurah says. "*Good night.*"

Randon goes to the bed and grabs a pillow, then joins Aurah on the floor. "Come on, Bryn," he says, patting the carpet on his other side. "Let's try and get some sleep."

I join them and lay down beside Randon.

The room goes silent again, except for the hum of the ship's engine, which seems to be running louder than it should be.

The floor feels warm beneath me. It makes me drift in and out of sleep. I speak, as though sleep-talking.

"You'll leave me behind too, one day," I say to Randon.

"Where would I go?" he says. "We're going to lead the Ruling Order together, remember?"

I nod, even though he probably can't see me.

Randon's hand finds mine in the dark and he clasps it tight. "I know you were mad your dad left you at the Academy when you were little."

I don't answer.

"And your mom left too, right?" he asks a moment later.

"She's just never around."

"I never knew my mom."

Aurah groans. "A conversation for another time."

Randon whispers more quietly. "I'm not going anywhere, okay?"

"Okay," I whisper back.

"Not without you."

"Okay."

"I promise," he adds. His thumb circles the back of my hand, lulling me to sleep.

Maybe Aurah was right, that people in dangerous situations cling to each other. Whatever the reason is, I've never felt closer to anyone in my life, as I do to Randon in that moment, and it's terrifying.

"We'll win this game and rule together," Randon whispers, then I fall into a heavy sleep.

one true attachment

I WAKE DRENCHED IN sweat, my arms and legs heavy with sleep.

I glance at the clock. 12:07!

I sit up too quickly and a dizzy spell knocks me back down.

We've slept in. A *lot*.

Why did the guards not come to wake us? Or to kick us out?

The air is dry and hot, and my tongue sticks to the roof of my mouth. I sit up again, slower this time and look around. Aurah and Randon are still asleep on either side of me. I can take a quick shower before they wake up.

I grab one of the five water bottles in the room and rip the lid off. I don't know where they got more bottles, but they're all we have. I can't seem to drink fast enough to quench my thirst. The water drips down my chin in my desperation to drink it.

The bathroom door doesn't slide open when I approach it so I hit the button. When it still doesn't open I remember that Cole is in there. I knock lightly and a moment later it slides open.

"Oh, it's you," Cole says when he sees me.

"You'll be calling me Master soon enough," I say to him, taking another drink of my water.

"I'll never call you Master," he snarls.

"We'll see." I push past him and walk into the washroom. "I'm going to have a shower, you can join me if you want."

Cole's face turns red. I smile. He's so easy to irritate.

I pull my shirt over my head and he quickly leaves, the door sliding closed behind him.

* * *

"Finally," Aurah says as Randon steps out of the washroom.

He has a towel wrapped around his waist and nothing else on, and his hair tousled every which way.

"Put some clothes on!" Aurah snaps at him. She covers her face with a pillow, grumbling something into it.

"It's so hot in here, I thought I'd stay with no clothes on for a while," Randon says with a playful grin on his face.

"No!" Aurah and I shout at the same time.

"Relax." Randon waves his hand at us and opens the water bottle he's holding. "I'll get dressed. But I don't want to get back into the clothes I was wearing yesterday and all night, they're gross."

"Do you want my clothes?" Aurah says, sitting up in the bed. Her tank top is damp and her skin glistening with sweat, drawing my attention. I quickly check to see if Randon noticed me looking. He didn't. I turn and stare at the wall instead.

"Where's Cole?" Randon asks.

"He went to get some more food or something," Aurah replies. "Why? Are you disappointed he didn't see you walk out in a towel?"

Randon chuckles, cursing under his breath all the way back to the washroom.

Aurah winks at me and I shake my head.

"What are we going to do with him?" she says.

"What do you mean?"

"If he really does have powers like you, then he can only have one true romantic attachment for his whole existence."

"I don't understand, what?"

"I know he has powers too," she continues, her expression serious now. "I'm not stupid. You called to him using your Gift when we were separated, and he *heard* you."

My pulse races. "Does *he* know?"

"No, but it's probably best if he doesn't know. He'd go crazy with that kind of power. I mean, he's self-controlled most of the time, but if he realized he had that kind of power, it would go to his head."

"You're right, we can't tell him. He can't know. Promise."

"Don't worry, I'm not in any hurry to be on the receiving end of his powers."

"What did you mean when you said, those who are Gifted only have one true attachment?"

"It's a myth. I read it in one of the ancient books at the Academy."

"You were reading about Gifted people?" I didn't even know the Academy library had books on things like attachments.

"You're my friend aren't you?"

I nod.

"Anyway," Aurah continues. "I wanted to understand it more. And I can just tell, with the history we were taught of the ancient Gifted people who went mad with power."

"You think I'll go mad with power?"

"It just looks like they all have one common theme, the death or separation of a loved one causing them to go crazy, or evil."

"Wait, where is this coming from?"

I suddenly remember the little girl I saw in Cole's thoughts.

Aurah fidgets with the water bottle in her hand. "Anyway," she says. "Attachments are strong and that's why Dukath always warned against them."

"He forbids them."

"And the level of attachment Gifted people are capable of, with the powers they have, can be dangerous. If we go by what history tells us, it always ends up in a lot of deaths. Sometimes the destruction of an entire race or planet."

"You think Randon is my one true attachment?" I ask. "What did the book say? Do I have a choice about who my attachment is? Or is it...some kind of fate?"

"I don't know. I think you have a choice and..." She stops abruptly. "I don't know if Randon is your attachment or if someone else is, but just be careful. I think *you* might be *his*."

"How do you know he's not mine?"

Aurah sighs. "I'm pretty sure the little girl Rue is."

"Rue?"

"If we're all going to die here anyway, I might as well tell you. The little girl you asked me about, the one the others saw you with all summer, her name was Rue."

"You'll tell me about her?"

"Maybe."

"But, she's just little."

"For now. She'll grow up."

I think back to what I saw in Cole's thoughts of me this summer. I looked really happy and so did the girl.

Rue...

"So you should back off Randon a bit." Aurah crosses her arms and frowns. "Don't encourage him if you're not serious about him."

"What? I'm not—"

"You're confusing him."

"*I'm* confusing *him?*"

The door to the bathroom opens and Randon steps out, dressed in a new set of Ruling Order clothes. "Washed and dried!" he says, striking a pose and winking.

Aurah rolls her eyes. "You'll get it sweaty soon enough."

"Always the pessimist, Aurah."

"Ready to go?"

Aurah stands up.

"What about Cole?" I ask.

"We can't just sit here and get bombed," Randon says, grabbing a water bottle. He drinks it all down.

"Hey that's my water!" I say.

"Oh." Randon wipes his mouth and throws the bottle aside. "You can have half of mine."

"Holy Galaxies are we really down to just five?" Aurah gasps.

"Three bottles. Cole must have taken one."

"No." Aurah grabs her hand-held blaster and tucks it into her belt. "I mean Dukath said if the numbers don't go down to fifteen by today, then he'll change the rules again and only five can win."

Randon and I don't respond.

"And," she continues. "If we don't get down to five by the end of today then…"

"He'll bring the number down to one," Randon finishes for her.

"How do you know?" I ask.

"It's what he would do," Randon says.

Aurah nods in agreement. She says something about the bombing of Aiden's group but all I can hear is the humming of the ship and the pulsating of the core reactor, radiating through me. My head pounds. Something is wrong, with the ship, really wrong. I can sense it.

"Hey guys," I interrupt. "I think the core reactor is un-stable." I shake my head to clear it. "It's overheating. That's why it's so hot on board, not because of the environmental controls."

"How do you know?" Aurah asks.

"I can sense it."

"You couldn't sense it before?" Randon asks, sounding accusatory.

"I guess not. But now our lives are in danger, so I'm definitely sensing it."

"We have to tell Dukath—" Aurah says.

"He's not here," I say, only now realizing it. My heart beats harder. "I don't sense him or any of the guards. That's why we slept in this morning and no one woke us. They've all evacuated the ship. It's only us and the other players left on board."

"Are you sure?" Aurah grabs me by the arms and gives me a little shake. "Is this part of the Game?"

"I don't think it's part of the game," I say. "None of us will survive if we don't do something about the ship's core reactor."

Hallucinations

"You okay, Randon?" Aurah says behind me.

I look back. Randon has fallen behind, which is unlike him. Now I'm the one leading as we make our way down the narrow service corridor. I stop to wait for Randon to catch up.

"Is it the heat?" I ask him. We're almost at the Engineering wing, where the engine core is. The heat is definitely coming from there and is becoming more intense the closer we get.

"We need to get some water," Aurah says.

"We will, once we figure out what's wrong with the core."

Aurah nods, giving Randon a worried glance, and we continue on.

The heat intensifies as we move forward, making it hard to take a full breath, as it burns the throat.

When we finally reach the service door to the Engineering room it doesn't open. There's a keypad on the wall.

"Aurah, can you…" I turn around but Aurah and Randon are not there. They've fallen behind again and are halfway down the hall. Aurah has her hand on Randon's back as though to comfort him.

Something's wrong.

I want to go talk to them, but I have to deal with the engine overheating, before we're all dead.

I turn back to the door. Even though I don't know anything about engineering, I have to believe my Gift instincts will guide me to fixing the problem with the engine.

I punch in the passcode Aurah set the first day we got here. The indicator light turns green and the door swishes open.

I don't have a chance to be happy it worked because the blast of heat coming out from the Engineering area stings my face. I raise my hand to block the heat.

Once the initial wave of heat passes, the temperature becomes slightly more bearable and I step through the doors.

The room opens up into a vast area with an opening at the center which drops down to the engine core below, a banister running around it.

I walk up to it and look down. The core pulsates with a blue light below, heat pushing up from it. I wipe sweat off my forehead and look around the room. There are buttons and consoles and monitoring equipment everywhere. I have no idea where to start.

I jump when I feel something touch my arm.

I turn to find Aurah with a concerned look on her face. "Come and see this," she yells over the loud hum of the core. I follow her to one of the control panels near the door. She shows me an information screen, but I can't make any sense of it.

"The core drive is on standby," Aurah explains. "Like when it is running at full speed but has been put on pause. It shouldn't even be on at all because we're not going anywhere. I think it's been on standby for days and that's why the core is overheating."

"Can you shut it down?" I ask.

"I don't have admin access."

"Try the passcode you set on the first day. It worked to get in here."

"I did. I tried everything."

"Everyone's left the ship. No one who is still on board, knows the admin codes."

"Cole might."

"Bryn!" Randon yells, running to the banister at the center and looking down to the core. He jumps up onto the banister ledge and my stomach drops.

"Holy Galaxies!" Aurah runs to him and grabs his shirt before he goes over the edge. I reach him a second later and grab him too. He tries to push us away. "Let me go, Bryn fell! We have to get down there!"

Aurah and I exchange a glance.

"I'm right here," I say at the same time Aurah says, "he's here."

We try to pull Randon back over to safety but he fights us.

"Let me go!" he yells.

"Randon, stop! Look at me." I try to get his attention. "I'm right here."

He ignores me. "Aurah, help me!" He's looking only at Aurah, as though I'm not there. He's breathing heavily and sweating profusely. "We have to find Bryn."

Aurah tries to turn his face so he'd look at me. "Bryn's right here—"

"Why aren't you listening! I saw him fall!" Randon's eyes are glazed over. "Please..."

I try to unclamp his fingers from the banister, but his grip is too tight.

"Aurah, help me," I say.

"Stop!" Randon's voice cracks. "We have to get down there. Maybe there's a ladder—"

"Randon, I'm right here," I yell, but it's futile. His mind is not working for some reason and he's delusional. Is Dukath tormenting him?

I suddenly realize I can use my Gift abilities on him. I quickly lock him in a hold and he stops struggling. Aurah pries his fingers from the banister and we all fall to the ground.

"No..." Randon says, his face crumpling into tears. I lift his chin so he'd look at me but he looks right through me. I try to read his thoughts but his mind seems lost.

"What's wrong with him?" Aurah asks.

I put my hand onto his forehead to try and search his thoughts again, but his mind is too overwhelmed with emotion for coherent thoughts. He really does believe I've fallen into the ship's core.

I let go of his forehead, which is burning hot. The heat is draining me of my energy. Randon's shoulders collapse forward and he covers his face with his hands.

"It's okay," I tell him. "Everything's fine, I didn't fall." I muster up my last bit of strength to try my manipulation powers on him.

"Listen to me," I command, setting my hands onto his shoulders. "Bryn didn't fall into the engine core. He caught the ladder just in time and climbed back out. I saw him. You're both safe now. He's here right now. Look up."

Randon lowers his hands from his face. His breathing slows as he calms down, but he doesn't look up.

I lift his chin. "Look at me."

He does, but his eyes are still glazed over. "I think he's drugged," Aurah says.

She continues talking but I don't hear her over the hum of the engine core. She motions to the control panel, then gets up and goes over to it.

I turn focus on Randon again. "It's me…"

He stares at me blankly and I sigh, leaning forward and resting my forehead against his. "Come on," I whisper. "Fight against this."

"Bryn?" Randon says, his voice hoarse.

"Yes?" I pull back and for a second he sees me, really sees me, and relaxes. I smile.

Suddenly his eyes open wide and fill with fear again.

"No!" he cries out. I grab him before he can get up and run to the banister again.

"Go to sleep, Randon."

"No—"

"Go to sleep!" I command with all the energy I can muster. "And don't wake up until I tell you to."

Randon's eyes flutter closed and he collapses into my arms.

Leader

"I CAN'T BELIEVE YOU carried him all the way here," Aurah says as she fiddles with the infirmary bio-scanner above Randon's head.

The temperature in sickbay is a lot cooler than being in Engineering, which I'm grateful for, but it's still uncomfortable enough to remind me that the engine is close to exploding.

"I wouldn't have made it without my Gift abilities." I look down at Randon. "What did he say to you out in the hall, before we went into Engineering?"

"His vital signs are stabilizing," Aurah taps the display on the wall. Is she avoiding my question? "The white blood cell pills are keeping him alive, but I don't know how to get this out of his system. I found the chemical composition of what he drank, in the computer. Basically it causes hallucinations, specific to a person's fears, like some hallucinatory anxiety. It's used in battle to confuse opponents and—"

"Aurah." I turn her to face me. "Before Randon almost jumped down into the engine, and you two were out in the hallway, what were you talking about?"

Aurah keeps her eyes on the monitor above. "He remembered everything Dukath made him forget."

I stop. How could he have remembered? Dukath's powers are not easily overthrown.

"How's that possible?"

"The effects of the drugs must have brought his memories back."

I frown and glance at Randon again. He looks like he's having a feverish dream. What did he remember, that Grand Master took away? "How long until he's better?"

Aurah turns back to the monitor and scrolls through the information. "I don't know. With the amount in his system it could...:" She stops and glances at me.

"It could what?"

"It could kill him, if it's not removed from his bloodstream."

"Are you serious?"

Aurah pushes the bedside screen aside forcefully.

"It was meant for me," I say, swallowing hard. "Randon drank from *my* water bottle."

We stand silent for a moment, listening to the beeping of the monitors. How many students are left now? And if Dukath is long gone, does it matter anyway how many are left or if we all die in an engine explosion? It just doesn't make any sense. But he's ruthless enough to kill all his students just to enjoy seeing them struggle and die.

"The decontamination chamber might help get some of the toxins out of his system, through his skin. But I don't know how to flush out his blood and the other things a medic would do."

"Then we need a medic."

Aurah frowns and doesn't answer.

"And we'll get one," I continue. "But first we'll do the decontamination chamber. And I'll try to get the admin password for the engine core." I let out a slow breath to calm myself. There's too much to do in a short time. I have to turn off the engine before it explodes. I have to get a medic. I have to save Randon.

Aurah nods, an angry expression on her face while her eyes are brimming with tears.

"Are we going to get through this?" she asks quietly.

"Yes." I stand closer to her but don't touch her, knowing she wouldn't like to be comforted in that way. "I'll get Randon into the decontamination chamber and you can stay with him until he's done. I need to go find Cole."

"Okay."

I pick up Randon from the examination table, and carry him to the detox chamber at the other end of the room. The door slides open and I step inside. A long bench runs along the wall. I lay Randon down on it, careful not to bump his head.

"He won't be happy later if he finds out we undressed him," I say.

"I'll do it," Aurah says. "He won't care if it's me."

"Okay." I step aside to let Aurah take over. "I'm going to kill them all. As soon as I get the admin password and turn off the engine. Then we'll get Randon some help. Okay?"

"Sure."

I turn to leave.

"Bryn?" Aurah calls after me. "Yes?"

"I can see why Dukath picked you as the future leader."

I nod, unable to take the complement when I hate Dukath so much at the moment.

"And…" Aurah reaches behind her. "Here." She tosses me her phaser pistol.

"No, you should keep it," I say. "In case anyone comes in here." I toss it back. "I want you to have it on you."

"I can lock the decontamination chamber from inside and the door is blaster proof."

"I'd still feel better if you had it while I'm gone."

Aurah nods then pulls out something else from her pocket. It's a rock, the same one I found in my room back at the school. "You left this in the bathroom in your quarters yesterday. I think you should have it with you."

She tosses it over and I catch it. "Was it Rue's?"

"I don't know."

I slip the rock into my pocket and head for the infirmary doors.

"I'm going to end this game," I say to Aurah as I step out.

She gives me a salute and run off before the doors finish closing.

* * *

I take my hand off the ship's wall. My Gift is stronger now, growing with my urgency to save Randon. The consoles around the ship aren't working but I have my own ways to find life signs on board.

They're in the Command Center, all of them, every life sign other than Aurah and Randon, all in one room. Perfect.

I run to the elevator. They might leave before I get there and Randon needs help. I need to end this, once and for all.

The hallways on Deck Two are wider, with a narrow window running along the left side. I see a large door to the right, which I now realize is the same Command Center we found the first day. I force the doors open with a blast of energy.

Inside, there are less boys than I expected. All heads turn to me in surprise. Where are the rest? Cole is standing in front of a console, his eyes wide with fear when he sees me.

"Didn't expect to see me alive, did you?" I say to him.

"Shoot him!" Aiden yells. He's standing at the head of the long command table.

Two of the boys hold up their blasters to shoot. I pull the blasters forward with my Gift. They fly out of the boys' hands, flipping through the air, then turn to face the other way so I can grab their handles.

The boys cower, dropping to the floor. All but Cole. He stands straight. My hands tighten on the blasters.

"You won't do it," he says. "You don't have the admin codes. You need me."

I open fire, shooting around Cole to startle him.

He raises both hands in surrender. "I wasn't joining their side," he stammers.

My hands shake as Cole continues to move towards me, his arms in the air.

The guns fall from my hands, dropping loudly to the floor. Cole grins. Sweat drips down my brow as I fall to my knees. My muscles ache. He's got the crystal, somewhere on him, the same one Randon had in the library that made me weak.

"How does it feel?" he snarls. "To be powerless?"

"You tell me," I say between clenched teeth.

Cole stops in front of me then crouches down, waving the blue crystal in front of my face. The light from it pierces my eyes and I force them shut.

"I don't care if you kill me..." I struggle for breath.

"Yes, you do."

"Randon needs help. He drank my water."

Cole doesn't say anything but the heat from the crystal moves away. I open my eyes and see that he's standing again, his arms crossed.

"I could save him. But I won't. I'm going to lead the Ruling Order myself. Master Dukath will be so surprised. He's greatly underestimated me." He wipes his forehead then flips the crystal in the air, catching it and smiling. "He never once looked my way, just stared right past me like I'm a waste of space, pretended he couldn't hear me when I spoke."

Cole crouches down again, his hot breath in my face. "He won't be able to ignore me now, not when he returns to find his two precious apprentices dead."

"We'll all be dead soon if we don't fix the engine."

"Don't you think I know that?" Cole stands, glaring down at me. My head throbs from the sight of the crystal and I look away.

"Where did you get that?" I whisper.

"From Randon, of course. He gave it to me."

I shut my eyes tight. "You're a liar."

"We were going to rule together. I suppose he told you the same thing. He says that to anyone he thinks can help him win, but he doesn't care about you. He's the one that had the idea to poison you. He put the Harvoth's fever in your water himself."

I know Cole's lying. Randon wouldn't have accidentally drank my water bottle if he'd poisoned it himself. He's a little more careful than that.

Bryn...

Randon's voice drifts into my head. The humming in the room stops and Cole's voice fades away until I hear only the sound of my own breathing. I see Aurah in the sickbay, rushing around in a panic.

"No, no, no!" she shouts, rushing from one monitor to another. Tears streak down her face. A high beeping sound fills the room. Randon is dead. But he's not.

Goodbye Bryn.

I can hear him. He's still alive.

Hold on Randon. I rush over to his hospital bed and run into Aurah, but her shoulder moves right through my arm and I realize I'm not physically here. It's a vision, or really happening but on the other side of the ship. I reach for Randon.

Please don't die.

Suddenly I'm back in the room with Cole. He's pointing a blaster at my head, still holding the crystal, but I'm not scared anymore.

I stand, Master Dukath's words coming back to me. There is no strength or weakness with the Gift. I now understand what he meant. It can surpass anything, if your motivation is strong enough.

Cole's expression falters when he sees my glare. Randon is dying and the ship's engine is failing. I need more strength and I now know how to get it.

I lift my hand and the crystal goes flying across the room. Cole tries to shoot me but he moves too slowly, or else I'm moving very quickly. He doesn't get a chance to pull the trigger. I grab his blaster, along with another one off the ground, and open fire.

I shoot at them all. The others don't have weapons and are defenseless, but Master Dukath was right. They all exist for me, even these players in the Game; for me to understand the power of my Gift. Randon, Aurah and the Masters, they're different. But Cole and these boys, they're just small hindrances in a bigger Game.

One by one they fall. My strength builds with each death, and my power grows.

When the blaster sounds die down, Cole is the only one left standing.

His hands are up again, only this time he is actually surrendering. "I wasn't really going to shoot you—"

I throw the blasters down. They land with a loud clatter, making Cole flinch. There's no time for questions, just answers. I reach my hand out to read his mind.

He found us using the ship's bio scanner, and four of Aiden's team members are on their way to sick bay with two blasters, to kill Aurah and Randon.

"You can't save them, Bryn," Cole says with a smirk. "They're probably already dead."

I get the access codes from his mind, then pick up one of the guns from the floor and shoot him.

***

I hear the phaser shots the moment the elevator door opens. The sickbay doors are open. I run in.

Four of Aiden's boys are in the room, shooting at the decontamination chamber door, the sound is so loud that they don't hear me come in.

I raise my blaster and shoot, one, two, three of them in the back, before they even know what hit them. It's so easy. Their energy gathers inside of me as they release their last breath. My growing strength makes their deaths worthwhile.

The fourth boy, a skinny brown-haired kid with dark eyes, is crouched down on the floor, covering his head and trembling. I didn't see him. His cowering position makes me hesitate before shooting.

"Please, don't kill me," he begs.

A calm fills me, one that I've never felt before with this Gift. It's the peace of the Dark Masters; the lack of emotion which allows them to be who they are, in their position of power. Something has shifted inside of me and I can feel it growing.

I look down at the boy. He's still shaking and keeps his eyes down, not daring to look at me. I step forward and he cowers, as though he expects me to strike him.

I crouch down and wait for him to stop cowering and look at me. When he does, I can tell right away that he's sick with some virus. His eyes are glazed over and his skin is ghostly white.

"Are you sick?" I ask him.

He trembles at my voice but nods slowly.

"With what?"

I recognize him now, short brown hair and lanky limbs, like a puppy not grown into its full size yet. Anthony or Andrew, is his name. From combat class. One of the smaller kids who would always get paired up with me in fighting simulations since I was the youngest. Now I'm a lot bigger than him. I guess he never grew. His eyes have dark bags under them.

"Harvoth's fever," he says. "I took the pills, but I'm not better yet."

I frown, suddenly reminded of the boy Randon killed, who never got the chance to recover.

"I don't want to die," the boy whispers, his breathing labored.

I put the back of my hand to his forehead. He's feverish.

"Wouldn't it be better to die?" I say. "And be free of your suffering?"

"No, please. I want to live."

He looks so helpless that I can't deny his request. But just as quickly as the sympathy comes, it's gone again, replaced by the strength now inside of me. The act of killing so many in such a short time has made me powerful, quickly. I think I understand now why Dukath set up the Games the way he did. It's the best way for me to come into my power. Not in the way my brother is powerful. He relies on meditation and self-discipline, but this is far more effective. I will be greater than him, and even Dukath, some day.

"What's your name?" I ask the sick boy.

"Anthony," he says in a raspy voice, struggling for breath. I could kill him too. Or not. There's a detachment inside of me now, which makes me not care if he lives or dies.

I get up. He can live, for now. If he doesn't prove himself useful later, I'll just kill him then.

"There's medicine here for your fever," I say, heading for the decontamination chamber. "You should take some right away." The phaser blasts have shattered a layer of the glass and I can't see Randon or Aurah inside.

I look back over my shoulder at Anthony, before going in. "You belong to me now, understand?"

He quickly nods.

I open the decontamination door, afraid of what I might find on the other side. There are only four of us left now, if Randon is still alive.

The Games are finally over.

Takano Rynn

ASTER DUKATH WOULD LIKE to see you, sir," a guard says, startling me from my vigil at Randon's bedside.

I look to the medic who is an alien species I don't recognize. He nods.

"He'll be fine now," he says to me. "It's just a matter of time."

"When will he be his normal self again?" I ask.

"Soon. He just needs a bit more sleep. By wake hours he should be feeling close to normal again." His accent is so thick I have to use a bit of mind reading to clarify what he's said.

"Good." I turn to the guard who addressed me. "Tell Master Dukath I'll be right there."

"Yes, sir." He nods, then marches off.

I start towards the door then turn back to the medic. "Have General Randon taken to the Captain's quarters to rest there for the night," I say.

"Of course," he nods to me again, bowing slightly.

"And if Aurah returns, let her know where he's been taken."

"I will do that. And I also recommend you return for a full body scan yourself."

"Maybe in the morning," I say.

"Very good. And, may I say, congratulations to you, on your advancement to Leader of this crew."

I don't respond but take one last look at Randon before leaving to meet Master Dukath.

* * *

"You've done well," Dukath says, turning his chair around to face me. The lighting in the briefing room is dim, the way Dukath likes it.

My nerves are still on edge from the Games and I can't look Master Dukath in the eyes. He abandoned us to die. I have a better understanding of how easy it is, for a Grand Master like him, but he promised me I'd be leader, and yet he didn't care if I died.

"Thank you, Your Leadership," I say.

"You're the Leader now, Rynn."

I nod but don't respond. There's a lot I want to say to him, but it's not wise to do so.

"I knew you would emerge successful," Master Dukath continues. "And Randon, how is he?"

My jaw clenches. "He's recovering."

Master Dukath nods slowly, watching me. "How did you turn off the ship's overheating engine?"

I stare over Master's shoulder, hesitating. I don't want to tell him the truth, that I was able to deactivate it with my new found strength. It's better that he not know to what extent my Gift has grown.

"I got the codes from Cole and Aurah deactivated it," I say.

"How does it feel, to be the leader?" Dukath grins and a chill runs down my spine.

"It will feel even better after some sleep, Your Leadership."

"Of course." Dukath nods. "I have a large army for Aurah to lead, which Randon will oversee as the new General. Do you think he'll be glad to be appointed General?"

"Yes, I do."

"Good." Master Dukath leans back in his chair. "I sense a change in you. Have you felt it as well?"

"I believe so."

"You've passed this test and are stronger now. You understand your priorities and don't get confused by emotion."

I don't agree or disagree. In one way, I do feel a lot more detached, yet in another I feel wildly protective of Randon and Aurah now. And increasingly angry towards Master.

"This is a driving force for you," he says. "Which can be used to transition you into a Dark Lord, as your grandfather was, when he fought to save those he loved."

My grandfather was a horrible leader who massacred many, even destroying entire planets.

"I don't understand," I say.

"We never truly understand these things, do we?" Dukath replies.

I remain silent, waiting to be dismissed.

"You will be called Takano Rynn now, the young Dark Master."

Dukath raises his hand towards me.

"I will give you my blessing," he continues. "And we will have a proper inauguration in due time."

I bow slightly. Dukath closes his eyes and I feel his presence in my mind.

What is he doing?

"You will need to sleep tonight," he says. "Your dreams tonight will be important."

"Yes, sir."

"Very well." Dukath lets my mind go and I start to breathe again. He didn't read my mind. I don't know what he did and it unnerves me.

"Go and take your rest, you've earned it." He dismisses me with a wave of his hand. "And tomorrow you and Randon will report to me. We have a lot to discuss concerning the building of our new super weapon."

"And Aurah?"

"She will have plenty to keep her busy, as the Captain of the army."

I nod.

Master Dukath sits back in his seat. "I'm proud of you, Takano Rynn. And I know your grandfather would be too."

I bow. That's as good as any dismissal to me. I turn and leave, not bothering to give the compulsory parting words.

* * *

"Bryn!" Randon yells, waking from a nightmare and sitting up fast.

"It's okay," I say, sitting up too.

Randon turns to see me and his shoulders relax. He rubs his face with his hands.

"I had a horrible dream," he says, sighing deeply.

I set a hand on his shoulder and he opens his lowers his hands. My chest tightens at the pained expression on his face. I don't know what I imagined it would be like, to embrace being a Dark Master and kill easily, without guilt. Maybe I thought I'd no longer feel love or physical desires or emotional pain. That I'd become hard and heartless. And in a way I have. When it comes to killing, I feel only a cold indifference to the deaths of those I don't care about. But when it comes to Randon and Aurah, I've never felt so strongly about protecting them before.

"It was so real," Randon shudders.

He looks a lot healthier now, after his blood transfusion and the medications. His cheeks are flushed now and no longer a ghostly white.

"And I remember..." He stops and looks around the room. His brow furrows. "Where are we?"

The captain's quarters are big, with three different sections, the sleeping area, small kitchen and the lounging area. The largest quarters on board. We're in the bed in the sleeping area, which has soft blue lighting turned on around the floorboards, for sleep hours.

A glass wall, with water trickling down on the inside, separates the sleep area from the next section, which has a small dining area with a table and chairs. The Captain's quarters even has its very own food replicator so I never have to go down to the mess hall.

"We're in the Captain's quarters," I say.

Randon rubs at his eyes. "What happened? I'm so con-fused."

"We won the game. You got drugged. And I killed the rest of them, except for one."

Randon turns to me. "You killed them *all?*"

"Yes."

"You couldn't even remove the heart of a bird just a few weeks ago."

I shrug. "It was easy. I didn't care about them."

Randon gives me a look which is either concern or admi-ration, I can't tell.

"You cared more about a bird?" he says, grinning.

"I..." A thought surfaces suddenly. "I think the little girl, Rue, cared about the bird. And I cared about her. So..."

My head begins to hurt and I stop trying to remember. "You're the new General now," I say to Randon. "We've got a whole crew. They're all older than us, but they listen to everything I say and never question me. They call me sir and know exactly what they're doing—"

"Bryn," Randon says. He looks at me so intently that I stop breathing for a moment. Then he seems to change his mind and lays back onto the pillows instead, his hands behind his head.

"I guess Dukath was right," he says. "You did it. You won the game. It's finally over."

"If I had been the one who drank the poisoned water, like Cole wanted, then I wouldn't have won," I say.

"*We* wouldn't have won," Randon corrects.

I look down at him. "I think you would have won."

He smiles. "Maybe. But I don't need to win a game, to become leader."

I'm not sure what to say. Is he planning to take over my leadership some day?

"So I'm the General now," He continues. "I think I'm ready to start giving some orders."

"Good, because I've got lots for you to do."

Randon laughs. "Do I have to call you Master now?"

I pretend to think about it. "No, but I am your Master."

Randon sits up again. "So do I get my own quarters, or are you my Master in the night hours also?"

I glance at him. Is he challenging me or just joking?

"I'm always your Master," I say. "And my name is Takano Rynn now."

"Takano Rynn," Randon says, as though trying out the name.

"It's the middle of sleep hours," I say. "I need to sleep." I lay down and quickly turn my back to Randon so he doesn't notice that he's making me nervous.

"Okay," he says. Then a moment later he adds, "Master."

I can't tell if he's mocking me, but I'm too tired to care. "Go to sleep," I mumble then drift back into sleep.

Memories of Rue

THE VOICE OF A child wakes me from sleep. I look up at the rounded ceiling of the Captain's quarters. Am I hearing things?

"Rynn... Are you here?" the child calls again.

I sit up quickly and look to the other side of the bed. Randon isn't there anymore.

"Randon?" Throwing the blankets off of me, I run to the door and punch in the code to unlock it. The door slides open but there's no one out in the dim light of the hallway. It's still sleep hours, which seems odd. I hear the gentle sobbing of a little girl.

My heart still pounds from being woken with a start, refusing to settle down. I would rather hear the voice of some terrifying monster, than the voice of a scared child. It's eerie in the empty hallway.

Then I see her, standing in the shadows at the end of the hall.

Her hair hangs down in front of her face, covered by her small hands as she cries.

Is this Rue? What is she doing onboard? And roaming the hallways alone?

I walk over cautiously, afraid this might be some sort of trick.

"Rue?" I whisper.

"Rynn!" She takes her hands away from her face and her eyes go wide. "You're here!"

She reaches her hands up to me and I immediately pick her up into my arms.

"I'm scared," she says, clinging tightly to me. "I don't know how I got here."

The hall suddenly fills with light and I shut my eyes against its glare. A soft breeze brings the smell of the outdoors and I open my eyes again.

The stone walls of the Academy chapel appear. We're at the front doors. The sun shines from its morning position in the sky.

"Do you want to meet my grandpa?" Rue asks, her cheeks are no longer stained with tears. She's wearing a dress now and her hair is tied back.

I remember this.

I was worried that she'd gone missing. This was the morning I found her at the chapel. The relief washes over me anew, just like it did then.

"The next time you go away," I say, as though reciting a script from the past, "tell me first, so I know where you are."

She looks at me with a serious expression and set her down. This is the moment when I moved her unruly hair away from her face and set it behind her ears.

I do it again, now, replaying the moment the same way it first happened. She smiles.

The chanting from inside the chapel drifts out on the wind that is rustling the treetops.

I relish the sights and smells. I want to stay here forever, with Rue. Where did she go, before I went to the Games?

"Am I your attachment now?" she says, her eyes bright.

I smile. "You're a smart girl, Rue."

"I know."

She shoves me playfully and I let her push me to the ground, only it's not stone that I land on, but grass.

I look behind me. There's grass everywhere.

We're in the large field, between the school buildings and the forest. Rue tumbles into the grass beside me and begins to hum a tune.

"What are you singing?" I ask.

"Something my mom used to sing to me. Want me to teach it to you? It goes like this. When the sun shines in, just lift up your chin. Frowners always lose, and smilers always win."

I laugh.

"What's funny?" Rue asks, giving me a serious look.

"Your song is."

"No it's not!"

"Dark Lords don't smile," I tell her. "And they *always* win."

"They smile!" Rue sits up. "They have evil smiles like this."

She tries to give me an evil smile, tilting her chin down and narrowing her eyes at me.

I push her forehead playfully and she falls back onto the grass.

"Can I read your mind?" I ask her

"Okay."

I rest my hand on her forehead to read her thoughts. She's thinking about Mr. Rock and how he's going to be lonely if she doesn't get back to her room soon.

"You love Mr. Rock a lot, don't you?" I say.

"Yes," she replies softly.

"You shouldn't, because it's an attachment."

"What's an attachment?"

"When you love something too much."

Suddenly her mind shifts to Ungar, an alien who oversees her father's trading business.

"Why are you scared of Ungar?" I ask. But before she can answer the field becomes dark and we are inside the cargo ship office. The smell of fuel and equipment brings back the emotions of this moment, in full force.

This is the day Rue was taken away from me. She's in my arms, her breathing ragged from crying.

"I don't want to go back to Kahnju!" she cries, the sound piercing my soul. "I want to stay here with you!"

"Rue," I say, my heart racing out of control now. It's happening all over again, but I won't let them take her away this time.

And yet, I recite the words that I spoke in this memory, as though I have no choice.

"When I'm ruler over the Galaxies," I say, "I'll come find you and we'll rule together. I promise. And you'll be my little sister forever, or we can get married when you're older, whatever you want. Just don't forget about me."

Rue's breathing is staggered and she hiccups as she replies. "You'll forget... about me."

I can't stop this scene from playing out as she is taken from me all over again.

"Rue!" I wake screaming and find myself back in the Captain's quarters.

Randon curses and sits up in bed beside me. "Bryn," he clutches his chest. "Are you trying to give me a heart attack?"

"No." I kick at the blanket around my feet, trying to get out of the bed. "I need to find Rue. I told her I'd go back for her, that I'd never forget her!"

"Wait... slow down," Randon grabs my arm. "Rue's got a family and parents. She's back home now."

"No..." I shake my head. "Something's wrong. I can sense it. I need to go. We need to go find her, now!"

space pirates

"**U**NFORTUNATELY, HER FAMILY WAS taken by space pirates that raided Kahnju," Dukath says, leaning forward on the smooth table of the command center.

"Space Pirates?" My stomach clenches. If Rue is sold as a slave by the pirates, she'll lose her identity and I'll never find her.

"Yes, they took many families from Kahnju, not only hers."

"Then we'll hunt the pirates down," I say, slamming both hands onto the table.

"Rynn." Dukath sits up straighter in his chair, his expression serious.

My heart pounds uncontrollably. Is he going to tell me I can't use the Ruling Order resources to chase after these pirates? That we have more important matters to attend to?

"This is your army now," he says, instead. "If you want to take the Ruling Order to war against a fleet of pirates, then do. But you will need some additional resources."

He gets up slowly from his seat and takes his cane. "Get your Commanding Officer to acquire additional fleet from our nearest base. The Urandrei Bandits have been around for a long time and I believe they've joined together with another pirate group to form a considerable opposition for you."

"All I want is the girl."

"Then I'm certain that is what they will try and keep from you," Dukath says, leaning heavily on his cane.

"Then I'll destroy them all and take what I want."

Dukath nods. "They aren't of any benefit to the Galaxy. If you feel they aren't of any benefit to you either, then by all means, destroy them."

"They are of no use to me. They're no better than my mother." The sudden anger at my mother comes out of nowhere. She's not a pirate, but might as well be one, trading and selling all over the galaxy for more than the goods are worth, not caring who she cheats and harms.

Dukath smiles then shuffles over to a key-coded safe box, fixed into the wall. "Retrieving slaves taken by force and killing space pirates is a fine first mission for the Ruling Order. I know you are eager to get started in this, your first act of righting the wrongs of the Galaxy, but we need more weapons and troops and power. We also must continue working on our super weapon and get the Galaxy under our rule."

"Yes, Your Leadership," I say, anxious to get going.

Dukath enters the code to the safe box and it opens. He reaches inside.

"Many feared your grandfather," he says. "His name still brings nightmares to children and is revered among even the darkest of Dark Lords."

He pulls out a black cape and my breath catches. It's just like my grandfather's, but new.

"And now, you will follow in your grandfather's footsteps. You are Takano Rynn, grandson of the greatest Dark Master that ever existed. You must stand before your enemies and instill fear into their hearts, and command the respect of those who follow you." He hands me the cloak. "It matters not that you are young, it is only your power and your name, which matter."

I take the cloak carefully, my hands unsteady. The door call button sounds and Dukath smiles.

"Come in General," he says.

Randon steps into the briefing room. He's wearing a black General's uniform with the Ruling Order insignia on the upper arm and gold stripes on one sleeve. He has black gloves, boots and a new belt, and his hair is combed back in a clean-cut way. He looks striking and it sends my stomach fluttering.

He gives me a wink before bowing to Dukath.

"Nice to have you join us, General Randon," Dukath says.

"The fleet is awaiting orders, Your Leadership."

"Don't look at me, your leader Takano Rynn has a new mission for the Ruling Order and I imagine you will need to ready your fleet and have Aurah ready the troops, right away."

Randon turns to me, giving me a slight bow. "Takano Rynn," he says, raising an eyebrow.

"General," I say in return, standing straighter.

"A new uniform has arrived for you." He glances down at the cloak in my hand. "Are we going to war... Sir?"

"Yes. But first we need reinforcements. How many troops and fighter planes can you assemble in a short time?"

"A lot." Randon smiles.

I give Dukath a hurried bow. "Thank you, Your Leadership," I say, then hurry out of the room, Randon at my heels.

* * *

"I am Takano Rynn, Leader of the Ruling Order," I say to the Pirate Captain on the view screen. I feel more confident now that I am wearing the new cloak of my rank. I keep the hood on, choosing to keep my face hidden, the way Dark Masters tend to do.

Randon stands beside me, looking up at the beastly Pirate with a smirk on his face.

"We've never heard of this Ruling Order before," the Pirate snarls down at us.

I don't care about him. We have more firepower than they do.

"We're looking for a girl," I say, ignoring his comment. "Taken from Kahnju, along with her parents."

"Kahnju?" The pirate says, raising his chin. "We plundered some loot in Kahnju. Why does this concern you? We submit to no authority but our own, and we answer to no one. The Galaxy does not *have* a ruling order."

I clench my jaw, resisting the urge to reply in the way I want to. They'll discover soon enough who the true ruling order is. "Tell us where the families from Kahnju were taken," I say.

"Those slaves are not with this fleet. The fleet who have them left to go trade them in other Galaxies."

"Where?"

"I have no obligation to tell you."

"Sir," Lieutenant Jaylon says to me. He's an intelligent looking man with gray hair and sharp facial features. "We can trace the warp signature of the ships that left from here."

"End transmission," I say to the Communications Officer. She quickly ends the link.

"Lieutenant Lucas, raise shields."

"Yes, Sir."

"Ready the Dual Cannons and fire at will," I say to the Operations Officer.

He nods and starts pushing buttons.

"Destroy them all," I roar.

I turn and walk off the Bridge. Randon follows close behind.

"Have the fleet follow the warp signatures of all ships that left from here, and Kahnju, once these pirates are destroyed," I say to Randon as he steps in stride alongside me. He grabs my arm to stop me from walking.

"Bryn," he says. The sudden informality of his tone sets me on edge. We have an important mission and I don't have time for friendliness, only efficiency. "I had Lieutenant Carle scan for life forms aboard all the ships in this pirate fleet while you were talking on the Comm System with the Pirate leader."

"And?" Could they have been lying about Rue not being with them? I just gave the order to have the fleet destroyed.

"There were no young, human life forms on board... but Bryn," Randon looks me in the eyes. "You should never simply trust what a pirate says. You need to slow down, before making decisions like destroying—."

I push his hand away. "I don't have time for this," I say, walking again. "Get the fleet on the trail of those warp signatures. And it's *Takano Rynn* to you."

Suddenly the ship shakes, startling us both.

"They're firing back," Randon says, then runs off.

DON'T FORGET WHO'S IN CHARGE

I WATCH THE BATTLE from the observation deck, instead of the bridge. Randon is in command. He knows more about battle and giving commands than I do. Besides, I don't want him to question my decisions in front of the crew. He can take this battle. I'm too impatient to be up there at the moment.

I pace in front of the large windows. Explosions light up the darkness as the Urandrei ships are destroyed, one after another. The Galaxy will have one less space gang to worry about.

I stop and watch the battle for a moment. Aurah is out there, fighting on the front lines. I haven't heard from her lately so it makes me worry a little.

I should be out there too, or on the bridge. But I don't care about this battle. It just needs to hurry up and be over. We have a huge advantage over the rustic pirate ships trying to fight back. What I care about is the locations of the disbanded fleet. One of those ships has Rue, but we don't know which one. I clench my fists.

The bright colors fade and the excitement dies down. A silence fills the room. Is it over?

I walk over to the nearest Comm unit and press the button. "General Randon, report."

"The Urandrei ships have been destroyed," Randon's voice comes through the speaker. "We are now setting a new course to follow the warp signature of the disbanded fleet as you commanded."

"Meet me in the briefing room with the other officers," I say.

"Yes, Sir."

I let go of the Comm button and hurry to the briefing room.

* * *

"How soon until we reach them?" I ask the Chief Tactical Officer, Lucas.

"About two hours, Sir," he replies. The officers are seated around the command table in the briefing room. I prefer to stand and pace the room.

"Can we go any faster?" I ask.

Lucas hesitates before answering. "We could, Sir, but the fighter planes and some of the battle cruisers wouldn't be able to match that speed and we would arrive without them."

"Then we'll just have a conversation with the last of the Urandrei, as we wait for the fighter planes to catch up. We can give them the news of their leader being destroyed. Then they can decide whether or not to cooperate." I pause. "Then we'll destroy the rest of them."

Lucas frowns and I can tell he doesn't like this decision. "Yes, Sir."

"General Randon, what's your report?" I stop pacing by Randon's seat.

He blinks and seems to gather his thoughts. "The Urandrei ships we attacked were destroyed but we lost eighteen fighter pilots in the battle and there's been damage to two of the battle cruisers, as well as to the hull plating on Deck Seven and Nine on this ship."

"Are the battle cruisers unfit for a battle?"

"No, we should have enough ammunition to defeat the disbanded fleet of the Urandrei, without needing to stop at a base for repairs, but—"

"Sir," Lieutenant Jaylon says. "We could approach the Urandrei traders under the guise of wanting to make a trade, the slaves for some alloy. Then, once we've acquired what we want, we can destroy them."

I nod. "Do you know where the last of the Urandrei are now?"

"Yes, Sir. They are in the Dalamoar System on the trading planet of Norgon."

I cross my arms. "Then we'll go to Norgon and make a trade for the slaves." I look around the room.

"You are all dismissed," I say. "Commander, Randon. Report to my Ready Room."

* * *

"An hour seems too long." I pull my hood off and run my hands through my hair. It's a relief to remove it. I wear it all the time now, when on duty, hiding my face and speaking from within its large covering. I prefer to address the crew with my cloak hood on, like a Dark Master.

Now that it's off, I feel exposed, but free.

I sit down on a rounded bench in the Ready Room and lean back against the wall.

Randon takes a seat beside me and sets his hand on my shoulder. "We'll reach them in time," he says. "Before they have a chance to sell her. Those trading shows take a long time."

I sigh. He's right. My mother trades took days to negotiate. "I wish I'd paid better attention in training at the Academy." I give Randon a halfhearted grin. "I'm worried I'm going to call someone Lieutenant, when they're actually a Commanding Officer, or say one of the technical terms wrong. Do we even have dual cannons?"

Randon shakes his head. "They're Plasma Cannons."

I roll my eyes and Randon laughs.

"I'm just joking," he says. "Dual Cannons are the same thing as the Plasma Cannons, they're Dual Plasma Cannons."

My muscles relax at the sound of Randon's laugh. It's my favorite sound in the galaxy. He's a lot more relaxed when we're alone and it makes me relax too.

"You know I can't treat you as an equal, when the other crew is round, right?" I say.

"I know."

"You're the only one who doesn't address me as 'sir,' when you speak."

A muscle twitches in Randon's jaw and he gets up and walks over to a console as though to check something, but I can tell he's just stepping away to calm down.

I get up too. "We've only got one hour before we reach them. Maybe I should call another meeting to discuss exactly how we're going to follow through on this plan."

"I think they've got it figured out," Randon replies, his back turned to me. "They're a competent crew."

I start pacing again.

How fast does the trading happen on these types of planets? Will Rue have been sold by the time we get there? Taken away by her new owners to some other Galaxy where I'll never find her?

"Bryn?" Randon says. "Can you please stop pacing."

I stop, annoyed that Randon feels he can give me a command *and* use my old name.

"Are you listening?" he says.

"To what?" I look down at my hand and realize that I'm holding Rue's rock, Mr. Rock. I don't even remember taking it out of my pocket.

"I was asking you if she's going to live on board with us, once we find her."

I put the rock back into my pocket. Rue was so worried about it going missing, and it's just a rock. How much more upset would she be if saw the battle that we had only moments ago, with all those deaths? This ship is no place for a small girl with a gentle heart.

"She'll go back to Kahnju, with her parents," I say.

"And if they're dead? Or we can't find them?"

I pull my hood up over my head again and turn to leave the room. "Contact Engineering and see if the warp drive can go any faster."

"It can't—"

"That's an order," I yell over my shoulder.

Randon doesn't respond so I turn around. He's glaring at me with an defiant expression.

"Did you hear me?" I say, glaring back.

He holds my stare for a moment longer, then looks away and nods.

"Don't forget who's in charge," I remind him, then continue out of the room.

* * *

I take out Grandfather's sword from its case. It gleams even in the flat lighting in my quarters.

It's reassuring to finally have it back. I had it delivered from the Academy. I can now command anyone to do anything for me.

Aurah and Randon also had things delivered to them. Aurah had her spices, massage oils and scarves delivered, but I can't imagine what Randon sent for. He's not one for material attachments.

I grasp the sword firmly in my hand.

"I know grandma died before you could save her," I say, looking at the sword and thinking of grandfather, the terrible Dark Lord I never knew but always felt the closest too. "I won't let that happen to Rue. I'm a Dark Master now, like you were." I lift the sword and it seems to get lighter in my hand.

A peace flows over me and the sword heats up. The energy I gained from the act of killing those boys stirs inside of me, growing and activating some power in the sword. For a moment, I feel invincible.

"I have the power now," I say, "to save Rue, and rule the Galaxy. And make you proud."

The floor shifts beneath me and I realize that we've dropped out of warp speed.

I set the sword down again, my hand vibrating from its power.

I've picked up this sword hundreds of times before, and never felt anything.

I wasn't ready then. But now I am.

"I'm coming, Rue," I whisper, then hurry out of the room.

Ungar the Alien

T HE TRADING MARKET ON Norgon is hectic with activity, even in the night hours. Endless rows of trading booths line the lower streets of Maladoria, the small planets largest city.

Heads turn in our direction as we walk down the center of the narrow road, Randon at my side and the three officers behind us.

I stop and turn to Lucas, who is looking down at his bio scanner.

"Where are the Kahnju families?"

He repositions the map on the small screen. "They are scattered throughout the trading market. But there's a concentration of them in that direction."

He points and I step aside to let him lead the way. I don't recognize any of the alien species that are buying and selling at the various booths, speaking in different languages.

They make way for us as we walk, and I think some of them sense that I'm Gifted or have powers. I keep my hood low so they can't see my face.

Lucas leads the way and Randon keeps pace with me, behind him. He is silent as he takes in the sights. He looks up at the metal buildings above. Maladoria has a Sky City, like most class system planets do.

Above the dusty trading lane, the lights of the Sky City shine like stars. It is where the wealthy live, away from the dirt and clammer of the working class below. Norgon is rich in resources, making the rich, richer, and the poor, poorer.

If I wasn't so worried about Rue, I'd be excited about being here. Fortunately, Randon knows a thing or two about trading and the class systems on other planets. He has already warned me not to make eye contact with the Maladorians and to avoid small talk.

The pirates are already here somewhere, doing their trading. Our battle cruisers are on the ready nearby, waiting at the outskirts of the Dalamoar sector, out of Maladorian's sensor range. Randon didn't think it a good idea to alarm the Rulers of our military presence.

We're here to find Rue and that's it. There should be no reason to start a battle with this planet or the Maladorians.

Rue...

I try to call out to her, but there's no response. I don't sense her here, not in this part of the city at least. It could be the large crowds and different species that are blocking me.

I glance around at the muddy tables and ill-kempt animals being traded. I hate of Rue in a scummy place like this, among all this chaos.

Lucas stops in front of a large cage with humans in it, clad in desert clothes.

"Interested in a human slave?" A large Ruleon man says to us. I recognize him right away, from Rue's thoughts. It's Ungar, the trades dealer from Kahnju.

"Ungar," I say in a low voice.

I reach for my sword but Randon grabs my arm to stop me.

"Where's the little girl named Rue?" he asks Ungar.

"Do I know you, Commander?" Ungar looks him over suspiciously.

"We are here to trade for the little girl from Kahnju," I say.

"I have many little girls from Kahnju."

"You know this one personally," I glare at the Ruleon from under my hood.

Ungar shifts from one foot to the other.

"Help us," a man from the cage behind Ungar yells.

"Quiet!" Ungar turns and snaps a whip in the direction of the cage. The man who spoke moves away from the metal bars.

I reach out my hand and grab Ungar in an Gift hold. He stiffens, his eyes widening in surprise.

I read his mind quickly, before we draw too much attention from onlookers or the market patrol. He knew the Urandrei were coming to Kahnju and he made deals with them, including selling off Rue's parents and betraying her father's partnership, with there being a high demand for humans in the trade market.

Her parents are no longer here. They were already sold and he doesn't know where they were taken, he only cares about the money he got for them.

Rue is still on Kahnju. Ungar didn't want to sell her, but keep her for himself now that her parents are gone, so she can be his personal slave. He left her with his brother, Karun, until he returns.

"You won't be returning to Kahnju," I say to him.

A few heads turn our way, slowing before they continue on. I Keep Ungar in a choke hold, cutting off his air. He struggles to breathe, his face turning red.

"I would have enjoyed making you suffer more," I say to him. "But I don't have the time for scum like you."

Ungar body spasms few more seconds, then he drops to the ground, dead.

* * *

"We've got affiliates in Kahnju who have reported seeing the girl," Anthony says. "She is living in an abandoned army hut near Naatir Trading Outpost, with Ungar's brother in charge of her."

He looks different now that he isn't sick anymore, all cleaned up in uniform. He has proven himself very useful in information gathering and I'm glad I kept him alive.

"That will be all," I say to him.

"Yes, Master." He bows. He's the only one on board who calls me Master, although I am worthy of that title now, the others address me as Sir. Technically, Dukath is still the head Master here, I like hearing Anthony call me Master.

"Anthony," I say to him.

He stops. I move closer and his expression turns fearful as I approach. I enjoy sensing his fear, which feeds my Gift somehow.

"You're very obedient." I raise a gloved hand to his face. "And submissive, too."

Anthony swallows hard and doesn't answer. I sense more fear. It travels from him, through my hand and into the rest of me, revitalizing me. His fear will be useful.

"I'm reassigning you to different quarters, on Deck Five," I say to him.

"M-may I ask why, Master?" Anthony stammers.

"To have you closer to my quarters." I watch as the fear grows in his eyes and I smile. I don't have any specific intentions for him, in reassigning his quarters, other than the boost I get from his nervous energy. His anxiety will triple just by having to reside so nearby to me.

He looks into my hood but I know he can't see my eyes.

"You're dismissed," I say, dropping my hand from his face and stepping back.

He bows and wipes at his forehead.

"Yes, Master," he says, then quickly leaves.

That's Not Rynn, That's a Monster!

THE DESERT HEAT PINCHES at my skin, way too hot even in the night hours.

My cloak is not the right attire for Kahnju weather, but I'm required to wear the clothing of a Master, no matter where I go. I'm covered from head to toe, even my fingers are hidden by black gloves, so that no part of my skin can be touched by another person. The heavy hood keeps the blowing dust away from my face, at least.

Karun gives me a suspicious glare as we approach the trading counter. I don't bother with introductions but go straight to reading his mind.

I reach out my hand and Karun's eyes widen, just like his brother's did when I killed him. Beads of sweat drip down his brow.

I search his thoughts. He's an unfair trader, like all those involved in trading, but he's not interested in Rue in any concerning way, finding her too willful to command, and too weak for hard labor.

I see an image of the abandoned army hut, where he left her to fend for herself. He doesn't care much about his brother and took all of his money and possessions the moment he got word he was dead. But he has been feeding Rue. He's waiting until she's older so he can sell her for a higher price.

I let him go and he falls forward, grabbing hold of the countertop in front of him for balance. He gives me an angry glare but is smart enough not to challenge me or call the guards. He simply snarls at me. He thinks I'm here to steal from him.

I turn to Randon and our two guards that came with us.

"I know where she is," I tell them.

Randon nods and we leave Karun at his trade station.

* * *

"You let him live," Randon says as we make our way to the army hut in the near distance. It sits in the shadow of evening, such a lonely sight that my heart aches for Rita.

"He's not like his brother," I tell Randon.

My pulse speeds up as we approach. I sense Rue's presence now, and it takes me right back to the Academy and our time together there. I didn't realize how much I truly miss her.

I don't know why Dukath chose to give me back my memories, the night he told me to sleep and pay attention to my dreams. It has only caused a war inside of me. The memories of the weak person I used to be, conflicting with the person I am now, killing for power and strength.

We stop in front of the makeshift door of Rue's humble home; an opening with a blanket hanging down in front of it. The guards didn't come with us. I didn't want to alarm Rue unnecessarily with their presence.

It's so quiet, with only the rustling of a light breeze kicking up sand around our feet. We may end up startling Rue after all, if we're too quiet and surprise her.

Suddenly, the curtain door flies open and a high-pitched battle cry startles us. Randon jumps and I step back as Rue lunges forward with a large stick in her hand. She whacks my head, making my ears ring.

"Rue..." I reach out for her but she smacks my gloved hand hard. "Ow..." I retreat, fumbling to pull my hood down, realizing too late that she doesn't recognize me in my new cloak.

She continues to smack at my hands, her little face scrunched up in anger. I finally grab her stick and pull it away.

She screams and runs to Randon, reaching her hands up to him.

He crouches down, looking bewildered as she throws her arms around his neck, pulling him onto his knees.

"Help me," Rue says to Randon, gripping him tight. "He's one of the evil aliens that took my parents away and he's going to take me away too." She buries her face into his shoulder.

"No..." Randon says, trying gently to pull her away from him but she won't let go. His hand hovers over her back as though he's not sure if he should touch her. He looks to me. "It's just Bryn, with a hood on."

"Rynn?" Rue lets go of Randon and turns to look at me. Her eyes widen in fear and she buries her face into Randon's shoulder again. "Tell him to take off the mask, it's scary."

"What mask?" Randon says.

My heart squeezes in my chest. She's never looked at me this way before, with such hatred and fear.

I reach my hand out to read her mind. She's terrified. She doesn't see me, she sees...

Rue lifts her tear stained face to me. "That's not Rynn," she cries. "That's a *monster*."

* * *

I stop slashing the control console with my sword to catch my breath. Everyone has left the Bridge, choosing to get out of the way of my anger.

The image of Rue's terrified face won't leave my mind. She saw what I've become, a Dark Lord, killing without mercy, feeding off the fear of those I intimidate. She once said her mother believed she had a gift for seeing people how they really are on the inside. That's why she didn't recognize me. What she saw was a projection of who I am now. A monster.

His name still brings nightmares to children, Dukath said, about my grandfather.

Now I am the one who brings nightmares to children.

I will never love anyone else the way I love Rue. But she is lost to me.

There is no longer anything holding me back from becoming like my grandfather and fulfilling my destiny. I'm ready separate myself from all attachments. I don't need my memory erased this time.

"Bryn?"

I turn to see Randon standing at the entrance to the Bridge. He glances around the room at all the damage I've done and frowns. "Dukath sent a message that we return to Base. He wants us to give him a full report."

I put my sword away.

"Can I tell the crew that they can return to the Bridge now?" Randon asks, watching me carefully. He can't see my face beneath my hood but I can see his. He looks uneasy at awaiting my reply.

My breathing slows and I take in the room—all the slash marks on the consoles, open wires sparking, smashed view screens and monitors. I turn abruptly to Randon and he startles, standing straighter.

I walk past him and storm off the Bridge.

THE MASTER'S HOOD

THE SHIP SPEEDS FORWARD, stars zooming past, outside my window in the Captain's quarters. Each star marks another chasm of distance between me and Rue.

The sound of my breathing is more pronounced within the confines of my heavy hood, like a beast ready to attack. Like the monster Rue saw.

As a child, I wondered why the Dark Lords kept their hoods on all the time, hiding their faces. Now I understand. It keeps the rest of the world on the outside. There is nothing for me outside of this hood.

I glance down at my grandfather's sword sitting on my night table. The call button to the front door beeps and I ignore it, knowing it's Randon. No one else would stopping by this far into sleep hours.

The beep comes again. I don't get up. He'll give up eventually. I've got nothing to say to him.

The ringing continues and I finally relent, and go to the door.

I square my shoulders, preparing to face Randon and tell him I'm fine. I don't need him questioning my emotional state or my authority. If I want to destroy the Bridge and wreck the ship, then I will.

The door slides open and Anthony stands there, in his uniform. I sense his fear immediately as he tries to look at my face beneath my hood.

Anthony's presence is unexpected. He bows slightly, stealing another quick glance at me before lowering his eyes. "I came to see if I could be of service to you, Master."

I don't reply, not exactly sure what service he's offering at this time of night. His fear is of a different kind, than the desperation that came from Rue, which only made me hurt when I felt it. With Anthony, it's intoxicating. He *wants* to be afraid, he invites the fear, as though he has no regard for himself or his safety.

"What do you have to offer?" I ask him, curious.

"Anything you want, my lord," he bows again.

"That will be all, ensign." The voice comes from behind Anthony and he turns in surprise. It's Randon, still in his commander's uniform. He does not look pleased.

Anthony scurries away.

I cross my arms, blocking the door.

"I see you're feeling better," Randon says.

"You're still awake."

"My night clothes and bags are still in your room."

I uncross my arms and step aside for Randon to enter.

"I don't trust him," Randon says as he passes by me.

I stand near the door, keeping it open as I wait for him to get his things. He goes to the hidden cabinets in the wall and stops.

"She's going to be okay on her own, you know," he says, turning to look at me. "She's a strong little girl. She attacked you without hesitation—a Dark Lord—with only a stick. She's fearless." He smiles a little. "I can see why you're so fond of her."

I focus on the sound of my breathing within my hood. I don't want to think about Rue. I've been trying so hard not to fall apart. She is no longer a part of my life.

"Why are you still wearing your hood over your head?" Randon asks, as though only just noticing now.

He walks over to me.

"I'm a Master now. I always wear it," I say.

"What was Anthony doing here?"

"He was offering to be of service?"

"At this late hour?"

"At any hour. He's mine."

"Yours? How's that?"

"I'm the ruler of the Galaxy now. The universe. Everything is mine and for my use, including you."

Randon furrows his brow. "Can you take off your hood, Bryn, so I can talk to you?"

"You will address me as *Takano Rynn*," I say, tired of his insolence. "Take your things and leave."

Randon's eyes flash. "Should I send for Anthony, once I'm gone?"

"Yes," I say, even though I don't mean it, because I know it will upset him.

Randon presses his lips together tight and doesn't move away from in front of me, as though challenging me. He tries to look into my hood, but light doesn't reflect inside my hood and I know he can't see my face. The cloak is enchanted somehow, with the power to keep me hidden.

He reaches up to remove it.

"Don't," I say, stepping back, angry that I suddenly sound like my childish self again. Only Randon can bring that part of me to the surface.

"Bryn, you have to sleep sometime. And you have to remove your—"

"I won't be sleeping tonight." I don't reprimand him for not using my proper title, when speaking to me. A fight for another time. Right now I don't have the energy.

"We'll be arriving at Base in the day hours and Dukath has meetings for us to attend all day, about the new super weapon. And the Landaenorians are pulling out of their agreement to supply the raw materials for the weapon, after they found out we brought battle cruisers to Norgon, they no longer trust us..." Randon stops talking and steps closer. He pulls my hood back and I don't stop him this time.

I blink at the overhead lights.

"Aurah's been asking to see you," Randon says, his eyes searching mine now.

I feel exposed and I can't keep his gaze.

"I told her you've been resting," he continues. "She's starting to think you're avoiding her."

"What did you have delivered here, from the Academy?" I ask.

Randon looks confused for a moment, then his face flushes and he looks away. I wait, curious if he'll tell me.

"I could order the inventory crew to tell me."

"Why do you need to know?" he asks, his expression turning angry.

"I'm the leader. I need to know everything that comes and goes on my ship."

"Melli," he says.

"Melli?"

"Yes."

"What's Melli?"

Randon shrugs, his commander's uniform moving up in the shoulders as he does so.

"She's an animal someone left behind on a visit to the school. An earth one, called a cat. I fed her once and then she was always at my window."

I smile at the image that forms in my mind, a small cat peeking in through Randon's window at the Academy. He kept that secret well. I never once saw a cat in his room. The pain in my chest eases a little.

"I'll see you tomorrow." Randon bows curtly then turns to leave.

"Wait."

He stops.

"Stay here."

"What do you mean?" he asks, his back still turned.

"Why should I be alone all night?"

He turns and raises an eyebrow.

"And that's an order," I add.

He tilts his head to one side, as though assessing me.

"You're turning soft again," he says jokingly.

I feel the anger rising fast inside of me. He's accusing me of being soft? After I'd killed all those boys? And had all the Urandrei destroyed?

I clench my fists, ready to send him flying against the wall.

"I'm your superior," I say between clenched teeth. "I'm tired of you acting like we're equals, or like you're better than me,"

"Then act like a superior," Randon snaps. "If it's a monster she sees, then *be* a monster."

"I'm not a monster." My hands begin to shake, too angry to say anything more.

"I'm trying to help you."

"I don't need your help," I yell. "Get out!"

Randon gives me an angry look. "I should have been leader," he says under his breath.

I sense his powers stirring, and my anger is suddenly gone, replaced by a fear—of what he might discover some day; his Gift abilities. Would he challenge my leadership, if he knew? I raise my hand, ready to send him out of the room by force.

"I said, *get out*."

He leaves and my hand drops as the door slides closed. The room goes quiet except for the hum of the ship. I really did want him to stay. Now what?

How can I hate someone and still need them so much, at the same time?

I pull my hood over my head again and walk over to the Comm Unit in the wall, opening a channel to the room beside mine.

"Anthony, report to my quarters."

are you serious?

T HE CALL BUTTON BEEPS and the door slides open. It's too early to be woken, after the night I had. I shouldn't have given Randon the passcode to my room. I'm not ready for another confrontation.

"Just getting up?" Aurah's voice catches me off guard. She enters the room and my shoulders relax.

I lay back down and sigh. "I thought you were Randon."

"And I thought he'd be here," she says, as though we just saw each other yesterday when in fact we haven't seen each other since the Games.

"Do you ever stop long enough to come speak to your Leader?" I say jokingly.

She chuckles. "Stop sending my fleet into battle, and I will."

"And you thought you could come see me at any hour you want?" I say.

She continues to walk around my room, inspecting everything. "Your quarters are massive!"

She makes her way around the corner to the kitchen area. "Noblyn tea, hot," she commands from behind the wall. I hear my food replicator start up. I get up, becoming frustrated with the casual way Aurah is treating me.

She returns with a steaming cup of tea in one hand and a small gadget in the other. She slips it into her pocket. It's from the kitchen and I hadn't even figured out its use yet, but that doesn't mean Aurah can have it. I'll have to keep my sword under lock and key, as well as change my room passcode.

"How is it that you and Randon feel you can disregard my rank?" I ask.

Aurah laughs. "Are you serious, Bryn?"

"It's Rynn," I correct her. "Takano Rynn."

She's about to take a seat in a nearby lounging chair, but stops to look at me. "Are you actually serious?"

"Deadly," I say. "I could have both of you dismissed, or put to death with a simple command."

"I see." She sets the tea down and walks to the door. "*Stars near and far*," she curses. "Randon was right."

"What is that supposed to mean, Commander?"

"You should keep your enemies close, *Sir*."

"Is Randon my enemy?"

"Is he your friend?"

I don't respond and Aurah walks out the door, not giving me the bow she's supposed to give, when leaving the presence of a Master.

THE NEW RULING ORDER

"You're weakening," Master Dukath says, from beneath his cloak.

I narrow my eyes at him, resisting the urge to say something I'll regret. I didn't get much sleep, but to be called weak, is belittling.

"Your attachments hinder you," he continues.

"Do they?" I respond. "I have no attachments anymore, Master."

"You do."

"They don't make me weak, they make me angry, and strong."

Master Dukath seems to think about this. "Perhaps."

He gets up from his seat and walks slowly around the large table at the center of the room, using his cane to lean on.

I'm still on bended knee, where I'm to remain until he gestures for me to rise, which he hasn't done yet since I've arrived.

"You can not rule the Galaxy, if you break down at the reaction of a little girl."

He comes to a stop in front of me and I look up into his hood. Is this what others see when they look at me? Nothing but shadow and intimidation?

"She did not break me."

"Were you not able to save her from the Urandrei?"

He's trying to anger me. He knows everything that happened.

"She is safe," I say.

"And you didn't destroy them? These space pirates?"

"I destroyed most of them. The rest are of no threat to us."

"Aren't they?"

I realize my mistake. I didn't take my revenge on the pirates, who were so insolent.

"I should have made an example of them," I say. "To instill fear in others and show the Galaxy that we're the New Ruling Order."

"Correct. They did not cooperate with us. Disobedience should not go unpunished."

Master motions for me to rise.

I get up, give him a quick nod then hurry out of the room.

***

I step onto the Bridge, glad to have a target to aim my frustrations at. There will be no more Urandrei in existence, once we're through with them.

The crew stand at attention as I enter. They've been given their objectives in advance, from Randon, and I'm only here to see they are carried out properly.

We pass through a meteor shower, then suddenly the expanse opens up into a display of colorful gases. We are headed to Urande, the home planet of the Urandrei. The pirates are away on another raid, and have taken most of their defense ships with them. They've left their planet vulnerable.

Randon steps up beside me and I tense.

"Tell me about Melli," I say to him, hoping to disarm him a bit. It's annoying how he can so arrogantly stand beside me, even after I've reprimanded him. He acts as though he's beyond reproach.

He clasps his hands behind his back, keeping his gaze forward to the large view screen.

My anger builds the longer it takes for Randon to answer.

Does he think he can ignore me?

"She demands a lot of attention," he says finally. "But when I give it to her, she claws me." He smirks. *Kind of like you, Bryn.*

I blink in surprise. Did he just speak to me using the Gift?

I wait to see if he makes any acknowledgement of it, but he seems oblivious to his unintentionally shared thought.

"Sir," the Navigation Officer says, interrupting my thoughts. "We're approaching the Urande sector."

I return to the Captain's chair and take a seat.

This is it. Our surprise attack will catch them off guard. The families on planet are defenseless.

"The fleet will attack all the major cities, at your command," Randon says.

We have to act fast. Once the Urandrei ships get notified of our attack, they will return and pose a worthy threat.

"Randon?" I say.

"Yes?" He turns around, then adds, "Sir."

"Contact the Base to ready our super weapon."

"It hasn't been tested yet, we're still in the beginning stages of—"

"Then this is the perfect opportunity to test it out."

"But—"

"Do as I say!" I yell.

Randon's expression turns dark. He seems to compose himself then shouts the order.

"Lieutenant Hydon, open a channel to Base."

"Yes, Sir," the Communications Officer says.

"We will destroy the entire planet in one shot. The Galaxy will submit to the Ruling Order!" Randon declares.

I clench my jaw and take a seat in the Captain's chair.

"Fire when ready," I say.

Randon turns to look at me. He winks and gives me a smile that instantly melts the tension of the last couple of days. My shoulders relax. We're in this together, just like we said we'd be. We've attained everything we'd hoped. Together.

I smile back, although I know Randon can't see it beneath my hood.

There is no one else in the Universe I'd rather have alongside me, to terrorize the Galaxies with.

ACKNOWLEDGMENTS

Special thanks to my daughter Jessica for all her patience in being quiet around the house while I would write, and then when she got older, accompanying me to Starbucks for our two writing/drawing sessions. Thank you Sorcha, Lorelei and Melina, for proofing the book, before it went out to print in its first edition.

To my writing buddies and critique friends Emily, Kaleen, Kirstie, Amber, Brittany, Linda, Joan, Amanda and Shannon, you ladies are the coolest friends a writer could have.

And thanks to my readers who have bugged me to get the next book out. Many hours, and emotional drama, went into completing this prequel!

To all the talented artists who drew fan art for Kylux and Huxlo, your art was the inspiration that became this entire novel!

And of course I have my breath, being and gifts from God, without whom I wouldn't have persevered through the process of writing this entire series.

BIANCA ROWENA

Bianca Rowena was born in Transylvania and moved to Canada at age five. She studied Writing/Producing/Directing at the Southern Alberta Institute of Technology, in the Cinema/Television/Stage/Radio program. She now lives with her family in Southern Alberta.

Visit her online at www.biancarowena.com

9 781999 204150